I0761930

A SPECULATIVE ROMANCE

WORLD WAR III

NATIONBERG, GATSBY, AND THE EXECUTION CAMP

JONATHAN GATSBY

BY JONATHAN GATSBY

The Wars Between Angels and Gods Series
Middle-Grade to Young Adult Mythological Fantasy

Book One:
THE BEASTS AND THE 4 DEMIGODS
Available at all major distribution outlets.

Book Two:
FORCED INTO HEAVEN'S WAR
(coming soon)

The Quest for the Forbidden Book Series
Adult Speculative Romance

Book One:
WWIII: NATIONBERG, GATSBY, AND THE EXECUTION CAMP
Out now at all major distribution outlets.

Book Two Coming Soon

The Quest for the Forbidden Book

Book One

WORLD WAR III

Nationberg, Gatsby AND THE *Execution Camp*

Jonathan Gatsby

SECOND EDITION
Hardcover
978-1-7361769-3-1
Also available in paperback and eBook.

Second edition published by Gatsby & Noel
(Jonathan D Dunham)
February 28, 2021, Fairbanks, Alaska
United States of America

Cover Design by Ricky Gunawan Book Cover Art
www.facebook.com/rickyillustrator
Line Edited & Interior by Emily Gleeson Editorial
www.facebook.com/emilygleesoneditorial
www.mountainponyliterary.com

Set in Century Schoolbook 12pt, Titles set in Baskerville Old Face

First published in the USA by Revival Waves of Glory Books & Publishing 2018

Get ready for

WORLD WAR III

CHAPTER ONE

"One of the officers was yelling from behind me as I tried to outrun the police. Between my thudding footfalls, I heard him over and over, 'Get him, get him!' The streets were so crowded, way too crowded for Fairbanks, and it was impossible to get away. There was this… event on, for the Native community. See, the government had voted to force their way onto Alaskan Native protected lands and national parks, against the wishes of the tribal elders."

He paused, shaking his head. "This government doesn't much care about people. All about the oil, isn't it? Was then too. They needed to get onto land that was supposed to be off-limits. Drill for oil. I guess they felt that a carnival in the snow was a fair trade off. All I could do was pray that I'd be able to evade capture… Even while I was running, I started making deals with God." He looked across the table at Manual Emotho, famous reporter from CGX Global News. Gatsby's hand wasn't quite steady when he picked up the glass of water, but he cleared his throat and drank.

Manuel watched him set the glass on the table, straightening the coaster it sat on with a subtle twist of his finger. The reporter inclined his head. "Please, continue," he said, reclining and clutching at his own deep brown, toned arm—he was intrigued.

Sergeant Stephen wasn't available for the interview, but Gatsby had assured Manuel that he knew enough about both sides of the story to tell it completely and, for Manuel, that was enough.

"Okay," Gatsby said, with a throat-clearing cough. "I was running away from the cops, praying I wouldn't get caught and, just as I thought I was going to be able to make a clean break through the woods and ditch the officers, I was cut off by screeching breaks and burning rubber. A patrol car blocked me in, and I was arrested. Since I was still a minor at the time, they took me to juvie."

"A minor?" Manuel interrupted. "How old were you when this took place? I believe the people listening to this broadcast would like to know."

Gatsby chuckled a little. "I was seventeen at the time, and this took place during the fall. I was arrested on September twenty-eighth, 2020. I remember it clear as day. Two police officers escorted me to the local juvenile detention center and left me in the custody of correctional officers." He shook his head. "I remember the head corrections officer was awful. She was a stern and ugly looking woman—big snarly face that put you on the back foot straight away." Gatsby shuddered. "I know they say there's someone for everyone, but her somebody must have been galaxies away."

Unbekownst to listeners, Manuel laughed.

*****

"Your name is Jonathan Gatsby, and it says here in your file that you live at fifteen-sixteen Gilliam Way, in—uh—apartment number three. Is that correct?" she asked.

"Nope," I replied smartly, with a lazy quirk of my brow. I wanted to show her that being locked up didn't bother me—not one bit. "That used to be my address. It looks like I now live at the Fairbanks Juvenile Detention Center," I continued with a smirk.

"Very funny," the corrections officer said in a sarcastic drawl, without any hint of a smile. "Now if you would please answer the question, Mr Gatsby…"

I stared at the paper in her hands for a few seconds before answering. "Yeah, it is. That's my address. I still live there."

"Thank you. I also have here in my file that you have requested to call your dad in…" There was a rustling of paper as the officer turned the page. "California. And you've listed him as your emergency contact." She pulled the phone from the shelf behind her, dialled in the number I'd put down, and handed me the phone to use.

It rang a few times, and I felt the nerves bunching up in my gut. I heard the click of it answering and gulped.

"How are you doing, son?" my dad asked on the other end of the line.

I'm normally a bit of a joker, but never with my dad. It just wasn't allowed. Growing up, he was very strict. Everything was yes sir, no sir, and we got the belt to our butts anytime we acted out.

"I'm doing okay," I responded, vaguely wondering how he knew it was me.

"You must not be doing that good if you're calling me from the jail, boy. What happened?"

Ah. That's how. "A re-formed KKK member threatened to shoot me," I said, trying to keep my voice steady. "He would've done it too, so I stabbed him—I didn't have a choice, Pops."

There was silence for a few seconds. "Boy, what is a *re-formed* KKK member?"

"It's the name they're going by now, Pops. It's a group of white kids that think white supremacy is right—they're trying to restart the KKK and—."

Dad cut in then, and I braced myself for what he had to say. "You don't need to tell me about their race, son. Don't need to sink as low as them. Trust me, Poppa knows a little more than you might think. I did grow up when the originals were about, after all. Try and explain this to me without using their color, eh?"

"Yes, sir," I replied. "Well, a racist group threatened to kill me, so I stabbed the guy in his neck, but the blade only went part way in because my friend Robert caught my arm."

"Dang it, son. You know Poppa would do anything for you, but I don't know if I can get you out of this one. I'll make some calls to my commanders, and we'll see if they can help Poppa out on this."

"Thank you, Dad," I said, hoping he could find some way to get me out.

"Okay, son. I'm going to pray for you and then I want you to hand the phone to the guard so I can make sure they know I want them to keep me informed about everything."

"Okay." I nodded into the receiver and we said goodbye before I returned the phone to the guard.

After the phone call, the detention center officers began to process me in. "I'm going to need you to stand over here and hold your arms out," a male officer said to me as he beckoned for me to come out of the office where I'd been sitting. "Now, before I search you, I gotta ask. Do you have any drugs, concealed weapons, or anything that might be considered a weapon or contraband?"

I replied honestly. "Not that I know of."

The search was clean and when it was over, the same officer handed me lime green scrubs and sandals and pointed toward a door labelled *shower*, just a little way down the starkly bare hall.

"You have ten minutes," he said. "When you've finished, knock on the door and wait for permission to come out. I'm going to ask you one time only. Do you understand the instructions that have been given to you?"

"Yes," I replied, gritting my teeth in thinly veiled agitation. I was starting to regret getting arrested, and as I looked toward the door I'd come in through, I almost began to toy with the idea of trying to make a break for it. In my imagination, I pictured myself beating up the guards and then buzzing the door open and escaping. The thought lasted less than a second, and I continued toward the shower.

I closed the door behind me and eyed the meager offerings. There were lime green tiles on the floor, and a small bench to keep your clothes dry. The sinks were clean, and the shower was private so nobody could see you. It was nothing special, but it wasn't the worst either. Nothing like it was in the movies, anyway.

I took a quick shower and dressed as fast as I could. I didn't want to give the guards any reason to try to sneak a peek. Some people say the only difference between a juvie guard and a Catholic priest is that one carries a rosary and the other a nightstick and flashlight. I wasn't prepared to take any chances.

I was escorted back to the office, and

the mean-looking officer was waiting for me, tapping a clipboard against her thigh and ready to continue my intake. We went through the things they'd taken from me when I'd been grabbed, and she had the gall to make me sign a declaration that it was all I'd had. I signed. It was getting close to eight-thirty, and I was ready to move into my new cell so I could sleep.

One of the officers handed me a blanket and a sheet but paused before leading me out. "Hold on a minute," he said to the room. "We haven't fingerprinted him yet—or taken his mugshot." He nodded at me, curt and demanding. "Put your clothes on the chair over there," he said, collecting his fingerprinting materials. "Hurry up now, come over here and place your index finger in this black substance and roll it on this spot I'm pointing to."

We did it over and over again, until they had neat little imprints of all my fingertips to go nicely with the mugshot they snapped before, at last, the guard escorted me through a maze of electronic doors to my cell.

We walked up a set of stairs and onto the second floor that overlooked an open common area below. There were scattered tables on carpeted floors, and the guards' desk stood right in the center, but pushed all the way back to the wall. We stopped at what was to be my cell—just mine, I had no roommate—and the guards at the desk buzzed the door open.

One of my escorts handed me a brown paper bag that he had been carrying. "You missed dinner," he said as he handed it over.

I looked inside it to find an apple, a BLT sandwich, some graham crackers, apple juice, and a small carton of two percent milk. "I can eat this in my cell?" I asked, eyeing him cautiously and raising my brow.

"Course you can. Wouldn't have given it to you otherwise." The guard chuckled. I guess he thought that was funny. "You can call me Mr Samuels," he continued, as he reached out to shake my hand.

I walked into my cell and had a quick glance around. It was a tiny box of a thing, with an even tinier window. The bed, directly across from the door, was bolted to the wall. I took one look at the water faucet and decided I'd never use it; it was connected to the toilet, and I wasn't about to drink toilet water.

I sat down to eat at the lonely desk resting against the wall. The chair was rock-hard and nailed to the floor. The officers nodded at me one last time and closed the cell door. I was alone, and I was tired. After I ate, I made the bed and then laid down, starting up at a ceiling I couldn't see in the dark—they'd cut the light off while I was still eating. The only remaining visibility came from an outside streetlamp that glimmered in through my cell window. Eventually, I fell asleep, but I woke up three times during the night because the guards were on patrol. I'd come to learn that they were going from cell to cell, shining a bright flashlight through the windows, right into the inmates' faces. Their job was to make sure that all inmates were in their cells and in their beds. Right then, I just thought they were being dicks. I guess I was right either way, really.

The next morning, I awoke to a guard tapping on my window. "Breakfast in thirty minutes," he called. "Get dressed, make your bed, and brush your teeth. Make sure your cell is clean before you come out!"

Damn, what time is it? I wondered. It was

still dark outside, but in Alaska, that didn't mean much; in the winter, it would be dark for most of the day.

I yawned lazily and stretched my arms before clambering out of bed. Peering through the window on the door, I tried to get a glimpse of the clock behind the guard's desk, but all I could see was its circular shape. I had very bad vision. The eye doctors had told me my vision was one hundred over twenty, which is almost as blind as a bat. I squinted in vain but couldn't make out the time.

With my bed made hastily and my teeth brushed, I waited patiently to be let out for breakfast. Man, time is sure going by slow, I thought. It seemed like an age had passed since the guard had woken me, and my growling stomach was making me irritable. I felt like I was trapped in a little box, and the promise of getting out for a while only made it worse. I hated being in tight spaces. I never figured out if I'm truly claustrophobic or not, but tight spaces bring with them gasping breaths and a violence that surges through me.

When the doors finally opened, I didn't need to be told twice. I rushed down the staircase to be first in line, but the first-floor residents had already beaten me, so I had to wait my turn. My excitement over breakfast was short lived, and I sighed when I finally made it to the front of the line.

You can't be serious, I thought. The 'F' word ran back and forth in my head, just dying to be unleashed. I wanted to cuss-out all the guards; breakfast was oatmeal—which I hated—and a miniature box of Cheerios with no sugar. *Who eats Cheerios without loads of sugar?* I wondered, as I dumped the whole tray in the trashcan, only hanging onto the orange and two single-serve apple juices that might be okay. That first breakfast was a solemn affair, and I was pleased to go back to my cell.

When the guards returned for exercise time, I noticed I was not dressed like everyone else. They were wearing black shorts, white t-shirts, and gray-ish tennis shoes, and I was still clad in my bright scrubs. One of the guards looked at me. "Gatsby, come down here!" he snapped. "And hurry. We better issue you some gym clothes."

I jogged down the stairs and signed a piece of paper to receive my gym clothes.

"Hurry, Gatsby," the officer yelled as I returned. "Everyone is waiting on you."

I jogged the rest of the way to my cell and changed quickly before lining up at my cell door like everyone else.

"For those of you who are new here, I'm Officer Haynes," the guard announced. "You can call me that, or Sir."

Some of the other inmates started snickering but seemed to be hastily cowed when Officer Haynes barked an order at them. "Stop all that laughing!" he growled.

"Yes, sir," a couple of the inmates replied in tandem.

Officer Haynes pointed at a couple of boys still smiling. "Alright! You already know—" He cut himself off, laughing. "Man, you guys are some straight-up haters. I'm trying to scare the new guys and you convicts are over here laughing. Well, as you can see," Officer Haynes continued, "since my plan to scare you is ruined... I like to have fun. And if you're respectful and do what you're supposed to, we won't have any problems. Now, if you decide to mistake my kindness for weakness, you'll find out real quick that it's not fun being on my bad side. Mr Johnson, in cell number thirteen, is it good being on my bad side?"

"No, Sir!" a boy yelled from inside his cell, his features flat against the glass of his window.

Everyone laughed at that, including me.

"Mr Johnson decided to be disrespectful yesterday, so he has a day of solitary today. He will eat in his room, have free time in his room, and will not be allowed out until breakfast tomorrow." Officer Haynes chuckled. "And that is only if he has his full, one-page apology written for me. It's easy! Be cool and we'll have fun. Be a jerk and *we'll* still have fun, but you won't."

Escorted by Officers Haynes and Samuels, we were taken to a basketball court. It was indoors too—probably because there was always snow on the ground. When we reached the gym, the officers made us get in a circle and do stretches, and then we played *Bump*—a basketball game in which the three lowest scorers had to bend over against the wall, while everyone else launched balls as hard as possible at their butts. It was easier in jail—the guards enforced the rules to keep it civil. On the streets, if you started the game, you couldn't quit. If you tried, or refused to take the hits, everybody jumped you. Not inside—the game was clean and fun, and afterwards, we retired back to our cells.

Once I was settled, a guard came by to explain the program to me. "In a second," he said, gesturing to the door, "you'll hear other doors open for them to go to classes. We have to find out if they're going to keep you here—see if you need to go to school or not."

I could hear the other doors popping open and nodded my understanding.

"While everyone else is in school, I'll allow you to come out of your cell and go to the library to pick out a book, if you want."

I nodded again. "I'm already bored," I told the officer, and sighed.

"Okay. Once we get everyone situated, I'll be back to take you to get your book. Oh, and just to give you a heads up so you don't get in trouble, you see that red button right there on the wall?"

"Yeah, I see it."

"Do not press that button unless it's an emergency. If you do, you'll be written up and lose privileges, and wind up like that boy in solitary. Not fun at all, trust me."

"I hear you," I said. I hadn't even noticed the button until he pointed it out to me. Now I was stuck in the cell with nothing to do, and I had to fight off the building temptation to press it.

*****

Gatsby chuckled at the memory.

"Hold on one second," Manuel Emotho cut in. "I want you to remember exactly where you're at in your story. We have to take a break so that Tremaine Sanderson can give America an update on the war—reckon there's some current news to get to, too."

As another reporter came on the set to present the update, Manuel and Gatsby stepped off. "This is really good," Manuel said, nodding at Gatsby. "I can picture it as if I was there." They took a seat in the staff room and listened as the reporter began to speak.

"Hello everybody, I am Tremaine Sanderson with CGX Global News, bringing you the *truthful news* from right across America."

Tremaine Sanderson was one of the news anchors at CGX, having only received his promotion two months prior.

"No good news today I'm afraid, folks. The war is taking its toll on the world. The Russian President has made a statement live on social media, saying that 'anyone who has not left the United States when the troops enter'—and trust me, they will soon be stepping foot on US soil—'will be at risk'. He has said that 'there will be no prisoners taken, and there shall be no quarter given. All Americans will be shot on site.'

"The Russian President continued on in his social media to say that 'the only sanctuary for Americans will be in Canada. If they're found anywhere else, they will be shot without question.'

"In other news today, seventeen Marines were killed near Iraq in a car explosion, and two hundred Army soldiers were killed near Syria, in Russia, and in Africa. Three Navy warships have been sunk overnight, and seventeen American Navy subs were destroyed. In addition, we have three hundred deaths in the air being reported by the Air Force.

"Let us have a moment of silence for our fallen troops, folks." Tremaine bowed his head, and Manuel and Gatsby followed suit where they sat.

"On a better note," Tremaine began again. "Our soldiers are doing very well in North Korea. They have boxed the North Korean leader in a cave where they plan to smoke him out. "Our troops have also defeated Iranian President, Jaha'Karr, and have at last seized control of Iran.

"Back on home soil here in the USA, we're reminded that, even while we're in the midst of World War III, the war between races has not been put on hold. Minorities are still refusing to sign up for the American draft and are firing at the police officers that are sent to arrest them.

Black Rights to Live organizations are still urging African Americans to attack Caucasians, police officers, and government officials.

"This is not fake, folks. This is not a joke—it's all real, and it's all happening. Since the election, many individuals in the Caucasian community have been shooting minority members—including *children*—at an alarmingly high rate. Those who are not involved are urging these shooters to stand down, after visuals of a Black father clutching at the lifeless body of his thirteen-year-old daughter emerge amid the rise of the *Make America White Again* slogan.

"I'm just a news anchor, but how is it that hatred for a color can be so strong that we can't even put it aside to win a war? This sickens me, folks, and this has been going on since long before the war began.

"Reports are coming in that large *Make America White Again* signs have been erected in many neighborhoods that are predominantly minority occupied areas, which has sparked further riots from within those communities. Word is that the sitting president has encouraged so much hate within our country—and around the world—that he's solely responsible for taking the world into World War III.

"We're hearing that some of the killings that took place overseas were inside jobs—Caucasian soldiers slaughtering the few minority soldiers who did sign up for the draft, and falsifying reports to say they went AWOL or were killed in battle. CGX cannot confirm these reports, but we can confirm that our source is a Caucasian soldier, so disgusted by what he saw that he left his unit shortly afterwards and became AWOL his-*self*.

"In response to these reports, the Army has made changes to its operations and the placement of US soldiers, deciding that segregation is the only way forward. It's been said many times, folks. We are fighting two wars at once. A world war, and a civil war between races."

As Manuel and Gatsby talked, the television crew cued them to return to the set, and they prepared to restart the interview.

CHAPTER TWO

"In five, four, three, two, one, and go." The director gave them the signal to begin. "Hello everyone. I'm Manuel Emotho from CGX, and for those of you just tuning in, we have Jonathan Gatsby here at the studio, giving his account of what happened to him leading up to his capture. Gatsby, who during his capture led as many as he could to freedom, is also speaking on behalf of Sergeant Dunham. For those of you who missed it, Mr Gatsby is still briefing us on the events leading up to his abduction and is right now telling us about his time spent in a juvenile detention center. Mr Gatsby if you would…" Manuel said, gesturing for Gatsby to begin.

"Okay," Gatsby said "Well, after the rules were explained, I went off to the library to look for a book. I looked for about twenty minutes before I found something wanted to read. It was one of my favorite books from elementary school, Johnny *Tremain*. The guard escorted me back to my cell, and I spent a few hours on the bed, reading."

*****

The buzzer for my cell rang annoyingly loudly and my cell door popped open. I walked up to the threshold but stayed inside because I wasn't sure if I was supposed to walk out without permission. "Mr Gatsby, come on down," the guard yelled. "You have a visitor."

Excitement shot through me, mainly because I was glad to be out of my cell again. Even though the book distracted me, I was still getting uncomfortable every now and then, and I'd switched reading spots quite often to try to prevent it. I hated being locked up in a small cell for most of a day. If it wasn't for the book, I would have gone crazy very quickly, what with my funny claustrophobia.

I walked down the steps to where the guard was standing. "I bet you're glad to be out of that cell, aren't you?" He asked me, laughing to himself. "I'm Officer Bojo Rafson," he said, and he reached out and shook my hand. "Your mom is here to visit you; you have one hour with her. When your time is up, one of the guards will bring you back in here and perform a thorough search to make sure that you're not bringing any contraband back into the center—not that we think your mom would try to do that, of course, but we have to follow procedure. You know how it is."

I shook my head and followed the guard as he escorted me to a room in a private part of the facility. When he opened the door, my mom was standing there, smiling at me, and I hustled in to give her a hug.

"Hey Jonathan, how are you?" she asked, as if I had just come home from vacation.

"I'm kind of locked up right now," I replied, flashing her a smirk. "But other than that, I'm fine." I shrugged. I couldn't help but notice a plastic bag on the table—it was just like my mom to bring me something.

"I brought you some snacks," she said, when she saw me eyeing it off.

Without hesitation, I picked up the bag and looked through it to see what kind of snacks she'd brought me. It felt like Christmas at the time, with a regular bag of nacho-flavoured Doritos chips, three small bags of Scooby Doo fruit snacks, a twenty-ounce Dr. Pepper, and a Twinkie. I got stuck into them quickly, while I talked to my mom, because I wasn't sure if I'd be allowed to take them back to my cell.

"So, I talked to your public defender and she said that the judge is going to release you tomorrow, but that the judge wants to talk to you before she does."

"About what?" I interrupted. "And if the judge is going to release me, why doesn't she just do it now?"

"Jonathan, you're lucky that they're releasing you at all. The judge initially wanted to charge you with attempted murder, but your dad talked her into letting you move to California with him. You'll be banned from the state for a year."

"Well, that's not really lucky, because Dad actually called his bosses at the DOD and they'll be forcing the judge to release me because I have the right to defend myself against racist terrorists." I scowled, the thought leaving a sour taste on my tongue. "Besides, they would have lost if they *had* tried to charge me with attempted murder, because that racist bum threatened to kill me right in front of the cameras, and a lot of witnesses."

"Yes, Jonathan," my mom sighed. "I agree with you, but the court does things differently. They're saying that, if he had pulled a gun on you, then it would have been self-defense, but since he didn't and he filed a police report and you didn't, that puts you in the wrong."

"Wow! You have to be kidding me," I replied, my frustration twisting my scowl into an angered grimace. "So, what was I supposed to do? Wait for him to kill me and then file a police report?"

"I know it's not fair, Jonathan, but I'm just telling you what they're telling me. Don't shoot the messenger, kiddo."

The rest of the visit was quiet while I ate my snacks. After an hour, I gave my mom another hug and was escorted back to my cell after Officer Rafson searched me for contraband. I started reading more of the *Johnny Tremain* book, and I enjoyed it so much that I hated having to put it down.

When five-thirty rolled around, the guards let us out for dinner, where we ate in what we called the dayroom. A few of the inmates that played on my basketball team sat next to me and explained how things were in the center, and the schedule for the rest of the day. After dinner, they told me we would have church service for those who wanted to go, and then we'd would have free time until ten.

For dinner, we had two large slices of ham, vegetables, a carton of two percent milk, and a pudding cup. I enjoyed the food well enough; it came from the hospital, which had the best in town—by far. Even though I was in jail, I enjoyed a king's feast while I played spades with the others.

After dinner, I skipped the church service and free time to read more of the book. I read until the cell lights went out, and when I had trouble sleeping—wired with excitement for the next day—I decided that I'd try to finish it, since I was more than halfway through. It was dark in the cell, but I found that if I stood on the bed, I could use the light coming in from the streetlamp to see the words stretching across the pages.

The guard tapped on my window while I was reading the seventh chapter. I held the book up so he could see that I was reading and not trying to escape, but he shook his head and gestured for me to lay down in bed. I did as I was told, but once he was away from my cell, I stood again and kept reading.

Somewhere around chapter nine, I heard the guard tapping on all the cell doors, yelling at each inmate individually to wake up, make their beds, wash their face, and get ready for breakfast. I skipped breakfast to read more of the book, more comfortable now I could sit at my desk.

The door to my cell popped open along with many others, and the guards began to call some of us out, one at a time. "Rivera, Jones, Gatsby, Conklin, Beard, Skinner, Shaver, and Alfredo, come on down and line up for court." I recognized the voice as Officer Samuels.

Officer Haynes accompanied him. "Come on, let's move a little faster. I know some of you aren't looking forward to being told you'll be here for the next two years, but you others heading home should be running at full speed because you're only hours away from freedom," he said, voice light with a friendly levity. "I'm begging you though, if you gotta stay here, don't go getting too comfortable and calling me Dad! Let's keep this professional."

I laughed along with the other inmates.

The officers cuffed each of our hands and legs, and then joined us to a partner by using a special chain that connected to the feet and the hands. They called it the Inmate Buddy

System. They then escorted us to a raggedy old school bus that they'd painted over to make it look better. It had the sheriff's symbol on both sides.

The ride was cold. It seemed the driver didn't turn on the heater even though it was minus twenty degrees outside. Once at the courthouse, the driver drove us to the back where more guards were waiting for us. They unloaded us, searched us, and escorted us to a big holding cell where we all had to sit until our names were called. My hearing was scheduled for eight-thirty a.m., which was good because I would be able to get it over with, even though I couldn't return to the detention center for release until everyone else's cases had been heard.

Shaver was called out first. When he returned, he said the court ordered him to serve three months of probation, and that he'd be released once he got back to the intake. I was called next. The judge gave me a good telling off for having a knife on a school campus, and for using it, whether I was threatened or not. I was given a one-year suspension from the state of Alaska, and told my dad had already paid for my ticket and I was set to head to California on the following Tuesday, which was eight days away. My record would only show a misdemeanor and the terms of my suspension.

CHAPTER THREE

"Wow," Manuel interrupted Gatsby's story. "If the ticket to California had been for the next day, you might not have been abducted! What are your thoughts on that? I mean, how does that make you feel?"

"To be honest with you, I'm glad that I was abducted," Gatsby said, watching Manuel with sincerity.

"Wait, wait, wait. So, you're glad that you were taken?" Manuel asked with a lopsided smile. "Just to be clear, you are glad that you were held as a prisoner of war in an *execution camp*, awaiting your own execution? No way; I don't believe you, you can't be serious. Because, as I just mentioned, you would have been executed, as in dead and not alive, if you hadn't escaped.

"If you will, please explain to me why you would be even a tiny bit glad about nearly being executed!" Manuel was grinning. He knew the answer but wanted the listeners to know as well.

"Well, it's simple really," Gatsby said, running a hand along the back of his neck. "If I hadn't been captured and made a prisoner of war, I would have never met Roxane. Roxane, whose last name is soon to be Gatsby." He winked at the reporter, taking another sip from his glass. "But she doesn't come into play until much later in the story, so you'll have to be patient."

"Well then, I think it best that we continue," Manuel said, "so that we can hurry up and get to the part about how you met Roxane."

"Right," Gatsby said still grinning—just the sound of her name brought a smile to his face. "Back to the story…

"After receiving my orders to make sure I was on that flight, I was sent back to the holding cell to await my moment of freedom. The guard there turned on the TV—turned on CGX News, and you were there, as the reporter." Gatsby nodded at Manuel.

"Yes, I'm aware," Manuel said, laughing. "As Ace Ventura said, 'you don't have to tell me. I was there.'" The two of them shared a chuckle.

"Just continue with your story as if I'm not here, so it will go smoother."

"Okay," Gatsby replied, "I'll do my best. Well, as we sat in the holding cell watching the news, an announcement came across the screen telling all stations to prepare for an important news update. Two of the guards even came into the room to watch it with us. It took about three minutes for the alert to go off, and then you popped up on the screen— "

"Real fast," Manuel interrupted, holding his finger up to silence me. "Don't say, 'you' when you're referring to me, because you have listeners tuning in every minute, and they need to know who you mean. Just say my name as if I'm not here." He settled back in his seat. "Sorry for the interruption, listeners. Please continue, Mr Gatsby."

"Okay."

*****

On channel forty-seven, Manuel stood outside the Global Headquarters of the World, surrounded by a growing crowd. He was waiting for the representatives of each country to come out and inform the world about the GHOW's decision about moving forward with Iran, North Korea, Russia and Syria who, along with many other nations, were threatening the United States. The hostile countries had good reason to be threatening us; the president was saying some jacked up stuff and it was spiraling out of control here at home, as well.

While everyone patiently waited to hear what the outcome of the vote would be, the television flashed back to the alert signal and the guards began chatting about what they thought the Global Alliance would do. Before they could finish talking, Manuel flashed back up on the screen.

"This is Manuel Emotho with CGX News. I'm standing here live at the Global Headquarters of the World where the Global Alliance, made up of leaders from nations all around the world, have met to discuss how to handle Iran, North Korea, Russia and Syria. North Korea and Iran have claimed responsibility for the recent attacks on Europe, Israel, and the United States, and Syria has proudly accepted responsibility for the attacks on London, India, and Australia.

"They have been in this meeting for several hours, but we have been informed that they have reached a decision and will soon be coming out to brief us on their solution. For now, we are as much in the dark about this as you are, viewers.

"What we do know so far is this: the FBI is not taking any responsibility. They have now accused Russia of hacking into our government servers. This comes on the back of recent accusations of the same against North Korea, and our ally, China. The biggest problem for me is what I think needs to be the main question. Was the president involved in the hacking that went on during his election, and afterwards, or not?

"This is beginning to get ridiculous. We, the American people, deserve answers and I'm not afraid to openly say that I, for one, would like to see a new president in the White House. President Brooks has accused immigrants from Mexico of being rapists and drug dealers. He has called Africans murderers, full of infectious diseases, and can be quoted as saying 'we need less immigrants from butt-hole countries like Africa and Haiti, and more immigrants from Norway.

"I'm giving the *Brookites* the benefit of the doubt here and hoping they didn't understand what he was saying—if they did, they'd have already been out in the streets, flying their confederate and Nazi flags in celebration.

"What the president really just said is that we need more white immigrants and less Black immigrants. I can't say if he's intentionally trying to start a race war, but he is definitely riling up the extremist crowds. We cannot tolerate that kind of speech from our president."

Manuel continued, and another half an hour went by slowly as we waited to hear what the Global Alliance had agreed to do.

"I wish they'd hurry up and show something," several inmates agreed, huffing in frustration.

"I'm telling you," one of the two guards replied. "Golf is more fun to watch than this with all the waiting!" As the alert screen flashed up again, conversation shot back and forth between the guards and inmates about what they thought was going to happen and. As they talked, Manuel flashed back into view.

"Hello again, viewers. My name is Manuel Emotho, and I'm reporting live from the GHOW headquarters in Antarctica. We are told that the president is about to give us a briefing on the current standings of the Global Alliance, as will a spokesperson or leader from each member country."

The reporters from across the globe were sectioned off by the countries that they represented to make it easier for the leaders to find them. The president walked onto the platform facing America's journalist, and approached the podium to speak.

Reporters began to shout questions at him, but with just a motion from his hand, they were silenced. "If I try to answer all your questions here today, one by one, I won't be able to leave this place for a week. So instead, I will just brief everyone on what went down in the meeting," he said. "To start thing's off, good evening." He—very awkwardly—picked up a bottle of water to drink from, holding it with three fingers on both hands and leaning his entire body away from it. He leant his face forward, stuck his sausage-like lips out, and took six really fast sips of water.

"To those viewers in the United States who have been waiting patiently to hear how we plan to stop these terrorist nations— trust me we have the best plan ever. No plan before, I tell you, has ever been as genius as this plan. Batman is probably sitting somewhere taking notes, our plan is just that good.

"Today friends, there is reason to celebrate, because I can bring you good tidings. It has been voted that the only way to keep our nation's citizens safe from more attacks is to annihilate the three countries involved in terrorist activities. No man, woman, or child is to be spared.

"The Alliance thought it best that we keep what we have planned secret, but I think everyone should be able to celebrate this victory with me. Twenty minutes ago, the news went up on my social media, so those who follow my Twitter account have already seen! If you don't follow me on Twitter, you're missing out on important presidential stuff. You can follow me at @Brookstherealpresident."

"Mr President, we're glad Twitter found out about it first, but for those who are still waiting, could you please elaborate more on the decision?" A reporter snuck in before the president could move on to talking about his Facebook friends.

"We have been killing terrorist after terrorist," the president began. "And all that ever happens is that their sons and their daughters are trained by their mothers to replace them! These kids eventually grow up holding grudges against the United States for killing their terrorist parents, and we can't risk them carrying out their plans for revenge!

"Right now, in the custody of our half of the Global Alliance, the leaders of these three terrorist nations are being held and will be executed at six o'clock in the morning. The executions will not be televised. I want to thank you all for your time and service to our great country. God bless you all and goodnight."

The reporters were once again frantically trying to pry more details out of the president, but he left without another word.

"Well, there you have it America. If you

want to be first to know important news about our country, add the president on Twitter," Manuel said, voice breaking in disbelief as he scowled in frustration. "I hope he doesn't plan to Tweet our launch codes," he added, right before the signal ended.

When we finally returned to the detention center, we all filed out of the bus in twos, some in more of a hurry to get inside than others. Once we were back inside, those of us who the court released were sent to our cells to clean them out, while they gave the rest of the inmates free time. Once my cell was clean, I sat around chatting with the others, waiting for my mom to pick me up. Because we were juveniles, we weren't allowed to leave on our own; we could only be released to a parent or guardian.

*****

"My mom eventually came, about an hour or so after everyone else had been picked up.

The sad part was that I knew she was going to be late, and I bet Officer Haynes a hundred push-ups that she would be. I believe in honoring bets, so I had to wait for him to finish the push-ups before I could leave."

Gatsby chuckled at the memory.

CHAPTER FOUR

"Hey, John!" My mom darted inside to collect me, and the excitement shone bright in her eyes.

"Hey mom," I replied as I walked out the door, leaving the detention center and planning to never return.

"Are you ready to get back out into the free world?" she asked, giving me two thumbs up and laughing at her own joke.

I didn't even reply. Instead, I just shook my head in shame at my mom's corny joke and walked with her to the car.

*****

"For the listeners," Manuel cut in. "Do you and your mom not get along?"

"We get along great," Gatsby said. "That was a corney joke." He laughed affectionately.

*****

The drive home was quiet except for a few random questions from my mom. Once at the house, things went back to normal real quick. My mom went into the kitchen and began baking; my brothers and sisters were nowhere to be seen, most likely still hanging out with their friends.

I sat down to watch a movie by myself on the living room couch. I don't know what time I fell asleep, but I woke up to my sister Natasha and her friends laughing loudly. I yawned and stretched before getting up.

"Johnny Baby!" my sister yelled, as she jogged over to me with her arms stretched out to give me a hug. Johnny Baby was a nickname my parents gave me when I was small, and it stuck. "When did you get out?" she asked.

"Well, I was supposed to be out at one-thirty, but mom didn't come get me until almost three o'clock."

Natasha let out a laugh, "Yeah that sounds like the mom I know."

"You would think after all that hard time I served she would have been early."

"What hard time?" Natasha replied, laughing even louder. "You weren't even locked up for a whole two days."

"Dang, Natasha," my brother Mark said, as he came up the stairs into our apartment accompanied by Benjamin and Athena—more siblings. "I could hear you from down the street."

Our apartment was on the second floor of a block, so once we walked through our front door, we had to walk up a flight of stairs to get inside.

"Anyways," Natasha replied ignoring Marks sarcastic comment.

"Oh my God, John when did you get out?" Athena asked with tears in her eyes. Athena was extra dramatic in everything she did, but we got along pretty good anyway. She watched me intently, waiting for a reply..

"Today," I said in a joking way. "And just so you know for the future, Athena, people normally cry when people go *into* prison. Not when they come out. That's like crying when a baby is born and then laughing when it dies." Laughter erupted across the room at my joke.

"Very funny, John," Athena said sarcastically as she wiped her tears and began sniffling.

Ben walked over and shook my hand with an air of professionalism. Even though he was only sixteen, he was super smart. He had a 5.0 in school and was in a program that allowed him to take college classes. I remember one time when he was sick, mom wouldn't let him go to school so he snuck out the window and walked himself there in freezing twenty-five-below weather.

Mark was different—more relaxed. He slapped me on the back and shook my hand with vigor. "What's good with you, bro?"

"Freedom at last is what's good with me," I replied.

Natasha did her scream–laugh again and I cringed. "I swear you be acting like you just finished a twenty year sentence, but you only did two days," she teased.

"Yeah, but don't forget. It was two days locked up with hardened criminals," I responded, looking at her pointedly.

Mark laughed again, shaking his finger back and forth. "No, no, no, bro," he said.

I scowled. "People don't start in the professional league, Mark. No. They start in little league and those that are good enough advance until they go pro. It's the same thing with inmates. They don't start in prison. They start in the juvenile system, and then advance to jail, and then prison when they're ready. As I said, hardened criminals." I said. "Really, the guy's in prison are nothing but advanced juveniles. You know what I'm saying."

"I'm afraid I don't, no", Mark replied, laughing more loudly.

I glanced at the clock on the microwave. It was seven in the evening. I yawned again because I was still tired, so I headed to my bedroom. The house had four bedrooms and, since I was the oldest, I had one to myself.

*****

"Mark and Benjamin shared one, Natasha and Athena shared one, and our mom had her own room, which she occasionally shared with Tony, or Ken, or a couple of guys named Ben." Gatsby laughed aloud while he was still in mid speech, "I'm just kidding. She's listening to this so I just figured I would mess with her a little bit."

Manuel busted out laughing, "You and your family seem pretty close. And you're the oldest, huh?" he asked.

"Yup. Nobody above me," Gatsby replied. "Just the way it should be."

*****

I fell asleep the moment my body hit my bed, and I had the weirdest dream as I slept.

I was walking down the street and, out of nowhere, a staircase ascended out of the ground. God's voice told everyone on Earth that only the first five people to make it to the top of the stairs would get into heaven, and the rest would be cast into the Lake of Fire. Everyone at once began to race up the stairs, trying to be in the first five. As I ran, I saw people tripping each other, and grabbing the back of people's shirts to slow them down. Fist fights were breaking out all around me. I only partially fought three people on my way to the top, because from the beginning I was at the front of the group, and I knew there was no time to waste on scuffles. I finished fourth, which was good enough to make it in. Once the fifth person made it to the top, the staircase began to disintegrate beneath everyone's feet, and they all fell into the Lake of Fire, just as promised.

The successful five entered Heaven, but it wasn't what I expected. It was a big hot tub, with only God and the winners present. A Bible was passed around and each person was required to read a chapter. One of the guys couldn't read, so God cast him out of Heaven and into the Lake of Fire in a glass cola bottle. If I bent in just the right way to look over the edge of the hot tub, I could see all the people in the Lake, and they were all in glass cola bottles. It was pretty weird.

*****

"God sent me back to Earth because I asked him to, after finding out that the world had not ended and seeing the girl that I was in love with. God gave me a choice; he said if I stayed in Heaven, I was guaranteed to remain in Heaven forever, but if I chose to go back to Earth there was no guarantee that I would make it back in—as a matter of fact, the stats were against me.

"I chose to go back anyway, as I was in love." Gatsby grinned.

"Suddenly, we were all standing outside at a school dance, but we never got in and I spent the rest of my dream with gang members chasing me. What can I say? I have a lot of action-packed dreams." He shrugged his shoulders.

"I see," Manuel responded, gesturing with his hands again for Gatsby to continue with the story.

*****

The next morning, on the way to the kitchen, I noticed my entire family were glued to the television screen. "What's going on?" I asked Ben, as I moved to stand beside him.

"We're watching the press conference. They executed the three terrorist leaders around six this morning, and speculation is that the Global Alliance will be splitting up over the executions. Also, Iran, North Korea, and Syria have recruited some of our allies—those who were against nuking the terrorist countries—and talked them into switching sides.

"Last night, India and Pakistan launched a heavy artillery attack on Israel. Cuba fired a nuke at New York City, which was intercepted, and Russia fired nukes at Great Britain, which were also intercepted. Currently, the countries still in the Global Alliance are in a meeting and we're waiting for news."

"Wait a minute," I asked, a little confused. "So, Russia has joined in with Iran and the other terrorist countries? After all that killing they did of terrorists themselves?"

"Well, that's what they're meeting for. To find out what's going on and who's in what alliance now that it's all changing."

As I inched closer to the television, I saw Manuel Emotho, the CGX News reporter, once again at his post.

"We're still waiting to hear more on this split treaty rumor that has been so widely spread but not yet confirmed. While it's not certain whether another worldwide alliance has been formed, it has been confirmed that several countries have left the treaty and have launched attacks on nations still in the existing Alliance." Manuel shared what he knew. "What should have been three swift executions of the leaders of three countries that have terrorized all civilizations across the world has turned into complication, and confusion abounds.

"If things continue on their present course, with countries sending missiles and bombs at each other, we may be stepping into a massive nuclear war that will be far bigger than anything we've seen before.

"If the countries that have left the Global Alliance have formed another, and are attacking countries in the original, we may be on the verge of World War III—here comes the president now!" Manuel yelled, cutting himself off in the middle of his sentence to try to have his question answered first by Brooks.

"Mr President!" he called. He could barely be heard over the shouts of the other reporters.

The President waved his arms to silence everyone. "There will be no news for now," he said. "Each representative will return to their country and break the news to their citizens. I will break the news from Air Force One. I believe that Manuel Emotho and the CGX News crew are here somewhere. If they would be so kind as to make their way up here to the podium and speak to the sergeant right here..." the president said, pointing to a man in a military uniform. "He will aid and escort you to Air Force One.

"Thank you to the viewers and media for your patience and for your time, and for hopefully coming to report the truth instead of trying to ruin my ratings with propaganda and lies. Have a blessed night everyone." The President waved again and then walked away from the podium in a hurry.

A man, who appeared to be Russian, ran up to the camera. He randomly handed Manuel his phone and instructed him to watch something on it. After Manuel stood silent in front of the camera for ten minutes, watching a video on the phone, he told the viewers that he would be going to commercial and would address us again within the hour.

"Wow, that was a big waste of time for everyone who's been sitting around waiting to hear what happened. Some people stayed up all night waiting for the executions and the news, just to hear that they have to wait longer to hear about what's going to happen," I said, as I walked away from the television and into the kitchen to eat.

After I had breakfast, I went back to sleep.

"John, John!" I heard Mark calling my name as he shook my shoulders to wake me up.

I just looked at him. I was so exhausted I didn't even have the energy to ask him what he wanted.

*****

"You know," Gatsby said to Manuel. "I never did get to hear what you watched on that video."

Oh, yeah, nobody did, I kept that info to myself. I guess I can give you a rundown on it now… The man that brought me that video was a rogue member of Secret Security. He resigned soon after, and it was rumored he suffered a mental break and wound up killing himself.

"The video showed some strange things—a lot of people of really high wealth, heads of notoriously powerful families...even some religious leaders. Most of them weren't country leaders, or even into the political scene.

"What was weird is that they were not orchestrating the meeting, but the leaders kept asking them what they felt the *Babylonian Alliance* should do. After I watched the video, the Secret Security agent told me that things are not what they seem, and that there are secret societies and powers that are really running everything behind closed doors. Before he could give me any more information, he grabbed his phone and took off running.

"I didn't follow up on any of it because he seemed a bit on the crazy side and I had trouble believing it. That's all that happened, though, so we better get back to your story, because time is almost up."

"Okay," Gatsby replied, starting right back from the spot he left off.

*****

"Come on!" Mark said. "CGX News just announced that the president will be explaining what happened with the Global Alliance meeting earlier."

"Oh, okay," I said, as I slowly rolled out of the bed, letting my feet fall lazily to the ground. It was difficult to walk from my bedroom to the living room. I only had one eye half open and bumped into the wall four times before taking a seat on the couch next to Natasha.

There was a commercial on the television, but as soon as it ended, the news came back on.

"This is Manuel Emotho with CGX News, and I have the honor of being the only reporter allowed to interview the president as he gives his report on what's going on with these bombings. We hope to also learn about what's happening with the Alliance, and whether or not there's been a new one formed. On that note, I hand it over to you, Mr President."

"Well," the president began. "The rumors are true. Another alliance has been formed, and what really chaps my butt is that the organizers of the new one are the three terrorist countries that we were supposed to nuke.

"That, however, is not the biggest problem. The biggest problem is that the number of bombings will be increasing, and the US is certainly one of their main targets. During the meeting, The New Alliance officially declared war on any country that is in alliance with the United States.

"They are blaming me," the president said, "for starting this war. They misunderstood my Tweets that said Muslims were terrorists, Blacks were uneducated and lazy, and China was taking advantage of us here in America. They misunderstood my comment about non-white countries being butt holes. But hey, it's not my fault that the Chinese are crooks, and non-white countries hobby in terrorism.

"They're trying to turn every nation against me for making statements that are facts. Yes, I'm the bad guy, because I pointed out China's corruption. So, in answer to the question looming over everyone's heads—" The President paused for a minute.

"Yes, World War III has begun."

CHAPTER FIVE

When the collective gasps began to die down, the president continued. "But," he said. "With my brains, believe you me, we will outsmart them and we will beat them around every corner."

"Surely you plan to go to intelligence meetings, Mr President?" Manuel asked. "Because up to this point, the intelligence agencies have publicly criticized your refusal to meet with them or listen to anything they have to say. Your insistence that *your* intelligence is superior hasn't earned you the confidence of the agencies, Sir."

"I don't know," the president replied, with a cocky rise of his brow and tilt of his head. "Intelligence hasn't really been reliable in the past, but we may meet a few times. We will see. What I will say is this," he said, making a sweeping gesture with his arms. "I have built up corporations, I have beaten many false charges against me, and I will lead our country to a victory. So, if intelligence can keep up with me, I am more than willing to keep them informed."

Manuel shook his head and sighed. Debate wasn't a productive option, so he changed the subject.

"Mr President, can you give us any information on which countries have left the treaty, and which countries remain?"

The President responded to Manuel's question with a blank look. "Well, let me see. There are hundreds of countries involved in the Alliance and naming them all would be impossible. But, I can give you the ones that I remember. The countries forming the opposing alliance include Germany, Japan, China, Vietnam, Russia, Pakistan, India, Afghanistan, North Korea, Iraq, Cuba, South Africa, Iran, Mexico, Turkey, and Syria."

Manuel's eyes widened even as he tried to hide his shock, and his forehead creased with worry. A touch of nervous excitement lit his expression, and he was able to continue. "Who in the hell do we have left then?" he asked, his professionalism lost in a swirl of trepidation.

"We have all the powerhouses on our side, don't you worry," the president answered. "Everyone who's anyone! Great Britain and France and Canada have declared themselves neutral, but we have Israel, South Korea, and most of the South American countries. We have more countries than I can possibly name still in the Global Alliance!"

Manuel inclined his head. "Wow!" he said, not even trying to hide the concern on his face. "Who declared war first, Mr President? You keep using the term opposing side with a smile, as if this is a chess game, or a board game. It doesn't feel as though you're taking this very seriously."

"When I used the term opposing sides just a second ago, I believe the word defined itself. The two alliances have both declared war on each other, and it looks as though the terrorists will finally get what they've always wanted: the world in complete chaos, destroying itself.

I take this war very seriously of course, but if you're asking... am I worried about an attack here? No, not even a little. Our country is the greatest country in the world. Our country has such great defense and such great offense; I can guarantee the war will not be fought here, but overseas. None of our families will feel the effect of the war, and I believe most of our soldiers will be safe. We have top of the line weapons. Top of the line bombs. We are like aliens to the rest of the world. That's how much more advanced we are than all those third world countries declaring war on us. If you look at history, outside the Civil War, a war has never been fought on US soil. We are impossible to penetrate."

"Mr President, there have been other wars fought on US soil, including the biggest one in our history, the Revolutionary War, where we won our freedom from England." Manuel coughed.

"Slipped my mind," the president replied, smiling smugly.

Manuel chose not to get into an intellectual debate with the president over the conceitedness and ignorance of the words he just spoke, and very wisely changed the subject. "How long, exactly, does the United States have to prepare for this war?" Manuel asked.

"There is no official set date for the war to begin, so we have to be ready to defend our country today. Like they say in boxing, *defend yourself at all times*. A draft will take effect immediately in every town across America.

Everyone from the ages of eighteen to sixty-five are required to join. There will be no test or any qualifications required. Just show up to the nearest signup in your counties."

"Why a draft if we're not worried, Mr President?" Manuel asked. "Do we not have enough soldiers?"

"Even though I feel we are safe, it's better to be extra safe than sorry. I doubt any of them will see any action but at least they'll be around if we need them."

"So, for the viewers that are just tuning in," Manuel spoke into his handheld mic. "Our country is at war, and every county will have a draft signup starting tomorrow. If you're wondering where to go for the signup, I would think that they would post it in the morning papers, or on your local news channel. This is not a choice, viewers. Everyone between the ages of eighteen and sixty-five must sign up." He turned back to the president. "Okay, next question Mr President. Why do you believe that the United States will be a main target in this war? Do you think that the new alliance will focus a lot of its firepower on the US, and try to knock us out of the war first?

"Obviously I believe that, because we are the most powerful nation on this planet. Other countries are envious of us, and they'll focus most of their firepower on us because if they can take us out the war will be over. I believe there is a lot of hatred and jealousy of me; of me being so rich.

"There's a lot of anger because I've pointed out all the very real corruption within other countries. We just need to be ready to defend our country. And since we're in this predicament, I'm declaring a State of Emergency, and assuming full control. I don't have time to argue and fight with all the little snowflakes that want to be heard."

"So, can you clarify what happens in a State of Emergency so that the viewers can gain a better understanding of what that entails?"

"Well, it's very simple. When a president declares a State of Emergency, he gains full control of the military and country. He no longer has to follow protocols for decision making. It means that I can do what I have to do to save the country without having to get permission. It means we will be operating it under Martial Law—"

Manuel cut in. "Martial Law doesn't automatically occur on the declaration of a State of Emergency, Mr President—as I'm sure you're well aware—"

"I will declare a State of Emergency *and* Martial Law! The right of *habeus corpus* has to be put on hold so that we can save our country!" The President stared at Manuel.

"Too bad that wasn't the case for the last president who tried to create jobs for our nation by taxing the rich, and was shut down by the very wealthy Republican Party," Manuel said.

"Exactly," the president quickly agreed with Manuel, "Speaking of that, I was just looking at that bill, and while in the State of Emergency, I will be passing it through, with the president's seal. Meaning, once the war is over and thing's return back to normal, the Republicans will not be able to touch that bill, and the rich will be taxed, and the people of America will have jobs."

"Are there any countries that the Global Alliance will be focused on during this war?"

"Oh, naturally we will be all over China, North Korea, and Iran. Those are the three main problems. I cannot tell you when, but we are going to neutralize those countries so bad they will be begging us to end this war within days of it starting."

"Now if the war does wind up being fought here on US soil, is there some kind of emergency plan in place to keep civilians safe from oncoming enemy soldiers?"

"I just found out about the war this morning, so I will have to get back to you on that issue. Once I'm back in the White House and I have had proper rest and time to think, I will come up with a plan."

"That's a fair answer," Manuel responded. "Now, I need to ask you this Mr President. You say once we're back, you'll be willing to raise taxes for the wealthy and rich, and lower taxes for the middle and lower classes?"

"Well, I wouldn't so much put it that way. My plan is to raise taxes on food stamps—like it or not, that's income. I don't believe it's fair that the lower-class workers barely doing enough to get by should have less taxes while the government babies them."

Manuel's mouth dropped open. He was definitely in shock at what he had just heard the president say.

"Also, the president continued, obviously not catching on to Manuel's facial expression. "I must meet with my staff before discussing raising taxes for the wealthy Americans, who work real hard to provide jobs for people who would starve otherwise."

"But you just said that you were going to raise the taxes on the rich, as soon as the war is over."

"No, I didn't, I do not recall saying that. I feel that you're putting words in my mouth—"

"Never mind," Manuel said cutting the president off in mid-sentence. "We'll just move on to the next question. I must've been mistaken." He was just about to ask another question when the president held his hand up.

"Hold on a second," the president said, as his cell phone rang right in the middle of the interview. "Hello— hold on just one second. Mr Emotho, I'm going to have to put this interview on hold and take this call. It's very important." He rose from his seat to leave the room.

"I understand," Manuel replied, rising to shake the president's hand and thank him for allowing him to do the interview. He turned to address the viewers. "Well, you heard it here first on CGX News. The world is at war. Remember to find out where the drafts will be taking place in your counties, and have a good night."

CHAPTER SIX

I stood up from watching the newscast and walked into the kitchen to make a snack. As I passed the microwave, I noticed that it was a two forty-five in the afternoon. "Hey, Mom," I said, as she brushed by me carrying a bowl of flour in her hands.

"Hey, John."

I walked around looking for something to snack on. "Hey mom, are there any of those little bags of chips left?"

"I don't know. I'm extremely busy right now, so you'll have to look yourself." As she answered me, she bumped into the kitchen counter, dropping the bowl of flour. "Dang it!" she yelled when it hit the floor and spilled all over the place.

I tried to help her clean it up, but whenever she was baking for a client every little thing was the end of the world. She grabbed the broom and dustpan from me and started sweeping vigorously, mumbling to herself as she cleaned. "Dang it," she continued. "This is just what I needed. I have a big order today, and I'm already behind. I can't do this. I need to get my own spot where I can work without distraction."

"You need to stop tripping, Mom. You're being over dramatic. That was just one bowl of flour and you have a whole ten-pound bag over there."

"Jonathan, please. Just leave me alone and let me work in peace without any more distractions. In fact, tell everyone else the kitchen is closed until I finish this order."

"You need to see a baking counselor," I said under my breath so she couldn't hear, as I walked out of the kitchen to warn the others. "Hey, just letting you guys know, Mom said to tell you the kitchen is closed until further notice," I yelled to my brothers and sisters as I passed through the living room. I walked to my room, content to lay around.

The weather that day was twenty degrees above zero outside, which was warm for Alaska in the winter. I didn't have the slightest clue as to where I was going to go, but I needed to walk somewhere. I walked to the Bred Meyer store, to Mal-Mart, the movies, and then back home. I laid around the house for the rest of the day, until I eventually went to sleep.

The next morning, I opened my eyes, yawned, and slowly crawled out of bed. I glanced at the clock to check the time. It was seven minutes past ten. I was hungry and wanted some breakfast, so I headed to the kitchen. Once again, my whole family was in the living room, glued to the television.

"What's going on in here?" I asked as I joined them. "Aren't you guys supposed to be in school right now?" I looked questioningly at my brothers and sisters.

"Aren't you supposed to be in school?" Natasha said back to me.

"No, you know that I don't go to school until after lunch," I said, smiling.

"They closed the schools down for the day," my mom answered me at last. "People were abducted from each country in the Global Alliance last night. The president received a letter from China saying that starting at noon today, a person from each of the countries will be executed every hour until the Global Alliance surrenders to the new alliance, which is going by the name of Babylon."

"That's crazy," I responded, shocked at the news. "Are they showing the executions on television?"

Before anyone could answer, Manuel began talking again. "To the viewers just tuning in," he yelled, trying to make his voice heard over the howling wind that was blowing so harshly it almost knocked him off his feet. "In less than two hours, the first execution is due to take place. From the information I've been given, it appears that the first victim is a young girl, no more than nine years old, from the United States. The US government says they will not be airing the executions but will honor and remember each of the victims whose lives will be lost on behalf of our country.

"The President gives his sincerest apologies to the families of the victims to come, but wants to remind the country that we are at war and surrendering is not an option for this country, or any other country in the Global Alliance. It looks like the ignorance will continue." Manuel shook his head as he stood in front of the camera, eyeballing signs that protestors were carrying.

"Turn the camera towards some of these signs so our viewers can see them," he said to his crew. "As you can see over here, the sign says, *White Immigrants Go Home*. And directly across the street," Manuel continued as the camera operator zoomed in on the signs. "One sign says *Make America White Again*, and another says *White Pride Needs Colored Slaves*. Here we are in the midst of World War III, and it seems we're gearing up for the second American Civil War at the same time" Manuel looked disheartened, but continued.

"These people on both sides need to leave America. If you're uncomfortable in a country filled with varied races, maybe it's you who should leave and go somewhere where your race is the only one, because here in America, all races are welcome.

"This racism has caused so many other countries to despise mainstream America. Even our allies speak against us because of it. The racism needs to stop. We need unity. We need it now if we want to survive this war." Manuel paused. "As you can see if you look up in the sky," he said, pointing. "The blue skies are already being blotted out by hundreds and hundreds of military jets flying over this windy city of New York—jets headed to defend our country against attacks from China and Cuba, who have war ships and jets on course to attack both the east and west coasts. If you haven't signed up for the draft yet, the time to do so is now.

"So much for the war not reaching the United States. I want every American that said we are too powerful, and that the war would never come to us, to look outside. Just yesterday, the president himself said the war would not reach us, yet here we are trying to defend our coastlines against oncoming attacks.

"Those who thought we were untouchable have been proven wrong. Rule number one:

never underestimate your enemy or overestimate your strength. The war ships were here to do a military show between countries, just four months ago. It would seem this war has been planned for a long time, because after the show, their ships remained docked for two months and then retreated just outside of the US territory zone, where they remained until yesterday morning.

"Get down to the draft sign up as soon as possible, viewers, because any person who has not signed up by the end of this week will face criminal charges. Once again, you have heard it right here on CGX News, bringing you live coverage of World War III."

After the news went off, Athena and my mom flipped through the channels to find a movie that everyone could watch.

*****

"The movie was about a rich girl whose family owned a very lucrative business, and a boy who was visiting his mother who was a maid for the family. The two fell in love, though their families are against their relationship. Typical chick flick," Gatsby told Manuel.

Manuel laughed, "My wife made me watch that movie and it's definitely a chick flick."

"Sure is," Gatsby replied, chuckling before he jumped back into telling the story.

*****

As we sat around the television watching the movie, the channel became fuzzy and we couldn't see anything for a few seconds. When the screen became clear, we could see a little girl standing in the middle of a room next to a table, which held an axe, a long knife, a whip, a blowtorch, a hatchet, and a rope. The little girl had tears running down her face and was pleading with the men who were in the room with her.

It looked as though there was an Afghan soldier, a Chinese soldier, and a Korean soldier—they were in full military uniforms. The leader of the group seemed to be an Iranian man, dressed in civilian clothing. The Iranian man began to speak to the camera in English, "We have given you plenty of chances and you have not listened. Maybe now you will take us seriously in our demands. In order to save this young girl's life, you must surrender to the Babylonian Alliance within the next five minutes, or else we will execute her on live television, with the entire world watching—including this young girl's parents. While we wait for your answer, we will allow her to explain who she is, and to plead with her country's government to do the right thing and save her life." He looked at the quivering girl before him. "You have four and a half minutes to convince your government to surrender and save your life. You may begin," he told her.

As the girl began to talk, my mom and two sisters began sobbing. I didn't cry, but I can't lie. I had to fight back my tears because you could feel the little girl's pain as she spoke.

"My name is Brianna," she said. "And I am nine years old and… and…" Brianna stopped as she began to cry harder. "Please. I don't want to die. Somebody please. Mom! Dad! Please," she yelled through her tears.

You couldn't help but hope that at any minute, a team of Navy Seals would show up and save her, but they never came. As Brianna cried and pleaded for her life, the men grabbed her roughly and forced her to the table in the middle of the room.

The screams that came from her mouth as they carried her were shrill with terror, and they cut right through you like a knife.

"No!" she cried. "Help! No! Dad! Please! I want to go home! Please!"

The man from China grabbed the nine-year-old's right arm and held it tightly to the table. Without hesitation, the Afghani soldier grabbed the hatchet off the table and hacked her hand clean off her wrist.

Her scream was deafening.

"What about now?" the Iranian man yelled into the camera. "What about now?" he repeated.

The Korean soldier grabbed the little girl's other hand and held it up as the soldier from Afghanistan high fived it with the severed one. They tried to make her watch as they cut the fingers off her severed hand but, mercifully, she fainted as soon as they began. They poured water on her head to wake her up, and once she had, they made her watch as they finished.

One of the soldiers grabbed the axe from the side of the table and swung it high in the air. She closed her eyes just as it fell towards her neck. Once, twice, three times it swung, and it became harder and harder to see what was going on as drops of blood smeared across the camera lens. It must have been a very dull axe, as it took nine swings to decapitate the girl.

*****

"I heard her family was watching, and the mom and dad were hysterical. Their family members had to hold them down as they screamed and cried."

"I remember that execution," Manuel cut in. "I was in New York, watching it at the headquarters for the Department of Defense. The government was doing all they could to kill the satellite signal—to stop the terrorists from transmitting the execution on everyone's televisions—but as you saw, they were unsuccessful.

"I'm truly sorry to cut your story short, but we're out of time, and will have to continue it tomorrow. For those of you who missed it, Gatsby has been telling us about the events leading up to his capture and, tomorrow, we will continue at the same time right here on CGX News."

Gatsby left Manuel and headed to the house where his mom and sisters were staying. He and Roxane were staying with them until the base could get a house prepared for them. They were told a house would be ready by the next afternoon. As part of the recompense for the time they were held prisoners of war, and for their rescue unit abandoning them, and as a reward for Gatsby taking on the job of guiding so many safely to a US base, the government was going to pay the mortgage on a house for up to three years and give them a weekly stipend for their first year back in the normal world.

*****

"Well, it's me, Tremaine Sanderson again, bringing you, America, *truthful news*. The only news for today is that the FBI still has not found any concrete evidence regarding who hacked our government's elections or their information grid. This is getting very frustrating. We need something soon, or they'll be forced to drop the case.

"Outside of that, we don't have any recent updates so we're going to walk back in time a little bit. We want to understand exactly what brought our country to the point that it's at right now.

"The whole Babylonian Alliance blame America for seeking war and has offered immunity to any country that pulls away from the United States. They have also offered immunity to all United States citizens, except for political figures and the president. That right there tells me that their problem isn't with America, but with our government, who I think the people of America also have a problem with.

"Leading up to his presidency, our President insulted African Americans, Mexicans, and the entire countries of China, Mexico, North Korea, Japan, Germany, and Iran. Although he first praised the Russian leader, he later called him unfit and insulted him with several social media posts.

"The Natives of this land were protesting the installation of pipelines on their land. They did not say that America couldn't build the pipelines, just that they couldn't do it on the small sections of land belonging to them, or over any rivers that flowed into their drinking water.

"The treaties made between the United States and the Native Americans long ago should have been the first thing to come up when this issue arose. If they just compared a map of the proposed pipeline and a map of Native territories, they would have seen that the land indeed belonged to the Native-American people and should be protected by a treaty made long ago.

"The police chief in North Dakota, very much a coward, called other states to support an attack on peaceful Native protestors. He had them shot with water cannons, rubber bullets, real bullets, shrapnel grenades, and tear gas, and then he sicked the dogs on them.

"The chief falsely imprisoned reporters for reporting the story—one reporter earned up to forty-five years in prison for trespassing on her people's land. *A dang news reporter*. Talk about ridiculous. Then they held the Native prisoners in dog kennels with no food or blankets. People died of hypothermia while in their custody. They need to be put in prison for that. I wish that sheriff would try to falsely arrest me—that would be the butt kicking of his life." Tremaine chuckled sadly.

"And what's maybe the saddest part is that our government allowed it to happen under the former President, and then again under the current President. Yet, we want to say that all the countries that stand against us are wrong about us; that they are the terrorist nations, and we are the best in the world. Racism makes this place terrible. We need to rid this country of those who can hate a person because of that person's skin color.

"It's my opinion that the other countries don't like us because we hated them first. Our current President ruined many relationships by making racial remarks, calling all Muslims terrorists, calling all Christians killers, calling all gays abominations, calling all Blacks monkeys, calling all media liars, and calling all countries not part of the United States third world countries. It was disgusting, and now we have to live with it.

"And now we find ourselves the main target of World War III. Those still keeping their alliance with us, with the exception of Australia and a few European countries, have mostly avoided attack. Most of the forces were directed at America or kept back in their home countries, and in their allies' countries, for strength at home.

"And we show our ignorance asking, 'Why?' Asking, 'How did this happen to us?' We thought we were invincible at home and it's that type of thinking that got us here to this point. Some people spoke up said that we need to stop making rude comments towards China and Russia. Others responded, "Oh its fine. Our Air Force is too strong, our Army is un-touchable, our Marines can't be beat, and we have the strongest Navy in the world.

"Our pride created our ignorance, and our ignorance is leading to the fall of our country. I want everyone at home to pay attention to how bad it is. With the exception of Alaska, we're darn near preparing to separate the states here in America by race, because different races don't seem to be able to live together any longer.

"Cops have been killing minorities since before the Civil Rights Movement, and I remember, in 2016, police killed seven hundred and eighty-three unarmed civilians and seven hundred and seventy-four of them got away with it.

"We've got Black Lives Matter, Blue Lives Matter, Native Lives Matter, and All Lives Matter movements. The one thing America cannot do is admit when they're wrong and unite together. It's really simple. There should have been no need for any of the Lives Matter movements. If a Black person commits a crime without a weapon, the cop's job is to take him to jail, so a judge can sentence him. If that Black person resists arrest, the use of batons, pepper spray, and tasers can be employed, as long as over-use and dangerous misuse is monitored. Trained officers should never use guns, unless a gun is being used against them.

"If a police officer kills someone unarmed or commits a crime, jail should be the only option for them. And if the courts upheld the law with corrupt police officers, things may not have gotten as bad as they have between minorities and cops.

"The President won the election on a racial platform, calling all Muslims terrorists, all Mexicans who come across the border drug dealers, and by saying all Blacks are uneducated and live in ghettos. On that platform, many whites and upper-class Latinos voted for President Brooks. Then, it got worse. His only endorsements came from the leaders of the KKK, which really heated things up between the president and minority communities.

"After he won, he elected KKK leaders to office, chose famous wrestlers for cabinet positions, picked a man who hated Native Americans as head of Native Affairs, and elected someone who refused to believe in climate change to protect the climate.

"Still, we here at CGX tried to calm things by suggesting that we respect that he's the president now, and that we should wait calmly for change. Obviously, people didn't heed our words. They began blocking highways with protests, resulting in many being run over. Supporters of the president attacked minorities, and minorities attacked supporters of the president—Brookites.

"The problem that came about was this. The racists knew who most of the minorities were, but the minorities decided to assume that all white people are President Brooks supporters and attacked them all. News flash—many white women did not vote for President Brooks. Many white males did not vote for President Brooks. Many white college students did not vote for President Brooks. Many innocent people were attacked.

"With all of that going on, President Brooks decided to use social media to insult multiple countries, which resulted in North Korea, Iran, and Syria committing the terrorist attacks that they did. Our country has had problems before with other countries, but the problems were always solved diplomatically. President Brooks' social media posts are what caused the biggest world war in the history of this planet, and man oh man are we are losing this war bad.

"We thought the enemy was backing off, but they weren't, they were just reconnecting with more enforcements. Three times the number of missiles are being shot at us right now than there were in the beginning, and some are actually able to get past our missile defense systems. This morning, people were killed right here, after President Brooks so arrogantly guaranteed that no blood would be spilled on American soil.

"That is all the time that I have with you. I want to say thank you for listening, and you and your families stay safe, and goodnight."

*****

Agent Smith walked past reporters, as they tried to get an answer out of him about the investigation into the Russian hacks. "Currently, we have several of the president's campaign managers in custody. It is clear that they colluded with Russians to hack our systems."

"I knew it was the Russians!" somebody yelled from the crowd.

"You're a liar!" someone else shouted. "The Russian leader did not interfere with the elections. He personally assured me of Russia's innocence, and I believe him!"

"Yeah!" a few people shouted together.

"Shut up, you idiot Brookites!" another yelled into the growing crowd.

"Enough," agent Smith said calmly to the crowd, holding up his hands. "We have confessions from four of the six people we have in custody, so we know for a fact that they're guilty. They're working with us to arrest others involved. The hacks they've mentioned so far, however, were smaller ones that focused on social media and the election. They were carried out by teens hired by the detainees, not the actual Russian government.

"We still need to find out if Russia hacked into our secure servers and stole classified information or not, and if it wasn't them, we need to find out who did it. This will be a very long investigation, and we'll let you know when we have more." Agent

Smith walked away from the press and over to his boss, Agent Conlin, who had assigned him the case.

"We need some results right now. Even with their confessions, I don't believe the Russian government is linked to these hacks. I need everything that you have on this case on my desk before the end of the week. No more delays."

"Yes, Sir," Agent Smith sarcastically replied to his boss. He was irritated because his superior knew how difficult it was, yet he was succumbing to pressure from the media and White House. Twice now, Agent Smith's job had been threatened. He wished that this damn case had never come across his desk.

Agent Smith went back to his office to see if he could find some answers. Over and over again, the same results kept reappearing. Russia hacked the election. It looked like they didn't do it alone though. His results also pointed to North Korea, Japan, Antarctica, the Secret Security Agency, China, and just about every country on the planet.

He wants results, does he? Agent Smith thought. *Fine, I'll just print off these results straight from the computer, showing that we were hacked by every nation on the planet.*

He printed the results but hesitated to take them to his boss's office right away. He had in his hands over three thousand pages of hacks linked to various countries, though most were linked directly to Russia and North Korea. Agent Smith could not figure out why, if the computer could tell which country they were hacked by, that it couldn't locate any specific server used to hack the system. This fact ate away at his soul. Something didn't seem right about it.

He had handled a similar case years prior, and he was able to find the IP address of the computer that was used to hack the US government's intel only seconds after locating the country. This time, for some reason, he had located the country months and months ago, but no IP addresses could be found.

"I wonder," Agent Smith said out loud to himself. He talked to himself a lot to solve puzzles. For some reason, hearing his thoughts out loud helped him sort out the facts. He went back to his desk and plopped back down into his chair. Following a hunch, he traced all computers—local and worldwide—connected directly to the US government's IP address.

"Wait, what's this?" he questioned, as he scrolled down the list. A few of the computers connected were not government computers but belonged to private citizens.

He hit the print button and, as the print job finished, he decided to take it to his superiors and ask about a few of the strange connections. He scrunched up his face in confusion as he scanned the printed sheet for the individual IP addresses he'd just seen; they were not there anymore. He quickly jumped back on the computer to try to re-print the list but, as he scanned the screen, he realised they were no longer there, either.

Agent Smith sat back in his chair; he didn't know what was going on but, whatever was happening, it was an inside job. He began wondering who he could possibly trust; who in government authorized private citizens access to the IP addresses for the Department of Defense and other top level departments. Who and, just as intriguingly, why? Whoever he was looking for had more control over his computer than even he did.

*****

As Gatsby walked through the front door, his arms flew up in defense as a room full of people jumped out from all around him, screaming, "Surprise!" catching him completely off guard.

Gatsby had been back for only a few days. His family hadn't even known that he was coming home until he showed up at the front door. When they saw him, his sisters and mom were hysterical, crying, and hugging him repeatedly. His dad called him on his mom's phone, and they had a long but great talk. It felt long overdue. His mom had been even more excited when she'd discovered that he had a girlfriend, and that he'd brough her home with him, and it looked as though she'd decided to throw him and Roxane a welcome home party.

He shook hands with a lot of government officials and soldiers. It seemed that the whole town was coming in and out of the party. He felt a bit out of place and even more uncomfortable when he couldn't find Roxane. "Where's Roxane?" he asked his mom, when he was finally able to sneak away from the crowd. "I haven't seen her at all during the party."

"I honestly don't know, John. I haven't seen her either," his mom replied.

He sighed and, after another twenty minutes went by unsuccessfully, left the party to find Roxane. He looked for an entire hour but had no luck. He was about to give up searching when he turned and saw her walking towards him. She had on a dark, ocean blue dress with a crystal-crested split line inching up her thigh. The gold and diamond jewellery that adorned her was sparkling enticingly.

She was beautiful.

Her straight, dirty-blonde hair was down, and it shined like pure gold in the lamp light. They didn't give out shampoo or brushes in the execution camp, so Gatsby never saw her hair in its purest form because it was always tangled and dirty. Her eyes sparkled more than a trillion stars stretched across the night sky ever could, and he stared speechlessly as she approached him.

"Your mom said you were out looking for me."

"Yeah, I didn't see you at the house," he responded, swallowing the lump that had risen in his throat when he saw her. "So I wanted to find you and make sure that you were okay."

"Aw..." Roxane said, blushing. "You always know how to make me feel special." Her hands grasped each other tightly, and her lips quivered in the cold as she pushed her hair back over her shoulder.

"Well, that's because you are special. If you weren't, I would have left you back at the execution camp," Gatsby said, smirking.

"Shut up!" Roxane gave him a playful swat on the shoulder as she laughed. "Come on," she said, as she grabbed his arm and pulled him in the direction that she wanted him to go. "Close your eyes."

"Where are we going?" Gatsby asked.

"Quit being nosy," she replied. "You'll see in a moment when we get there."

"Um, okay, but it's cold out and I was walking for over an hour looking for you. I might know a shortcut to where we're going," he said, hoping Roxane would fall for his cleverness and tell him where she was taking him. Gatsby hated surprises. He hated not knowing stuff. Even during Christmas, ever since he was little, he would always want to sneak a peek at the gifts.

"Sorry, but not telling you. You'll just have to suck up your impatience and wait and see," Roxane replied. He couldn't see her face because she was forcing him to walk with his eyes closed, but he could tell by her voice that she was smiling.

"Well let me give you my jacket," he said. It was thirty degrees above zero, which was warm enough for Alaska at that time of year, but their bodies were still adjusting to the cold.

Gatsby opened his eyes to take his jacket off and hand it to Roxane, who slipped it over her arms, blushing as she smiled at him. Her hair sparkled in the moonlight, as if it were enchanted, and he couldn't help but admire it. He pushed it from her face with a reverent finger and smiled back.

Her silly smirk broke the tension and she noticed that he was looking around. "You'll find out when we get there, so just close your mouth, close your eyes, and get to walking," she ordered.

He did as he was asked, but he wondered what she was up to and where she was taking him. The two of them walked to the other side of the base, to a shutdown high school.

"What are we doing here?" Gatsby asked with a look of confusion on his face. He had opened his eyes for a peek.

"Close your eyes," Roxane said again, giving him a warning look and a hard punch in the shoulder.

He did so reluctantly.

As she walked him into the building, he tried to peek a few more times, but she was keeping a close watch. If he so much as blinked, her hand was rushing to cover his eyes. "Calm down, Jonathan. We're almost there," she said gently, when he asked if they were far away.

Gatsby heard a door open in front of him and he was dying to open his eyes and look. "Can I open my eyes now?" he asked.

"If it will stop you from asking a million more times, then yes," Roxane answered with excitement as she giggled to herself.

Gatsby opened his eyes and looked around. They were in the gym, but it had been changed into a diner. In the middle, there was a table with a purple tablecloth lying across it. There were two lit candles and a large projector screen hanging down from the ceiling. "Wow, this is nice," he said as he looked around. "What's going on?"

"It's our first date," Roxane answered, grabbing his hand and pulling him towards the table while the slight hint of a blush colored her cheeks..

He looked at her, one eyebrow raised quizzically. "First date?" he asked, confused. "We kind of have been dating for over two years now."

"No, we have been boyfriend and girlfriend for two years now but have never been on a date, because we were either in that awful execution camp or running through Africa from all the people and animals trying to kill us."

"I never even thought about it like that," he said, smiling.

"Of course, you didn't. You're a man, and men don't think." She smirked at her joke flirtatiously.

As they sat down at the table in the center of the gym, Gatsby's mom walked in holding two menus. "One for you," she said as she handed them out. "And one for you. I'll be your waitress this evening. What would you like to drink? And I do take tips." Gatsby's mom and Roxane laughed at her joke. Gatsby laughed too, but he was laughing at them laughing and not the corny joke.

"You guys have no sense of humor," he said as he chuckled to himself. "I'm going to have to put you both through a comedy class." He looked at the menu to choose a drink. "Mom, really? The menu is blank!"

"I know! I couldn't find a pen, and we only have spaghetti and lemonade anyways..."

Gatsby looked at his mom, biting his lip trying not to laugh. "I'll have the lemonade, please," he finally managed to get out."

"And for you?" Gatsby's mom asked Roxane.

"I'll have the...," Roxane paused to look at the blank menu. "Yes; I will have the lemonade as well, please."

Her beauty was too much for Gatsby to bear. He couldn't believe that something as tragic as becoming a prisoner of war, waiting to be executed, could have resulted in the best thing that had ever happened to him: Roxane.

He shook his head at Roxane and laughed. "I see that you and my mom are going to get along perfectly."

"Okay! I'll get your drinks. Just let me know when you are ready to order."

"I like your mom," Roxane said as Gatsby's mom walked off. "She's sweet."

"Yeah, she is," he agreed. "Although, she could have just brought the drinks with her the first time." He smirked. "So, you went to all this trouble for me, huh?"

"Not any more trouble than you went to for me. You wanted us to leave the camp earlier, remember? But I wouldn't leave everyone so, instead, you stayed. If it wasn't for you, we'd all be dead. I wanted to find a way to do something special for you, and this is what your mom helped me come up with. I know, it's a cheap date, but I'm having fun and to me it's a memory. And a good one."

"I know you love me," he said. "And you actually saved me. You saved both of us really. If just the two of us had left, the lions would have eaten us both because we would have been the only two targets. Not saying, I'm glad the others were eaten… I'm just saying we would both be dead right now if we'd escaped without the whole group."

"Oh my God. I'm responsible for them dying!" Roxane said, holding both sides of her face in shock.

"Roxane, slap yourself. We didn't escape on our own. That Army guy came and got us, and then abandoned us. If he hadn't abandoned us, we wouldn't have gotten lost and nobody would've been killed by the lions. I was trying to pay you a compliment!"

"That was an epic fail, then," she said, giving him a weird look that made him feel guilty. "But yeah, you're absolutely right. It was his fault, one hundred percent! And I hope he gets court marshalled," she said angrily. "Or eaten by a lion himself." Her eyes glowed with introspective mirth and for a second, Gatsby stopped to imagine what she was thinking.

"Yeah, but back to the present," Gatsby said. "I really appreciate you going to all this trouble for me. It's amazing."

"Thank you," Roxane replied, staring into his eyes. He stared right back into hers like he always did, as if it were the first time he ever saw her.

"I love you," he said, voice thick with emotion. "And I want you to be my wife."

"Are you asking me to marry you?" she asked, shock lighting up her face.

"Yes, I am. And, although I don't have a ring for you, or money, and we're... in the middle of a war, I have been in love with you since the day they placed us in the same vehicle to take us to the execution camp. I would rather have stayed there and been executed than to have escaped without you. At least there, I would've died knowing that I had found a love that most people search their whole lives for, in vain. They'll never find it now, because that love belongs to me. Roxane, please be my wife?"

"You fall in love too easy," she said, smiling.

"Yeah, it seems to run in my family."

"Yes, I will marry you." Roxane's eyes started to get watery. "I will marry you," she declared, rushing to his side of the table to wrap him in a great big hug.

His mom returned and ruined the moment as they kissed. "Here come the drinks," she said loudly, as she entered the gym with two plastic cups full of lemonade. She hadn't noticed the intimate way they were hudled together.

Gatsby and Roxane sat back down in their seats at the table.

"Thank you," Roxane said as Gatsby's mom handed them their drinks.

"You're welcome. Are you ready to order?"

"Sure thing," Gatsby answered, with a big smile on his face. "I'd like to order the spaghetti for both of us," he said. "And give us a bottle of your finest lemonade. We have reason to celebrate!"

"Really?" Gatsby's mom asked. "And what are we celebrating?"

"He proposed to me, and I said yes!" Roxane exclaimed joyfully.

"Really? Wow! I would say it's fast, but I guess it only feels like that to me because you guys just got back here. It's easy to forget that you've been dating for quite a while now. Oh! I am happy for you both!" She gave them each a kiss on the check. "So, now you two have a wedding to plan."

After dinner, Gatsby, his mom, and Roxane, cleaned the gym together before heading home. This time, they rode in a car with Gatsby's mom, so they didn't have to endure the weather walking back to the house.

Gatsby looked at the clock on the wall as he entered the house. It was late—almost three in the morning. He was exhausted and told his mom goodnight as he and Roxane walked to his room.

After some time, he fell asleep. He had to be at the newsroom by nine in the morning to do what had become his daily story time with Manuel.

He awoke the next morning at around seven-fifteen and began to get ready as quietly as he could. Roxane was still sound asleep, and he didn't want to wake her. He watched her for a few minutes as she slept. She was his everything.

He wished desperately that he didn't have to go in for the interview. He wanted to get back in bed and spend the morning cuddling with his girlfriend, but he knew she'd be there when he got back so he left for the newsroom.

"Man, its cold out here," he said to himself. "It has to be at least thirty degrees below zero. He walked right back into the house and layered on as many clothes as he could to stay help him stay warm on the way to the studio.

*****

"Smith, I read your reports this morning," FBI Director Conlin said, slamming a stack of papers on Smith's desk. They're one hundred percent contradictory of each other. Half your reports say Russia has been hacking into our nation's security, while the other half accuses China, North Korea, Iceland, and just about every other nation I can think of! I even saw Antarctica on the list, and the Secret Security Agency—what's that about?"

"Sir," Agent Smith began. "All I did was copy the information right from the computer so you could gain an understanding of what exactly is causing this investigation to take so long. I put everything that popped up on your desk. Trust me, Sir, I noticed that issue as well—along with few other things—which is why I am researching it right now."

Director Conlin looked at the numbers on the computer screen. "Okay," he said, after a moment of silence. "Get in touch the minute you find out anything I need to know. This country is in uproar and we need to find out who's hacking our government, before we wind up in a government shutdown."

"Sir, I'm doing the best I can. You see all this mess on this computer that I have to sort through. I can tell you this: so far, out of everything I have gone through, I cannot find any signs of our system being hacked at all."

"What do you mean?"

"Well." Agent Smith ran his fingers through his hair and began to answer his boss. "Normally if we're hacked, if we can track the country, we can track the IP address as well. Well, not in this case;

there's no IP address at all showing up. So I looked further and I noticed that there were private IP servers connected directly to our government's IP address, and when I tried to print it, nothing showed up. I went to print it again, and those addresses were gone from the computer, too."

Director Conlin thought to himself for a minute before responding. "As soon as you find something, I want it on my desk. The media and congress are jumping down my throat, demanding I find something sooner rather than later, and the president is threatening to fire me just about every other day if I don't put an end to this investigation. You can see the need for swiftness, I'm sure."

"First thing sir, it'll be on your desk," Agent Smith responded with a curt nod to let the director know that he did indeed understand the pressure.

"You're on to something, Smith, and if it is an inside job you need to be careful; there are people and organizations that are nearly untouchable."

"I understand, Sir."

"Not yet you don't," Agent Conlin replied, "and I pray you never do."

Agent Smith stayed up late into the night, researching every social media post he could find, and attempting to trace them to a domestic IP that someone was using to unite the people against the government. Halfway through his research, his screen went black. A message popped up on the screen.

Your mom and dad have just been killed. Your wife and kids are next. We are above your pay grade, above your government, and that is all you need to know. You will pretend to keep looking and will report that Russia is responsible for the hacks if you wish to protect your family.

Agent Smith frantically searched his pockets for his phone and scrolled down his contacts .

Ring… Ring… Ring—Ring… Ring… Ring… his mom's phone kept ringing, but nobody answered.

He ended the call. His hands were shaking, and his heart felt like it was slowing down and dying. Quickly, Agent Smith pulled himself together and called Director Conlin.

"Hello?" Director Conlin answered his phone. "Did you find something?"

"Sir," Agent Smith cut him off. "I need to leave for a bit. I need to go check on my parents."

"Why? Has something happened?"

"I don't know yet, Sir." Agent Smith hesitated to tell Agent Conlin about the message. What if he was in on it? Or worse, if they'd been able to get into his FBI computer—which was encrypted with the highest level of security—they'd likely already tapped the phone. He took a deep breath. "Sir, I have reason to believe that they're dead, but I need to go and see." He spoke quickly, unspent emotion crashing over him in waves, leaving his stomach roiling.

"Agent, use your head. You're in the middle of one of the most important cases ever to come across your desk. Someone is trying to shut the American Government down. See how you called me? Call someone to check on your parents. Better yet, call the police so you'll know for certain, before you waste precious company time that's greatly needed right now."

Agent Smith nodded into the phone. "Yes Sir," he said, swallowing. He had no idea why he didn't think of calling the police to check on his parents. He decided to call nine-one-one, because his parents' local police station would be closed.

"Nine-one-one. What city and state? Is this an emergency?" the emergency line operator said when they answered the phone.

"Yes, it's an emergency," Agent Smith responded, "and this call is for Idaho Falls, in Idaho."

"Is this for the police, fire department, or do you need an EMT?"

"The police," said Agent Smith, irritated even though he knew the questions were protocol. He couldn't help but feel it would help if the operators would start shutting up and just letting the caller tell them why they called.

"Okay," the dispatcher's voice came through the phone, "transferring your call now."

"Nine-one-one, what is your emergency?"

"My name is Alex Smith. My badge number is FA7654. I work for the FBI, and I'm calling from Washington, DC. I have reason to believe that my parents have been murdered and I need officers to immediately head over to check." His hands shook and the line crackled.

"Okay, what's the address?"

"One-three-triple-four, Martin Luther King Boulevard, Idaho Falls."

Agent smith listened as the dispatch made the call to on duty officers. "This is dispatch to all cars, we have a ten-forty-two on the family of a law enforcement officer. He believes his parents to be dead." He gave them the address.

The phone went silent for a second as dispatch waited for an officer to respond.

"This is car thirty-seven. We are in proximity to the address and will proceed with caution to the family's location."

"Sir?" Dispatch came back to Agent Smith's call. "We have a unit heading over there now, and they will do a check. If you can leave a number that you can be reached at, we'll notify you as soon as our officers let us know something."

"Okay, thank you," he replied. He wanted to stay on the phone, but he knew they had to free up the line for other emergency calls. He decided it would be best if he stayed off the computer, since it had been hacked. In the back of his mind, he felt his parents were still alive and that someone was just messing with him.

Ring... Ring... Ring... Soon after, his cell phone began to ring. He quickly picked it up, seeing that the number was from the Idaho Falls area. "Hello?—Hello?" he said and then repeated, before the person on the other line could answer.

"Hello, Agent Alex Smith?" a voice responded.

Agent Smith replied. "Yes, that's me."

"This is Detective Brandon Simple. I'm here at your parents' house—"

"Are they okay?" Agent Smith cut Detective Simple off in the middle of his sentence. "Is everything okay?"

There was a pause for a moment, and Agent Smith felt the blood rush from his face.

"No," Detective Simple said at last. "No, I'm sorry Agent Smith, everything isn't okay. As you already surmised, your parents are dead. What I need to know is how you knew they were going to be killed. I'll be the lead detective on this case, and any information you can provide me with right now will help us find who did this much faster. I'm going to need you to come in and make a statement."

Agent Smith sat frozen in his chair. It was no prank; his parents really were dead. He really did not want to know how.

"Are you still there? I know it's a lot to process," Detective Simple's voice came through the phone, after a long moment of silence.

"Yes, I am," Agent Smith finally responded. "There isn't much I can tell you. I received a tip that they'd been killed, and I immediately called nine-one-one because I'm out of state. I don't know who did this, but whoever it is, I think they're above both our paygrades. Be careful, Detective. Take more caution than I did. I was warned to be careful by my boss, and I didn't listen and got my parents killed."

"Well, Sir, I appreciate your concern, but I would appreciate it even more if you allowed me to do my job," said Detective Simple.

"No offence to you, or any local police officers, but if we—the Federal Bureau—cannot find these guys and they can do this to an FBI Agent, I highly doubt your department will be able to handle the case any better."

"It's funny, isn't it? How someone always says no offence to excuse something offensive that they're about to say," Detective Simple replied. "Well, I figured you'd be difficult, because we basic police officers know how you FBI look down on us, so I've already gotten a warrant from a judge to bring you in. You can come on your own, or officers will be down there to bring you in by force."

"Damnit!" Agent Smith yelled into the phone. "You don't know what you're getting into! They're going to kill my wife and kids next! I need to do my job down here. We're in the same field, so I know you can understand."

"Well, Agent, we have a double homicide here in our peaceful city of Idaho Falls, and the only lead we have right now is you, so I'm sure you can understand why I need to bring you in for questioning. You can get back to your job afterwards."

"You do what you have to then, because I'm going to do what I have to here to protect my family."

There was a crash as Agent Smith thumped his hand against the table, hanging up the phone in anger. His parents were dead, and it looked like he was soon to be a wanted man. He needed to get his family to safety, and then go off the grid for a while.

He rushed out of the office, stopping to make a withdrawal at an ATM on the way home. He had to pick up his wife and kids.

"Get up!" He yelled as he entered his home. "Everybody up!"

His wife came rushing down the stairs. "What's wrong?" she cried, with a frightened look in her eyes as she watched her husband rush around in circles, covering every piece of electronic equipment in the house.

"No time to explain right now. We have to go. We're going to get on a plane and go to your mom's in Rhode Island."

"Wait, what?" His wife asked, confused. She was about to say more, but her husband gave her a very stern and scary look, shaking his head and signaling for her to be quiet.

"Not the time to talk, Deborah," he mouthed to her quietly.

The kids came down the stairs rubbing their eyes. Their expressions soon became bewildered as they noticed the television, computer, laptop, and video game systems had been covered with thick blankets.

"Kids, bring me your phones!"

Janice, who was eleven, and Malachi, who was thirteen, both ran upstairs to get their phones. As they handed them over to Agent Smith, he turned to his wife.

"I'm going to need yours, too."

His wife, Deborah, hesitated but slowly handed her husband her phone. Agent Smith next took his phone out, adding it to the pile. He placed all four of them into the microwave and turned it on, setting the timer for thirty minutes.

"Okay, let's go."

"Where are we going?" Malachi asked.

"I can't tell you yet," Agent Smith said to his kids. "A bit of an adventure."

"Don't the kids need clothes?" Deborah asked.

"Trust me when I say we have no time."

A siren sounded very quietly in the distance,

and Agent Smith knew in his heart exactly where that police car was heading—right to his house. The kids and his wife quickly got into their car and he jumped in the driver's seat. He backed the car out of the garage as quickly as he could, leaving his headlights off to avoid having the satellites above spotting their vehicle.

As they began driving away, at a rather fast speed, his wife looked up at him, concern etched into the way she studied him. She started to ask again where they were really headed, but before she could get two words out, he cut her off.

"I'll tell you later," he told her, as he pulled up to another ATM. He withdrew a larger amount this time. That should be enough, he thought to himself. He'd pulled a large wad of cash from the emergency stash he kept in their basement too, and calculated that they had almost ten thousand dollars on them. That would definitely be able to hold his family over until the situation cleared itself up. Also in his emergency stash were fake IDs, fake social security cards, and fake birth certificates. Agent Smith had long prepared his family for a day like this, in case it ever came.

He pulled up to a warehouse and, without a word, he got out of the car, telling his wife and kids to stay put. Twenty minutes later, he came out of the warehouse driving a beat-up Dodge Chrysler van with an intense look on his face.

"Get in—hurry up," he said to his wife and kids. They did as they were told, and he went to his car and unloaded all the camping equipment from the trunk into the van he had just purchased.

"I'm scared," Janice said to her mom. She was sitting in the middle section off the minivan.

"I know baby, it'll be okay though."

Agent Smith drove away quickly, leaving the keys to his car behind.

"Okay," he finally spoke to his family, "here

is what's going on. I couldn't tell you at the house or in the car, because anything electronic can be traced and used to eavesdrop on conversations. "I've been working on a top-secret classified case at my job with the FBI, and I don't know who it is that I'm investigating yet, but they found me and killed my parents."

"Grandma is dead?" Malachi said softly, as tears poured from his eyes. His sister was crying too.

"No!" Deborah's hands flew up to cover her mouth and stifle a shocked sob.

He swallowed and nodded. "Yes, and they said they were coming after you guys next if I didn't cooperate. Somehow, they've set it up so I'm now a wanted man for the murder of my parents, so I need to get you guys to safety—away from any electronics. Think of it as a long camping trip."

Agent Smith drove away from the chop shop. As he pulled up to the first traffic light, a Toyota truck stopped right in the middle of the intersection and a man shaking his balled-up fist and sweating profusely got out of the truck with his phone in his hand. "Take this!" the man said, holding his phone up to Agent Smith's rolled-up window. "It's for you."

"We told you what to do," a raspy voice said into the phone. "Shoulder shot," the voice said, and a bullet pierced the window of the van's middle section and passed through eleven-year-old Janice's shoulder.

They all saw the glass shatter and, at first, they thought it was a warning shot, but blood began to pour from the little girl's shoulder. Deborah screamed when she saw it. Janice was silent, and within a few seconds, she had fainted. Malachi whimpered beside her and threw up on his side of the car, all over his clothes. The man who owned the phone took off running, leaving his truck and his phone behind.

"Do we have your attention?" the man on the phone asked.

"Yes, you do—you have my attention," Agent Smith replied. "Please just leave my family alone, I will do anything you want, but please don't hurt my family, please." He was racked with guilt, frightened tears spilling down his face as he looked back at his daughter.

"Okay, let's try this again—except now the game has changed a bit. You guys can take your daughter to the hospital, and on the way there you are to explain to your wife what's going on and make her understand that if she speaks, both your children will be tortured, raped, and then finally killed. You will be imprisoned, and you will be beaten and raped over and over again."

"Prison?" Agent Smith questioned.

"Yes, Prison. You will say that you colluded with Russia and North Korea to hack the US Government, and that they sent contracted killers to kill your parents when you tried to back out of the deal. You were tired of all the corruptness, and one day just snapped. The Secret Security Agency figured it out, and your daughter got shot in a shootout as you tried to escape. The shot was fired at you, but you turned your car as it was fired, and it hit your daughter instead.

"This is your last chance. If you mess this up there will be no more chances. We will do those things to you and your family. We will capture your wife and let the wild ones have her. I hear they're into women having sexual relations with animals. They like it when they drink blood, and eat the hearts of sacrificed babies, too. She will wish for death, but it will not come."

Agent Smith nodded his head rapidly. "I understand. I will explain it to her, and I'll turn myself in. I colluded with Russia and North Korea." He was crying so hard that he had to repeat himself twice to be sure that they heard him recite his lines. Deborah was looking at him in shock; her mouth was open and her face was still like a waterfall, as tears cascaded down her cheeks and onto her chin.

Agent Smith hung the phone up. "Deborah, listen. If I don't lie and say that I colluded with Russia and North Korea to hack the US Government, they will abduct you, and force you to do horrible things."

Deborah heaved and threw up out the passenger side window.

"I'm not done. If you say anything about anyone forcing me to say this, they'll make sure that I'm beaten to within an inch of my life every day in prison, and they'll torture and kill the kids.

"No!" she cried out before she fainted, nearly falling out the open door of the van. Agent Smith caught her by the arm. By the time she opened her eyes again, they were pulling up to the hospital.

Deborah looked back over her seat and saw her daughter, who looked faint and was still bleeding profusely. She started crying again. "Why are they doing this?" she asked her husband.

"To cover up what they're up to. I just wish I knew who it was, so I could go after them."

"So you have no idea who it might be?"

"No, I don't," Agent Smith answered his wife. "The only thing I know is they are not hacking into our government; they have open access."

"So it's our government doing this?"

"Again, I have no idea."

Agent Smith and his wife rushed their daughter into the hospital. While they were upstairs, Agent Smith received a text message on the stranger's phone. It said that the Secret Security Agency were downstairs waiting for him, and that he would be allowed exactly three minutes to say goodbye to his family.

"Baby," he started. "I have to go."

"What? Why?"

"The Secret Security Agency are downstairs, waiting to arrest me."

Deborah began to cry all over again.

"Listen, I need you to be strong for the kids. You guys need to forget about me. My life is over. It's been taken from me. You have my permission to marry again; be happy again." A tear rolled down his face as he spoke.

"No," his wife responded firmly through her tears. She shook her head fiercely.

"You have to. If you don't get the kids to forget me and they slip up and say something—or you do—they'll know and come after you. Please just forget I ever existed. Now I have to go." He turned to go and cussed under his breath. "Damnit. They could at least let me stay to see if she if she makes it through. As he spoke, a text came through, demanding that he begin heading down to the lobby with his gun out, where they could see it.

He hugged his wife and kissed her goodbye one last time. He gave his son a soft kiss on the forehead, careful not to wake him because he was asleep in a chair in the family waiting room. Walking to the elevator, he pulled his gun out as he'd been instructed to do. A few of the nurses and visiting family of patients screamed when they saw it. Two took off running.

*****

Agent Smith had left the stranger's phone with Deborah, so she'd have it if she needed it. It beeped twice, alerting her to a text. She didn't want to look, but curiosity got the better of her. What if it was those people, and her refusal to respond got her husband or her family killed? She steeled herself and read the text against her wishes, clenching her jaw against her panic.

Your husband messed up and did not follow instructions. We hear everything you say and see everything you do. If you do not wish to have bad things happen to you and your kids, you are never to discuss anything you know, regardless of what happens with your husband. If you talk about it in your sleep, we will be coming for you and your kids.

As she finished reading the text, alarms began to go off in the hospital. One of the nurses ran over to Malachi and shook him awake. "Ma'am," she addressed Deborah. "There was a shooting downstairs!" She brought Malachi to his mother and said, "Please follow me."

At that point, Deborah was numb. Everything was too much for her. She no longer registered anything in her mind, the recent events overpowering her. She was in complete shock. She knew they had just killed her husband, her daughter was dying on the surgery table, and her son was crying and asking where his dad was. Their entire lives had been destroyed in one night.

Her mind went completely blank and she just sat in the hospital room's visitor chair, not hearing her son's cries, instead just rocking back and forth.

CHAPTER SEVEN

"Hello America and good morning. I am Manuel Emotho with CGX News, and sitting here with me again is Jonathan Gatsby, who was a prisoner of war. Yes, I said it. *He was a prisoner of war*. Gatsby was taken by enemy troops to what he describes as an execution camp. After two years imprisonment, Gatsby and many others escaped to freedom. However, Gatsby and the brave group that followed him found that the road to freedom wasn't easy. Many who were with him died on the way, and only the lucky ones survived to make it back here to the United States.

"The ones that did survive the journey gave account, upon being rescued, that the man sitting beside me was the leader, and that none of them would have made it back to America without him. I can't tell the story in the same way that Mr Gatsby can, so I'll leave that to him.

"Yesterday, he did a marvelous job of giving our listeners a breakdown of the events which led up to his capture, and today he'll start from the very day that he was caught and take us into his life in the execution camp. His story is one of incredible endurance and hope.

"Well, listeners, I've said enough. Take it away, Sir," Manuel said to Gatsby, as he moved to find a more comfortable position in his chair to listen to the continuing story.

Gatsby coughed to clear his throat. "Before I begin," he started. "If you don't mind, Mr Emotho, I have an announcement to make. There's no date set yet, but my girlfriend, Roxane, and I are now engaged. We want to get married before the end of the month, but we'll see how things go."

"Wow," Manuel exclaimed, standing briefly to pat Gatsby joyfully on the back. "If you'll allow me to say a few things on this, I'd really appreciate it." He paused and waited for permission to continue.

Gatsby laughed, gesturing for him to go ahead.

"Well," he began, enlightening the listeners, "Gatsby hasn't reached this part of the story yet, but Roxane is one of the captives who escaped the execution camp with him. They began dating in the camp, which has a lot to do with the reason they could escape. They weren't sure if they were going to live, but they agreed that they needed to be together anyway.

"You can say it's corny or you can say that their focus should have been elsewhere while waiting to die but, to me, theirs is a true story of love."

"Thank you, Mr Emotho," Gatsby cut in with a grin on his face. He rested his hand on his chin as he sat, recounting in his mind what happened the day he was taken. As he thought, his face filled with anger, because a memory he had suppressed was brought back to the forefront, and it had everything to do with why he was taken.

"What's wrong?" Manuel asked, seeing the change in his guest's demeanour.

"I'm fine," Gatsby replied. "It's just that the worst thing about the day that I was taken wasn't me being abducted. It's the reason why I was abducted."

Manuel sat on the edge of his seat. He didn't

want to miss a single word of what Gatsby was about to say. The emotion in the room was palpable and he knew this part of the story would be good.

"On the day I was abducted, I was supposed to meet Brandi, who was my girlfriend at the time, at a place in Alaska called the Lathrop Woods. We were going to spend the night there. I brought the blankets, candles, and sodas, and she was supposed to bring the food and dishes. I sat in the woods alone and freezing my tail off waiting for her to show up. In the back of my mind, I knew she wasn't coming.

"After waiting for two hours, I considered walking back—and should have—but it was a long walk back home from where I was, so I decided to keep waiting, even as the temperature began to get worse. I started a fire in one of the stone pits that the government had built to keep civilians from starting forest fires by accident.

"Once the fire was lit, I unrolled the blankets and laid them as close to the fire as I could, so I would be warm. At some point I fell asleep, and I woke up to a sound in the woods. When I looked around to see if it was Brandi, I realized I couldn't see anything at all, because the fire had gone out.

"As I reached for my flashlight, I heard something rushing towards me. I became scared because there was a rumor about a monster in the Lathrop Woods, and people were known to wind up missing. The newspaper had once mentioned that thirty-three people had gone deeper into the woods, but none of them ever came out. I, of course, didn't believe the monster rumor, which is why I had suggested to Brandi that we spend the night there. I figured she'd get scared at every noise and we'd wind up in the same sleeping bag—where I could protect her in a romantic way, if you get my point," Gatsby said with a boyish wink.

Manuel laughed.

"When I heard something rushing at me, I quickly changed my mind about the monster and panicked. My chest ached and I was panting hard before long—it felt like I was having a heart attack. I tried to hurry up and shine the flashlight on whatever was rushing at me but the next thing I knew, about twelve men dressed in US Army uniforms were all over me... At first, I didn't know what was happening but, once they began talking, I worked out that the men were Russian soldiers—their US impersonations were good, but not that good.

*****

You must be kidding me, I thought, as the soldiers tied my arms together and pushed me forward, with their guns pointed at the back of my head. I don't believe this. First, my girlfriend stands me up, and now I'm being abducted by Russian soldiers.

Without any warning, one of the soldiers struck me with the butt of an assault rifle, and I guess they must have put a blindfold on me. By the time I regained consciousness, my journey had begun. We were headed out of the United States and, as I'd later discover, on route to Africa. I remember being forced up a flight of stairs, where the rumble of the engines informed me that I was getting onto a large airplane. After that, I slept. The plane made a few stops and, finally, we were loaded onto a boat, where once again, I slept—until we reached our destination. Africa. Where it all happened.

When my blindfold was removed, I could see that there were hundreds of soldiers standing around with guns—in various uniforms, as they represented many countries. There were lots of large passenger vans—about eleven of them—and that caught my interest. It was night-time, and dark, with the only lights coming from a few spotlights they'd set up, and from the headlights of the vans.

One of the soldiers grabbed me with a rough hand and marched me towards the vans. I yelled a few insults at him as he pushed me forward. He didn't say anything back, but he did at least give me an angry stare as we reached a vehicle.

"Get in," the soldier said to me. His English was clear, but I detected a German accent as he shoved me inside.

There were already a few people in the van and, nervous, I crept my way to the back and sat down. They loaded it to capacity very slowly, and there wasn't much to do except to wait patiently, which isn't one of my strong points. Instead, I sat in my seat quietly, plotting. I knew I had to escape, but I didn't yet know how, or where I would go when I did.

At that time, I didn't know where I was, but the unfamiliar landscape told me that I was no longer in the United States. I wondered what had happened to Brandi, too. Why hadn't she shown up? I couldn't help but wonder if something bad had happened to her as well. I couldn't help but think the worst, and soon my mind was whirring with possibilities. *If she doesn't know what happened to me already, she'll know when they execute me on TV*, I thought, trying to chase away my concern.

I didn't have a watch, so I didn't know how long I'd already been sitting there, but it felt like I'd been in there forever. Frustrated, hungry, and tired, I went to sleep to pass the time, and didn't wake up until I felt the van moving. I opened my eyes and had to squint against the sharp glare of the sun as it flooded in through the window. It was out in full force, and ready to produce a triple-digit sweltering day. I pressed my head against the glass and noticed a woman in front of me. I don't know what it was about her because all I could see was the back of her head, but she had my attention immediately.

I tried to see what her face looked like in the reflection of the van's windows, but I couldn't get a good look because the sun made it hard to see anything other than her profile. Eventually, I gave up and went back to sleep. When you've been in an uncomfortable, overfilled van for as long as we had, there's nothing else to do but sleep, daydream, and listen to people's stomachs growling in aggravated hunger.

When I next awoke, I wiped my eyes as I yawned and looked out of the window. The sun had risen much higher, and the heat was becoming unbearable. The van began to smell like sweat and booty cologne. As I made myself more comfortable in the seat, I heard the girl in front of me crying to herself. I wanted to ask her if she was okay, but I didn't. I was too worried about being embarrassed or looking stupid. She leaned back in her seat, wiped her tears, and didn't make a sound for the rest of the trip. I started staring out the window again—taking in the view—as many thoughts wandered through my mind.

The van pulled up to a clearing and stopped. A soldier got out and engaged in rapid conversation with another—part of a group that stood in the clearing, obviously awaiting our arrival. They were close enough that I could hear every word. A Caucasian man was speaking in another language. His accent sounded French, but France was in an alliance with the US, so he couldn't have been a French soldier... but he was. When I looked more closely at him, his uniform clearly identified him as French. I scanned the group and discovered that they were all French soldiers. When they finished talking, they approached the van as a group.

It was clear that none of them spoke English, but they motioned for us to get out. When nobody moved, they began shouting and pointed to the ground. I cringed when I saw that one of them had an AK47 pointed directly at us—to help us understand that not obeying was not an option. As quickly as we could, we dropped to our knees and placed our hands behind our heads. The soldier knocked all of us unconscious, by hitting us in the back of our necks with the handle of his assault rifle.

We were awoken with a cascade of icy water, lined up by size, and given a change of clothes. None of us wanted to change in front of everyone—especially in front of the soldiers—but when they aimed their guns at us we stripped and changed quickly. We all looked the same in a t-shirt, pair of pants, and sandals. At least they gave us shoes.

While we were changing, one of the soldiers grabbed a girl by the arm in a bruising grip and dragged her towards the nearby woods. We couldn't see her face, but her terrified pleading and the overbearing stature of the soldier gave us a window into her fear. We didn't see what happened, but we could hear her tortured screams. She came back with a bruise on her cheek from where she'd been backhanded, and we couldn't miss the steady trickle of blood streaming down her leg or the awkward way she rocked on her feet.

Roxane St Claire, who was the girl I noticed in the van, paled when she saw the girl return. She knew she'd been raped. Roxane was clearly terrified, but she ignored her own fears and tried to console the girl the best she could. Sensing an impending uproar, the soldiers knocked us all out again and the next time I woke up, we were in the execution camp and surrounded by African soldiers. They were mean as hell and had clearly been well indoctrinated into their Army. "Get on the ground!" one of them yelled at us. "Do not move or I'll shoot." We all fell to the ground at once.

"Get up!" the soldier yelled, and we jumped back up.

"When I say jump," he said, "don't ask how high. Just jump, and you better hope it's high enough, because here, you belong to me. The more you listen, the longer you live." He ran his pointer finger across his throat. "You… boy. Come here."

The boy, who looked no older than eleven, hesitated and pointed at himself, to confirm that he was being spoken to. The soldier shot several bullets into him and he fell.

"You," the soldier said, pointing at a girl who looked to be around… maybe twelve? She started crying but ran forward anyway—she'd already seen what would happen if she didn't. Everyone in the section that the soldier was pointing towards ran forward as well, just in case he was talking to them.

"Much better," the African soldier said, his smile exposing the missing teeth in his mouth. "I see you want to live," he said, pointing to the group. "Now get back in the line. These are the rules. You work in the fields, in the mines, and where we tell you to work. Once a month, one of you will be executed.

The harder you work, the longer you live. It is very simple.

"There is no escape. There are one hundred African soldiers here at this base, and between you and freedom. We're surrounded by water on all sides—this base is much larger than is visually present to the eye. There is only one way out of here without swimming across a river that will kill you in a thousand ways, if you find a way past the soldiers here on this secluded base and somehow make it past the crocodiles and the snakes in the river, and they don't kill you. Beyond the river, if you make it that far, are even more soldiers, so you will die one way or the other."

After the long speech, we were given a tour of the execution camp. There were seven small buildings and two long buildings. One of the long buildings was for eating and the other was to be our living quarters, which was where we slept. The soldiers stayed on the outside of the camp on every side, in barracks that blocked our path to the river. They showed us where we'd be working; some were assigned to the kitchen, some to the fields, some to the mines, and others to deliver food to the workers. The guards assigned Roxane to be a deliverer, and they assigned me to the fields.

Once darkness had fallen upon us, we were led to our sleeping quarters. I thought they'd at least have one guard in the building with us, but they didn't. There were no separate rooms in the building. Just one large space, with seventy-five nasty, dirty hardwood beds with no mattresses; one for each person. I was hoping to get a bed next to Roxane, but she wound up on the other side of the room. There was no electricity, so everyone had to feel around to find an empty bed.

My eyes eventually adjusted, and I looked at my bed. There was no sheet, no blanket, no pillow. I knew, just by looking at it, that I wasn't going to get any sleep. Sure enough, I rolled around all night trying to get comfortable, but I couldn't—all I managed to get were a few splinters. The beds were as hard as rocks, and I discovered that sleeping on the floor was a slight improvement, as it wasn't as itchy as the bed.

CHAPTER EIGHT

"My biggest fear is of spiders. I feared the spiders here in America enough, but the spiders in Africa were much worse. I remember this one kid got bit by a little spider that was hard to see in the water, and his body disintegrated on the inside—like his bones melted or something. He became rubbery—like a rubber suit, almost. I nearly threw up when I saw him."

"I've heard of those spiders," Manuel said. "I believe they're called fishing spiders."

"Yeah, well whatever they're called, that's not something that I ever want to see again," Gatsby replied, still feeling disgusted by the memory of it. "The soldiers left the victim with us for a while and then, just before sending us inside, tossed his body into the river for the crocodiles."

Manuel looked a little green. "Okay," he said, "so what happened next, after you all picked beds to sleep in?"

"The next morning," Gatsby continued, "the soldiers barged into our sleeping quarters, banging on metal trash can lids and yelling, "Everybody get up!" They sent us out to the mines and fields to work without any breakfast. Once in place, we were instructed to dig irrigation ditches and plant food in the fields connected to them—the fields were surrounded by twenty-foot-tall stainless-steel fences. We were also ordered to gather the crops that were already ripe and ready…"

*****

On the first day, everyone worked on the same irrigation ditch. The ditches went further than the fences, all the way to the river that was two miles away from the base camp. On that first day, we lost a lot of people. A few in the river, the one I mentioned earlier to a fishing spider bite, and another was taken by a crocodile. He was trying to cool off and decided to swim a few extra feet out into the river from where he was standing. I swear he wasn't even swimming for more than a few seconds before there was an almighty splash and a thump, as a crocodile dragged him under the water.

"Oh my God!" a girl screamed, as she jumped back from where she was standing in the river. The attack unfolded not even five feet away from her. The shrieking and screams from the other prisoners went on and on, and it still haunts me now. The guards just stood by and watched, laughing between themselves.

From that point on, whenever we were digging the irrigation ditches near the river, we kept a close eye on the water. The only good thing about seeing the crocodiles was that it gave me a clue as to where we were. Not America, I thought to myself. What other places have crocodiles? It came to me quickly: South America, Africa, and Australia.

We were surrounded by jungle, and I knew that Australia is mostly desert—rainforest at the edges— so I ruled it out straight away. That left Africa and somewhere in South America. Although alliances were shifting, I still believed that most South American countries would be loyal to the United States, so I made the assumption that we must be in Africa—it was a lucky guess, perhaps, and I did eventually start to doubt my conclusion—it wasn't impossible that South America had switched sides. So, I still had no real idea as to where we were.

The higher the sun rose, the hotter it got. They gave us some water, so I poured some of mine on the dirt, turning it into clay. Then, I rubbed the clay on my arms, neck, and face to keep from getting sunburn. The heat was very dehydrating and caused a lot of people to nearly faint as we slaved away, but the guards were making rounds and beating anyone who was caught not working. It pushed everyone to keep going. Many succumbed to the cruelty of heatstroke over our time there. They'd become vague and disoriented, and their deaths were often almost as awful as the crocodile attack had been.

They too were cast in the river for the crocodiles.

At some point, early on, while we were out in the fields working, the deliverers brought food to us. Roxane was among them. While passing out the food to the other workers, she looked up and saw me looking at her. She scrunched up her face and gave me a look back that said, "You can stop staring now," before walking in the opposite direction to pass out the food she had.

I could tell that, at this point, she was in no way interested in getting to know me. Slowly, I ate the raw turnips that had been given to me by another deliverer. They were completely disgusting. I remember hoping that we weren't going to be eating only turnips the entire time we were there.

I sat silently by myself, strategizing a plan to escape. I did this until lunch ended and we were sent back to work. We worked until it became too dark to see. The soldiers would randomly hit us and knock over our barrels, making us have to reload everything. They knocked my barrel over three times.

When we returned from working in the fields and the mines, we were directed into the eating area where the deliverers fed us again. I tried my best not to look at Roxane, but I couldn't help myself. She caught me glancing at her again, but before she could give me the same cold look that she gave me earlier, I turned my head and looked away.

"Here," a voice said as she put my bowl of food on the table. I looked up and stopped in my tracks. It was her. It was Roxane. Despite being in such a nasty place, her face was clean; she had rosy cheeks and a narrow face that depicted the very meaning of beauty. Her eyes were a light blue color and, though her skin color was white, she was tanned from being out in the sun.

"Thank you," I said, as I gave her a quick glance and a half smile, before pulling the bowl closer to me. I sighed when I saw the turnips, but the addition of beans meant there was at least some variation in our meals.

"You're welcome," she said, returning a half smile over her shoulder as she very gracefully walked away.

After dinner, we were sent to the sleeping quarters. I was exhausted, so I sat on the floor straight away, leaning against my bed. Before I closed my eyes, I thought I saw Roxane looking at me from across the room. I quickly re-opened my eyes to meet her gaze, but by then her eyes were closed, and her head was turned in the other direction.

Am I going crazy? I thought to myself. I was sure I hadn't imagined it, but it was late and I wanted to get some sleep, so I figured I could find out in the morning.

I have no idea what time it was when I woke up because there were no clocks, but my back was hurting from sleeping on the ground. I got up and walked around the building, staring out of each window and looking longingly at the stars in the sky. A decently sized spider scurried across one of the windows, causing me to step back, but it wasn't interested in me—it just continued out through a crack in the window.

The stars were all I could see because everything else outside was completely dark—I'm talking pitch black. The soldiers lit a few torches for us to be able to see inside the sleeping quarters, and probably so they could check on us if needed.

How can I escape from here? I thought to myself, tapping my knee with compulsive fingers. I didn't want to die like the girl I'd seen on TV, who was tortured to death. As I stood staring out, I heard someone move in behind me.

"What are you doing?" I heard Roxane's voice, and smiled despite the situation we were in.

"I couldn't sleep," I replied. "These beds are extremely uncomfortable—nearly as hard as cement, I'd say—and the floor really isn't much better."

"I know." She nodded. "That's why I'm up, too. It's driving me crazy. My name is Roxane," she said, looping her finger into her hair. "And you are?" The look she gave me was mesmerizing, even then.

"Jonathan," I replied, still looking out the window. "Where are you from?" I asked.

"I'm from Rhode Island. I know most people complain that there's not much there but farmland, but I liked it. My family owned horses, and I'd go horseback riding every chance I got. I miss it already."

"Really?" I asked, at last turning towards her. "I've always wanted to go horseback riding, but never got the chance. And from the looks of things, I might not ever get to." I said, smiling. Roxane didn't laugh. "I'm only kidding," I said. I actually didn't find the joke very amusing either. "I have no intention of dying here. I will find some way to get out of here, one way or another."

"I hope you do, because I don't want to die."

"I will." The longing on her face only strengthened my resolve. "I've been going over multiple plans in my mind. I don't know exactly how yet, but I'll figure something out. The problem is that I don't know where we are. I know we aren't in America, but don't know where we are exactly. If I'm to plan a successful escape, I must know where we are, and where we're going to escape to."

We'd wandered all the way around to her side of the building, and Roxane sat on her bed and patted the space beside her. I took that as a sign that she wanted me to sit next to her. As I sat down, a few of the people around us sat up in their beds and made their way over to us. They were lonely, I'm sure, and they joined in our conversation. Their names were Amy, Amber, Cameron, and Sarah. The six of us stayed up most of the night getting to know each other.

Sarah was from Arkansas, and an only child. She was taken while walking home from work at night. Cameron was from New York. He was in the middle of a drug deal—also at night—when he'd been taken. The soldiers killed the people he was selling to, too. I had no sympathy for him being captured. Drug dealers, to me, are the worst kind of scum, getting kids hooked on anything and everything. I purposely kept conversations with him to a minimum. Amber worked as a bank teller in Oregon. She was a mother of four children and was taken right in front of her kids. The soldiers shot, and killed, her oldest son, just because he tried to help her.

Amy was a mother also. She had two daughters and a son. The soldiers seized her while she and her husband were taking a stroll through the park at around two in the morning, enjoying the fresh, early-morning clean air. Amy's husband saw the soldiers before she did and took off running without saying a word to her, leaving her to be taken.

Roxane had been at home with her parents, celebrating her mom's fortieth birthday. The soldiers broke their door down around four in the morning while everyone had been fast asleep, and lined Roxane and her family up on their knees. They shot them in the back of their heads, one by one. Roxane thought they were going to shoot her too but, instead, they took her prisoner.

I didn't want to tell the story of how I had been taken because I felt like my story was nowhere near as terrifying as their abductions had been. Nobody had been there to die beside me when I was kidnapped. The worst part of my abduction had been being stood up by my girlfriend.

As we talked in the dimly lit room, there was a sudden flash of bright light in the distance. We fell silent as we watched the lights come closer and closer. After a few minutes, a Jeep parked in front of our sleeping quarters. The rumbling engine noise set us on edge, and a bad vibe tore through the group. We all felt it. Something bad was about to happen. I motioned for Roxane to hide under her bed with me. Many of the others who had been in the conversation with us followed suit.

The room door flung open and in walked a general who stood in such a way that made him seem far larger than his actual stature. He was followed by ten soldiers—all holding AK47s. I recognised the African Soldiers but was unsure about the ethnicity of the general until he got closer.

Then I saw it. The North Korean flag embroidered in stark relief against his uniform. This was something new; something we hadn't experienced yet, and I felt my blood run cold when he pointed at a little girl in the corner of the room. In perfect English, the general said "There—that one."

It was the first time I'd seen the little girl, and she looked no older than five. From under the bed, I shook my head in disgust at the guards. Beside me, Roxane shook with fury and fear, and through her tears she whispered to me, "We have to help her."

A lump formed in my throat, but I bit it back. "There's nothing we can do," I said. "They will kill us, and still do whatever they're going to do to that girl. We have to pick our battles wisely."

"Do you think they're taking her to be executed?" Roxane asked. I could feel her desperation in the way she held her breath.

"Most likely," I replied.

Roxane covered her face with her hands and continued to cry softly. Many people in the room were crying. Before leaving, the general walked around and grabbed one of the women. Nobody moved until all the soldiers were out of the room.

"What the heck? I thought they were only executing us one at a time?" one of the boys shouted from the other side of the room.

"They are," another of the male captives replied. "The second one isn't being executed. She's most likely going to be raped."

He was right. When the girl came back, her face was swollen and bruised. She walked to her bed with tears pouring down her cheeks, lay down, and began to sob in earnest.

I thought Roxane was going to cry again, but she didn't. Instead, she walked over to the girl and let her cry in her arms while she rubbed small circles against her back. I sat on the wooden floor next to Roxane's bed, wishing that I were back home in Alaska. As I sat on the floor, Amy, Amber, Cameron, Sarah, and a few others came and sat next to me.

"When we were talking to you before the guards came in, you said that you were going to get out of this place. You told Roxane that you were going to get out, and that you had a plan, but what about us? Do you think you can get us out, too?"

"I don't know," I said, avoiding the many hopeful gazes burning into me. "That's asking a lot. If I escape by myself, I can find help and let the US Military know where you guys are. I can send them straight to you. It would be a lot easier for one person than it would be for over two hundred people to escape undetected, you know."

"It probably would be easier for you, but if you do succeed in escaping and they can't find you, what if they assume you're going for help and move us to another location, or decide to kill us and leave our bodies for the US Military to find?" Cameron asked, putting me on the spot.

"Wow. Really?" I responded. I was tired and hungry and afraid for my life; I was annoyed. "I appreciate the guilt trip. I just want to get out of this place, and if I take everyone I know, I won't succeed. Think about it. The little ones would slow us down, as would some of the others. We won't be able to feed everyone. What about keeping warm? If we light a fire, we'll give away our position. It would be impossible for everyone to escape from this place."

"Let him go," Roxane joined in the conversation. "We'll just have to find our own way out of this place."

When the others were laying guilt trips on me, it made me feel bad, but when Roxane joined them, it stung. Surely she knew how I felt about her.

"Roxane," I started, raising my eyebrows as a reminder that I'd told her I was going to take her with me—I didn't want to say it aloud in front of everyone. By now, all the captives were gathered around and listening to our conversation.

"No, I won't go with you," she said firmly, making my heart jolt. "Not unless everyone goes. Look around the room. Some of these kids here can't be any older than four. There are mothers here, taken from their husbands and children. Children taken from their parents. I wouldn't feel right leaving them here to die while I escaped to freedom, knowing that I didn't at least try to save them. So, if you're going to go, then go. But me? I'll escape with everyone else."

I looked at the ground. I was pretty pissed off at that point. Roxane was hindering my possibilities of creating a perfect plan of escape. There was no way in hell that I was going to be able to get everyone out with any plan that I, or anyone in the camp, could come up with.

*****

"The plan that I was going to originally construct would have been designed for one person, but after Roxane started speaking to me, I was going to design a plan for two. But to get everyone out, I was going to need to have the same powers as God. You know," Gatsby said, looking at Manuel. "Looking back, I'm glad I stayed, obviously, but never in my life have I put a girl in front of my own safety or needs. Roxane must have placed some kind of spell on me, because the man I was before I met her would have left on his own that night.

"I mean, I knew nothing about her. She could have been crazy or some depressed, jealous, insecure—I forgot where I was going with this, but my point is that I, Johnathan Gatsby, took a big chance and stayed because of her. There're plenty of good-looking women in the world, so it wasn't her beauty that made me stay. She had some kind of hold on me. I may not have known it then, but my heart knew that I would never find another like her. Ever."

*****

I threw my hands up in the air. "Okay," I said with a sigh. "I'll do it. I'll get us all out."

"So, what's the plan?" about four people asked me at the same time.

"I have to come up with a new plan," I said. "The old one was only designed for me." I wanted to make everyone feel as guilty as they'd made me feel. "I'll let you know as soon as I come up with a new one."

"Just try and get one before thirty days are up. Please? Because any of us could be next," a girl pleaded with me.

"You guys better try and come up with a plan too. I never said I was Rambo. I'm a victim here, just like all the rest of you," I responded, trying to be stern without allowing too much of my frustration to show.

A few people cracked a smile at that.

Daylight shined through the windows of the sleeping quarters, but no one was surprised to see that we'd been up all night. We were ready long before the soldiers came to wake us and take us to the eating area for breakfast. As usual, the eating area was filthy and smelled of rotten food and remnants of meals past, but we knew better than to let that put us off our food. We were given our daily assignments and were happy to be heading off to work full of rice, instead of working on empty stomachs as we'd had to do before.

CHAPTER NINE

"As I prepared to head to my work assignment, I took one last glance at the cafeteria. It was so dirty in there that when I walked outside, I wiped my feet so I wouldn't get the scum on the ground."

Manuel laughed as quietly as he could, so not to interrupt Gatsby's story. "That's funny," he said. "I'm going to have to write that one down and use it sometime."

"Well, as I was saying," Gatsby continued. "Just as they had done previously, they sent some of us to the fields, some of us to the mines, and some to the kitchen—same as where they had assigned us before."

*****

At first everything was fine but, by noon, everything took a turn. Three more people were taken by crocodiles, and the soldiers would not let us leave the area. They shot and killed a seventeen-year-old while trying to push us back towards the water. Revolted, everyone refused to move then, staying where they stood and looking defiantly at the soldiers. Despite the efforts, the soldiers were enraged, and began unloading their guns on us. People tried to run for the water, but about nine were killed instantly by flying bullets, and six others were injured.

The soldiers knocked the injured prisoners unconscious and tossed them in the river for the crocodiles to devour. One of them was taken by an anaconda; we saw its ugly head gliding across the water. It lunged at the unconscious girl floating in the water, wrapped itself around her, and took her beneath the surface. After that we all stayed clear of the water the best we could. The soldiers tried a few times to scare us back in, but even after they shot another captive, nobody moved. I think we were all in agreement that we would rather be shot than eaten alive by a crocodile.

At some point, the commanding officer came running over to the river yelling at the African soldiers in English. "Stop, you idiot!" he cried. "We need them for executions, if one more is killed, the Russian leader will find out, and any soldiers involved will be executed in their place. Is that understood?" The Korean commander stared them down as he yelled.

The African soldiers did not respond to the commander, but they did listen, and stopped forcing people into the river. They stopped killing captives as well and, for a while, we had a reprieve.

Within the next few days, they brought in another small group of prisoners—ten or so, not a lot. We were able to relax more, now that we knew the soldiers couldn't kill us at their whim and had learned to keep our distance from the water. After a while, though, everyone began to get musty and we knew we had to at least go to the edge of the river to bathe. I saved a turnip from my dinner and used it to scrub myself, like a bar of soap. It actually kept me clean and smelling decent, so others began to copy me.

We only bathed by the river at night, when we could see the glare from the eyes of any crocodile in the surrounding area; we only took baths together as a group. We'd go to the river's edge one at a time, while the others kept their eyes on the water, looking for eyes glowing in the moonlight.

I tried to work hard most days, but there were many times that I moved at a snail's pace. I just couldn't shake the heat of the day—I mean, I'm from Alaska; heat isn't exactly in our wheelhouse, if you know what I mean. I knew I had to start moving faster to keep myself safe, but I was exhausted. I should have slept more at night instead of staying up and talking until the early hours, like I did in our regular group meetings.

I saw a soldier write something in his note pad and point me out to his colleague. The colleague walked up to me and shoved me, yelling fiercely in an African language I was still largely unfamiliar with. I assumed he wanted me to work faster because he kept shoving me hard in the shoulder. He kept gesturing for me to hurry, so I pushed my barrel up the hill a little faster.

One morning before lunch, the blazing heat caused me to be a little lazy in my work and one of the guards bound a few cords together into a whip and lashed me across the back. I fell to the ground but when I jumped back up, I was ready to fight. My mood changed quickly when I saw the other soldiers making their way towards me, and I put my boiling anger aside to pick up my barrel and refill it with the potatoes that had spilled out during my punishment.

I tried to continue up the hill, but I was stopped and bent over the barrel of the wheelbarrow, where I was struck twenty times against my back with the whipcords that seemed to be their new method of control. I was in such a bad mood that when the deliverers came out to feed us lunch, I kind of took my frustrations out on Roxane and answered all her well-meaning questions with a sizeable helping of bad attitude. I was in pain from the whipping, and anger was the only way I knew how to deal with it. Roxane was infuriated and walked away. She wouldn't even look at me the entire time she stayed out there with us, doing her job.

Do they expect us to eat this crap? I wondered, as a deliverer handed me two turnips. I really would have rather eaten stale bread and water. If I hadn't been so hungry I would have tossed the turnips, but I was starving so, reluctantly, I ate them. As a soldier passed me, he paused and watched me sitting next to my food for a second. I pointed towards what was still in my bowl. "Look," I said. "I understand if you guys can't afford food but come on now. Are you too good to apply for food stamps?"

To my great relief, the soldier laughed. "Food stamps! That is a good one!" he said to himself as he walked away. That was when I realized that some of the soldiers spoke English and that I had to watch what I said in front of them.

That evening, at sundown when we were escorted to the eating quarters for dinner, Roxane served me first. "Here you go, Gatsby," she said, placing a bowl of beans in front of me with a shy smile.

I reached out and touched her hand. "Thank you," I said. "I know you're mad at me, and I want to apologize for earlier. Some stuff happened and I was upset; my body was hurting; I was acting out of frustration."

"I'm not mad at you," Roxane replied. "In fact, if you want, when we go back to the sleeping quarters, you're more than welcome to come to my part of the room and talk with me."

"Yeah, I'd like that! See you at dark o'clock, then," I said, cracking a smile.

"See you then," she said, with a dip of her head and the beginnings of a smirk.

Once we were back in the sleeping quarters, I slowly made my way to Roxane's bed. The soldiers had lit lamps outside of each of the windows now, instead of using the usual torches, so it was easy for me to find her. As I approached, I could see a look of worry on her face.

"What's wrong?" I asked, as I sat down next to her.

"Let me see your back," Roxane said, without looking at me.

"It's nothing," I replied. "I got into a little trouble today, because I wasn't moving fast enough."

Without another word, she lifted my shirt and gasped in horror when she saw the deep gouges left by the whip. She wiped frantically at her eyes, but I caught her gaze as a single tear rolled down her cheek.

"It doesn't hurt," I said, lying through my teeth. The truth was, I didn't even want to lie down, and was ashamed because everyone that was working in the field had seen tears come to my eyes as I was beaten. I only hoped that whoever told her about it had left that part out.

Roxane looked at me for a minute. "Please don't get yourself killed. Even if you don't feel like working, please work. I do not want to see you be the next one to be executed.

I could only nod my head.

I needed to shake off the way I was feeling, so I grabbed her hand and turned to face her properly. "Tell me more about you," I said.

"What do you want to know?"

"Well, for one, do you have a boyfriend?"

"Yes, I do," she answered with a wistful smile. "We're engaged to get married in May. We've been together since the eighth grade!"

"That's a long time to be with someone," I said, feigning happiness for her.

*****

"Wow. She was engaged. You had a girlfriend. This is getting very interesting," Manuel said, interrupting Gatsby briefly.

Gatsby shook his head and chuckled. "Interesting indeed," he said.

*****

"What about you? Do you have a girlfriend?"

"I think I have a girlfriend. She stood me up the night I was taken," I answered.

"Oh my God," Roxane replied, her hands flying up to cover her mouth. "Well, I hope she feels bad about it now that you're here."

I just shrugged. I really didn't want to talk about Brandi. I was still pissed off about her standing me up. "If you don't mind," I said, "let's change the subject. You don't have to answer this question if you don't want to, but I was wondering if you would tell me about your parents?"

"No, I don't mind," she replied. "My dad was a scientist and an archeologist, and my mom was a rancher. My dad's amazing. He would go off on incredible adventures to other countries, finding old artifacts for museums. When I was a kid, it always felt like he was a treasure hunter—I guess maybe he was. He always came home with remarkable stories of things he discovered in his work…" she trailed off and, for a while, seemed to be lost in her memories.

"Some of the stories were not so good. I remember him telling me that women in many countries are not allowed to go to school or to work. Then, five years ago, he came back and told us the Global Alliance was forcing the countries to change. They obeyed—on paper— but changed laws that made it nearly impossible for any practical changes to take place. They made it so a college degree was required for even the simplest of jobs, and made the prices of girls' schooling far higher than boys', so that only the children of the wealthiest families could attend.

"One wealthy family in Uganda was able to send their daughter to school and she was raped and tortured on her third day, about a mile from the school. She never went again, after that. I would love nothing more than to go to Uganda and get funding to start a grade-school-through-college program just for women and offer them the protection that their government does not." She paused for a moment, and I was struck by her giving nature and generous ambition.

"My mom loved horses," she began again,

"and she raised horses and other animals on a ranch. She also loved to travel and was always going somewhere. My parents forced me to focus on school, and they allowed me to do a lot, but they did all they could to keep me from having a boyfriend. For most of my life" —she grinned— "I had to hide my boyfriend from them. I wasn't able to tell them about him until the eleventh grade. They loved me and tried to protect me from all the heartaches of the world. I really miss my mom and dad." A tear rolled down her cheek.

"If it bothers you to talk about them, you don't have to."

"What about your parents?" Roxane asked, as she wiped at her tears.

I nodded. It was my turn. "My parents divorced when I was young, and I've spent most of my life since going back and forth between them."

"I'm sorry to hear that," Roxane said softly, curling into my side.

"No need to be sorry. It happens," I replied. "I was living with my mom when I was taken. She owns a catering business and ran it from the kitchen in our house. She worked hard to get it off the ground. She was getting a lot of clientele, and her business was very successful. I hope she can get her own building someday. I wanted to do something to help her, and when we escape I will." I yawned as I spoke. "So, how old are you?" I asked.

"Seventeen," she said. "I'll be eighteen on March twenty-third. What about you?"

"I'm seventeen too, but I'll be eighteen on August fourth. You know what?" Something occurred to me suddenly. "I don't even know what today's date is," I said, realizing that I wouldn't even know when it was my birthday.

*****

"Gatsby," Manuel interrupted. "Hold on one second, we've got someone here to talk. "Hello? Hello, Brandi are you there?" he asked, and Gatsby's eyes widened as he recoiled into his chair.

"Yes, I am," Brandi's voice filled the room, as if exploding from the speakers that hung from the ceiling.

"Brandi." Gatsby mouthed to himself, confused, and completely caught off guard. Luckily, Manuel had the situation under control.

"To all the listeners and, of course, Mr Jonathan Gatsby, we have a surprise! Brandi, the girl who stood Gatsby up the night he was abducted, is calling from Arizona and would like to clear a few things up." He chuckled. "Go ahead, Brandi."

"Jonathan," Brandi said. Her voice was very shaky, like she was about to cry. Gatsby didn't know what to do. He was getting married to Roxane and talking to Brandi wasn't the best start to their engagement, but he wanted to hear what she had to say, so he answered her.

"Hey."

"How are you?" Brandi asked in the same shaky voice.

"I'm doing well. How are you?"

"I'm okay," came her reply.

"So, what's up?" Gatsby asked, taking care to speak in a tone that suggested he didn't really want to talk. He still hadn't reconciled his anger with her; some part of him thought that she was the reason he had been taken. He could hear her crying softly on the other end of the line.

"I'm sorry I wasn't there that night. I was on my way to Lathrop Woods to meet you when my car slid off of the road. I had to wait for five hours for a tow truck to come and pull me out of the ditch. When it finally came, the driver examined the car and noticed the front tire had gone completely flat and my axle was bent beyond repair... He had to tow my car to my house."

She took a deep breath and continued, as though she had to get through the speech she'd prepared. "I figured I'd be able to borrow my mom's car and at least go get you and bring you back into town. But when I got to my house my mom wasn't there, and she didn't return until around one in the morning. I tried calling you all night, but your phone went straight to voicemail every time. When my mom got home, I drove straight to your house to see if you'd gone home, and when your family said you weren't there, I drove to the woods.

"It was pitch black, so I used a flashlight and walked to where we said we would meet. As I approached to the area, I saw all your stuff, including your phone, lying in the snow, but I didn't see you. I decided to wait for you, so I sat in the snow, and wrapped your blankets around me to stay warm. After an hour, I started getting scared because I kept hearing noises in the brush that surrounded me. I started to panic, wondering if that monster thing that everyone always talked about had actually gotten you, and was getting ready to get me.

"I sat in the snow crying, scared to move. I grabbed my phone and called the police. They searched the area for you, but you weren't there; no further trace of you anywhere. It wasn't until another officer came that they decided something was really wrong."

*****

"How many did you say were missing?" the newly arrived officer asked.

"Just one," the initial officer responded.

"Well, if you look here, there are a lot of

footprints in the snow. Only one set belongs to a pair of sneakers, I'd say the rest are military boots. I served in the Army for twelve years before I got out and became a police officer. We had to jog through the snow all the time during training, and those prints are the same ones our boots made.

"If you look closely, many of these boot prints are in different sizes, which means that more than one person made them. Look over there," the officer continued as he pointed to footprints heading into the woods. "You see the same boot prints in the snow heading into the woods, but no sneaker prints past that point halfway to the trees." As the officer said this, he noticed blood in the snow. "There," he said pointing at the bright red stain. "They must have knocked him out and carried him, which would explain why you don't see his footprints going all of the way into the woods."

The officer radioed the police station. "This is Officer Johnson to Headquarters. We have another abduction and are requesting back up to the Lathrop Woods. Please respond."

"This is Headquarters. Is anybody hurt?"

"No," the second officer responded. "But note there is blood on the scene. Possibly from the victim who was taken."

"Noted, Officer Johnson," the voice came through the radio again. "Back up will be there shortly."

"Thank you," Officer Johnson said into his radio.

*****

"Officer Johnson rushed to his car and signaled for us to follow. As we jogged over, he briefed the other officer, and me, about what was going on.

*****

"There have been seven abductions today," he said. "No clues were left during the first six but during the seventh, a witness saw a Russian soldier—in an American uniform—putting the victim in the back of a yellow sixteen-wheeler truck. Judging by the boot tracks left in the snow, these are the same soldiers, and I suspect this makes this their eighth victim today."

*****

"Once we reached the car, he pulled out a map and searched for a road that went away from the woods in the direction that the prints were going."

Gatsby sat in silence, listening to Brandi's story—the story of his kidnap.

*****

Within seconds, Officer Johnson was back on the radio. "I need a helicopter to fly over the Richardson Highway going south towards Anchorage. I have reason to believe that a yellow, sixteen-wheeler truck is on the road, and the vehicle is believed to be the one identified as part of the abduction earlier today."

"Copy that," came the voice through the radio. The same voice, seconds later, sounded from the officer's car radio. "We need all officers to the Richardson Highway heading south towards Anchorage. You are searching for a yellow sixteen-wheeler big-rig truck with a large white storage container on the back of it. I repeat, the color of the vehicle is yellow. Proceed with caution. The vehicle is believed to be driven by heavily armed Russian soldiers.

Keep your distance and follow the vehicle. Hostages are confirmed to be on board."

*****

"The officers then sent me home where I impatiently waited to hear if they'd found you. I called the police station every hour, hoping to hear something, but each time I heard the same answer—there's no new information, please stop calling, we'll call you when we have news.

"They never called me though. I wound up seeing it on TV, along with everyone else. I saw you, along with many others, walking blindfolded up a flight of stairs onto a Russian plane. The plane was huge. The reporters kept asking the same question, 'How did the Russians sneak that plane through US airspace without detection?'

"The soldiers stopped the last person in line and made them face the cameras. One of them held a gun to the captive's head and said, 'If you follow us, this will happen to the rest of them.' The captive was shot in the head. I watched as they fell over the side of the stairs and onto the ground. Even on the TV, we could hear the cracking of their skull; see where their brains splattered all over the place. It was awful. I cried and cried because I thought it was you."

Brandi stopped speaking and there was a long moment of contemplative silence.

"I just wanted to clear the air," she said, finally. "I didn't stand you up, John. I know you're getting married, and I'm not trying to break you guys up, but I thought it was important for you to know that I didn't stand you up. I loved you then. I've moved on since—I had to move on, as you also have—but I needed you to know what happened."

Gatsby waited for Brandi to continue, but no words followed.

"Hello? Hello?" Manuel tried to get an answer, but Brandi had hung up.

Gatsby sat in his chair, speechless and staring blankly at nothing. He felt that the only reason Brandi called was to clear her name. He almost said fuck you out loud, filled with rage. After all he'd been through, he couldn't stand that she'd brought up their past just so that the nation didn't think negatively about her.

"Okay, listeners, I think we'll be taking a little break," Manuel said, as he motioned for Tremaine Sanderson to take over.

"Well, hello again everyone. I am Tremaine Sanderson with CGX News, bringing you *truthful news* and, apparently, random news at random times!" Tremaine said, laughing to himself. A few of the equipment operators silently laughed along with him.

"Let's get into it, shall we? I'm hearing that the US Navy is being overwhelmed—and possibly destroyed— off the east coast. It may be only a matter of days before the war is being fought right here on US soil, which is exactly what the Nationberg Group want. They need to destroy every government branch, especially the United States, in order to bring in a One World government.

"For those who don't yet know, we've discovered that the Masons, the Illuminati, and the Nationberg Group, are all different branches of the one organization. Each of those branches has different branches—or levels, whichever term you prefer—of their own.

"The wealthiest families in the world are at the head of each branch, without a doubt, and we've reached the point where I can be killed just for mentioning them over this radio broadcast, but that's a chance that I am willing to take.

"Now, every time I talk about those groups on my social media, I get flooded with negative comments. Ignoring that they exist will not change the truth! Ignoring that leaks from their meetings have not only confirmed their agenda but have also shown us meeting notes and a list of their members will not change the truth—it just makes you ignorant to what's really going on. They have their groups on video, showing the allegiance of political powers, religious powers, royal powers, rich lobbyists, and the wealthy elite.

"President Brooks has been moved to Colorado, far away from the east coast, just as a precaution. They're currently attacking hard on the west coast. Here in Alaska, they are, as of now, being kept at bay, though rumors abound that suggest they're going to make another attempt to breach Alaska through Prudhoe Bay, while they're still trying to enter through Anchorage, Kotzebue, Point Hope, and Little Diomede... all small towns by the Russian border."

Manuel and Gatsby walked back into the room after their cool-off period. Tremaine looked up, and mouthed, "You guys ready?"

Manuel nodded and Tremaine mouthed back, "Okay."

"Well just one more thing before I go, folks," he said. "Agent Conlin of the FBI has been fired, due to recent events with one of his own, an agent Smith, confessing to colluding with Russia and North Korea, hacking into our American government's security system, and into many American citizens IP addresses. In an underhanded attempt at launching an American civil war, this group targeted ads at individual cultures, in attempts to breed discord. They have nearly succeeded in doing this, folks, and if we're to avoid falling into their trap, we need to take the higher ground.

"Agent Smith was killed in a shootout with the Secret Security Agency, inside a hospital where his daughter was being treated for—and get this—a bullet wound. Apparently, the SSA had tried to arrest Agent Smith earlier that day, but he wound up fleeing the scene and firing upon agents, forcing them to fire back in self defense. Smith's daughter was shot in the shoulder during the getaway. The shot was meant for Smith, but an abrupt turn of the vehicle caused the bullet to miss him and hit his daughter.

"Okay. That's all for your impromptu *truthful news* with Tremaine Sanderson. Make sure to stay tuned because you never know when you might miss something big."

Manuel immediately put Gatsby back on the air to continue his story.

"To start things off," he began. 'I have to right some wrongs. For those of you who were listening when Brandi called before the break and explained what happened on her part, it's important that you know this.

"I really did care for you on the night that I was taken, Brandi. I owe you an apology for getting into another relationship while in the execution camp. Obviously, you also moved on—which I found out while I was in the camp—and I feel you only called to clear your name. I think you were more concerned about just trying to cover for yourself, rather than just admitting you didn't show.

"Roxane, I love you, and I didn't know that Brandi was going to pull that crap, I apologize to you, Roxane Gatsby," He smiled. "Now that I've hopefully cleared that up, I'll get back to the story. I might as well skip to the night that Roxane and I got together. December the twenty-fifth.

"We had been in the camp for about fifteen months, and Roxane and I had become good friends. I knew everything there was to know about her, and she knew everything about me. We never crossed any lines because she had a boyfriend, and boy was she faithful to him. I even told her one time that if I escaped, I'd make sure to find him, and tell him to come save her," Gatsby laughed as he told his joke. "I said it jokingly to her, but at the time, I think I half meant it."

CHAPTER TEN

On December twenty-fifth, the soldiers pulled a shocker. They announced that it was Christmas day, and let us speak on the phone with our families. It sounds kind, but they did it with bad intentions. They were hoping our families would put more pressure on the United States but all they did was give the families assurance that we were still alive.

Tim's family, God rest his soul, had assumed that he was dead in a ditch somewhere. They had the city searching high and low for him. The family didn't even know he'd been abducted. They were so happy to hear his voice and to discover he was alive that he never got the chance to tell them he was in an execution camp, waiting to be killed.

*****

"So he was executed?" Manuel asked, on behalf of the listeners.

Gatsby put his head in his hands. "Well, no, not really—he was one of the ones who were eaten by the lions."

"Wait, what? *Lions*?"

"I'll get to that later, trust me," he replied, before jumping back into his story.

*****

I talked to my mom for a while, which is how I found out that Brandi had a boyfriend and had moved out of state with him. I remember walking back to my bed feeling pissed off. I didn't want to talk to anybody at all. Roxane was standing in line waiting for her turn to make a call, but when she saw me moping about—and those are her words not mine—she got out of line and came over to me—to see if I was okay.

Of course, I put on a front and pretended that I wasn't hurt, but the truth is that I felt alone and unloved, but Roxane giving up her spot in line to check on me, when she could of have waited until after her phone call, reminded me that I wasn't because I partially had her, just not as much of her as I wanted.

Get back in line," I told her. "All you've done is talk about your fiancé, and you're probably about to miss your only chance to speak to him."

"No, I won't miss it," she said gently. "I'll get back in line, but only after I find out if you're okay because it looks like you had a bad phone call. What happened?" she really did look concerned, so I gave in and told her.

"Brandi has a new boyfriend, and she moved to Arizona with him a month after I was abducted."

"Oh… I'm so sorry. She didn't waste any time, did she? Yeah, I would say that definitely qualifies as a bad phone call," Roxane finished, leaning over to rest her hand on my shoulder.

"Yeah, you could say that." I tried to wipe the grimace off my face when I spoke.

Roxane shot me a dazzling smile. "I'm glad to see you're starting to feel a little better."

"That was a fake smile," I replied, as a real one crossed my face unbidden. "You better get back in line to talk to your ex." I joked. "Before they take the phones away." I had noticed the line was getting down to the last handful of people.

"He's not my ex," she reminded me, as she always did when I said it. "We're still engaged. Now, are you sure you are going to be okay?" she asked one more time before leaving.

"I'll be fine, and if not, I'll still be here when you get back, so go make your phone call."

She left me and got back in line to make her call. I watched, waiting, and wished in my heart that God would make her mine. I also cheated just a little bit, and said a quick prayer, asking for them to break up, or for something to happen that would give me a chance. Once she was on the phone, I walked over to the window that was closest to me, and I stared at the stars for a while.

Roxane returned to her bed without a word to me and concerned, I hurried back and tried to engage her in a conversation, but she just rolled over and ignored me. For three days, the two of us didn't speak. She saw me in the field when she and the rest of the deliverers came to bring us food, but she would just turn and go the other way if I tried to speak to her.

I wondered what happened on the phone call that made Roxane stop talking to me. Maybe she told him about me, and he told her to stop talking to me. Maybe she felt guilty about becoming friends with me while she was engaged to him. I mean, it's not as if we had done anything, but we were becoming closer and closer all the time.

I wanted to hate her for ignoring me, but couldn't, and it was then that I knew I was not only in love with her, but that I had been in love with her from the moment I saw her.

Instead of allowing hate to enter in my heart, I became depressed. Roxane was all I'd had in the execution camp. It felt like I had nobody while we weren't talking. My work became even more slothful than it already had been, and I received three beatings from the soldiers in those few days. I was in so much pain from the beatings I didn't even eat dinner. I went straight to the sleeping quarters.

I stood by the window, and just stared out into space. The stars were beautiful. The moon was a full circle. Memories that I had of my family raced through my mind, helping me focus on ignoring the pain. I wondered how I would feel, once I was dead.

Would I be conscious in my body in the grave, and just not able to move? If so, would I feel uncomfortable? Would I be unconscious of it all? When I died, would I close my eyes one second and then open them in Heaven or Hell a second later? I wondered if I would come back as someone else, with zero memories of the life I'm currently living.

All of my unanswered questions had festered over time, and I became very scared to die. My body felt weird and uneasy; I felt extremely weak.

"Jonathan," came the voice of one of the captives. Her name was Mao.

I turned to face her but instead of looking her in the eye, I stared at the filthy flooring—as if I was hypnotised by it.

"Hey Mao," I said, quietly.

"I brought you some food, and some wet rags for your back," she said kindly. "What happened out there? I heard you got three beatings today."

"Yeah," I replied. "I did, and I don't know… I guess I just didn't feel like working today."

"Oh my God. Turn around."

I did as she said and could feel her eyes boring into my flesh as she stared at the blood streaking my skin. I heard Roxane gasp from across the room, and she was beside us in a few seconds.

"Jonathan, what did you do? Why did they do this to you?"

I kept my eyes on the ground as I answered her. "Today just wasn't my day I guess," I said coolly. "The guards got mad because they didn't feel I was working hard enough, and because I was mouthing off a bit. One of the soldiers was antagonizing me—he knew I was in a bad mood—and I punched him for it. They beat me a few times, then."

"You are a selfish bastard!" Roxane cried. I expected her to be angry, but not at me. "If you get yourself killed, I…" she stopped in the middle of her sentence, grabbed the rags from Mao, and began to clean my wounds herself.

It hurt twice as bad while being cleaned as it had before. She worked in silence, but she was pressing very roughly. I looked over my shoulder at her, and she looked back at me for a second.

"I haven't spoken to you for the last couple of days, because I had to do some thinking about a few things," she said.

"Like what?" I asked.

"About you."

"Me?" I said, confused. "What did I do?"

"Will you shut up and let me finish?" She pushed down a little harder on the largest of my wounds.

"Ouch, alright!" I yelled. "I'll shut up. Please continue."

She did. "I was mad at myself and needed some time alone. I found myself so confused when I was on the phone—so confused that I called my fiancé Jonathan by accident."

"A mistake," I started, wincing as she applied more pressure. "It could've happened to anyone—"

"As you can guess," she interrupted, "he got mad. And before hanging up, he confessed that he'd been cheating on me with another woman—for years before I was abducted. At some point in our relationship, sometime when we were still in middle school, he started dating someone else. Jonathan he—well, he's now married to her. I must be real stupid to be with someone and not realize that they were serious with someone else during most of our relationship."

I didn't know how to respond; I was tongue-tied. Luckily, Roxane wasn't finished.

"When he told me that he was married, I was so upset that I didn't want to talk to anyone; I went to my bed and cried myself to sleep. Through the night, I thought about the phone call and realized that if I had a choice between the two of you, I would choose you, which made me get upset with you—for making me like you—while I was engaged to be married to someone else.

"Then I realized that I couldn't blame you—I could only blame myself. I had given my heart to you without realizing it. I stayed away from you for the last couple of days to pray to God, to ask him what I should do."

"And what did he say?" I asked jokingly, a grin splitting my face despite the pain in my back.

"He showed me to trust my heart." She smiled. "But I need to know how you feel about me before I make any decisions."

"You already know that answer," I responded, sitting up. "I like you and I haven't tried to hide it."

She held my gaze for a moment, but soon turned away from the intensity. "But we haven't known each other that long, and don't you think it's a little weird to get into new a relationship while we're being held here, waiting to be executed?" Her voice was soft, as though she was truly nervous.

"Look. I'm not going to beat around the bush. If you like me, then you like me," I said. I was beginning to get frustrated. "If you don't, then you don't, and there's nothing that I can do about it. Who cares how long we've known each other? We're in an execution camp! How much longer do you think we have?"

"I do like you—of course I do," Roxane quickly responded, before I could say another word. "That's not the issue. But you said it! We're here! We're here to die and, if we don't manage to escape, what's the point in us starting a relationship?"

"What's the point be?" I repeated. "There's no great point really, other than to satisfy our hearts. I honestly truly believe that I'm in love with you, and I need you to say that you'll be my girlfriend, regardless of why we're here, or how much time we may have before one of us is executed."

"You love me?" Roxane blushed as the words escaped her lips.

"Yes, I love you. I don't know why I love

you, but I don't need to know why. There are many things that I don't know—like I don't know why just on this one planet, there are so many different races and languages, but we both know that there *are* different races and languages. I don't know why the world is round—think about it! On a round planet, that's constantly pinning, the wind should blow everywhere at the same time, never ending.

"If it is windy in Texas, it should be windy in California as well, yet it's not windy everywhere at the same time! But despite this, we know for a fact that the world is round, because if it wasn't, somebody would have found the edge by now.

"I don't even know why humans exist at all; our existence makes no sense. Whether you believe in God or don't believe in God, it makes no sense. At some point, something came from nothing, and created everything else. Nothing logically should exist, not even emptiness. Darkness shouldn't exist, light shouldn't exist, and yet here it all is real as can be. Here we are, existing. So, I may not know why I love you, but I know I *do*, because I've *felt* it! Right here!" I said at last, touching my heart.

I stopped to catch my breath and she smiled. "Yes," she said, nodding. "I will be your girlfriend."

"Really, you'll be my girlfriend?" I asked, wanting to make sure that I heard the words correctly.

"You've grown on me quite a bit, you know," she said, chuckling. "I fell in love with you, too. I just didn't want to put myself out there, or do anything stupid, because I thought I had a fiancé, so I wanted to be faithful to him. But since I don't, I'd love to be your girlfriend.

"Please don't get it confused though. We've only made ourselves vulnerable by liking each other, because we're stuck here in this execution camp. If we don't escape, I'll break-up with you before either of us get executed.

"Also, I hope you know that even though I caught feelings for you, I would never have cheated on my fiancé. I'm not like that."

"Ex-fiancé," I replied, smiling. Roxane punched my arm. "And I know you aren't like that," I replied. "Trust me, I know, but I think we fell for each other because, deep down, we were drawn to each other."

"No," Roxane cut in. "More like you were drawn to me and suckered me in." She laughed as she spoke, so I knew she was joking.

She hugged me and gave me a soft kiss in front of the window, with the moonlight shining right on us. We snuck out of the sleeping quarters and made up our minds to go to the cafeteria area. As if by magic, it started raining just as we stepped outside.

It was the first rainfall in a long while, so I knew the rainy season was probably just around the corner. The last rainy season was great, at first, but it brought the crocodiles very close to camp as the river rose. We stopped to enjoy the rain for a brief moment, enjoying the cool droplets soaking through our clothes. I remember it so clearly. She leaned in and kissed my lips so softly that I could've sworn she was an angel. She stole my soul, and my legs became weak; my heart raced. I could hear each and every breath and each and every heartbeat, thudding in my chest.

We slowly made our way to the cafeteria. Once we were inside, Roxane twirled in place, offering me a coy smile as she began to remove her shirt. I reached for her instinctively, and my breath caught when she pushed herself flush against me. She caught my bottom lip between hers as I wound a hand into her hair. Kissing her for the first time was divine.

She backed me into the wall and continued to kiss me. I was lost to her then, returning her kisses with fervent passion. We made our way to the ground and I could feel my grip on reality weakening with each little noise she made…

*****

"I probably better stop there," Gatsby said, chuckling as he turned to face Manuel. "I don't want to go into too many details on the air."

Manuel smirked but raised his hand. "No, no, trust me," he said. The listeners certainly want to hear this. Nothing attracts listeners like a good sex story."

Gatsby nodded. "Okay, but if I get in trouble, you're getting in trouble as well." He poked Manuel in the arm and readied himself to continue. "I closed my eyes and drew her closer, inching my fingers over her delicate ribcage…"

*****

She arched her back, rocking against me when my hand found her breasts, and I shuddered in anticipation when she moaned against my neck, dropping a line of kisses down to my collar bone. Her nipples peaked at my touch, and I could feel the pressure increasing around my groin as she reached up to unbutton my shirt. As I shrugged free of the sleeves, she rolled us over and found the fastening on my pants. Within a moment, I was lying bare on the floor, staring up at her in rapture.

I hesitated when her eyes fell on my growing erection. She gasped. "Oh, wow," she murmured, eyes widening. "You're going to have to go gentle on me."

I grinned and nodded, swallowing hard. Pulling her towards me, I peppered needful kisses across her collar bone and allowed my fingers to roam the curve of her inner thigh. At her nod, I entered her slowly, relishing in her enthusiasm—

*****

"Hold on a second!" Manuel cut in, "we have a call."

"I can already tell you who it is," Gatsby said, shaking his head as a feeling of dread encompassed him. "And we're both about to get in a lot of trouble, I'm telling you." He turned to back to the mic. "He made me say it! You heard him!" he said, trying to head off the lecture he knew was coming.

Manuel chuckled and shook his head. "We shall see. Hello?" he addressed the caller. "Please state your name and where you're from."

The voice on the other end of the line erupted. "Jonathan was right! It's me, Roxane, and I'm from *you better sleep with one eye open*. Both of you!"

"Oh, shoot," Manuel said, cringing and looking to Gatsby for information. "How on earth did you know it was her?"

He shrugged. "Let's just say it's the intuition of a man in trouble."

Roxane interrupted before they could move on. "Yeah, our sex life does not go on the radio, and I hope I'm clear to both of you on that subject!"

"Loud and clear," Manuel replied, with a dip of his head.

"Um, I didn't hear you, Jonathan," Roxane said, her voice sharp with attitude. She was fierce when she was riled.

"That's because I'm a grown man!" Gatsby replied, attempting a front for the listeners.

"Excuse me? What did you just say to me?" The threat in Roxane's voice was very clear.

Gatsby sighed. "I said," he began, changing tacts, "that I love you, and that Manuel and I are going to have a talk about him coercing me into telling that part of the story."

Roxane was silent for a beat before she huffed. "I'll—I'll just see you when you get home," she replied angrily, and hung up the phone.

Gatsby's mouth dropped open. "Dang," he said to himself, knowing that he had messed up.

Manuel was fidgeting with his water glass. "Let's just skip past that part of the story, shall we?" he suggested nervously, "and continue on where it picks up afterwards."

"Okay," Gatsby said, taking a deep breath. He was not looking forward to going back home. "Here it goes." He had to push himself to continue. "I began holding meetings every night, trying to come up with an escape plan."

*****

"Listen," I said. "We're close to them in number. We have sixty-seven right now, but will only have sixty-six after they execute someone this month. But here's the thing—while they *do* have a hundred armed soldiers, after an execution a lot of them sneak out during the night. And... the General always grabs a girl to rape, so he's occupied.

"So, on a night after an execution, we'll likely outnumber them. The problem is, while we outnumber them, they'll still have weapons and we won't, so we need to find a way to get a hold of some. A girl named Reba raised her hand. "Yes?" I said and pointed to her.

"I just wanted to point out that we do have sixty-seven people, but twenty of them are kids under twelve, so technically it will be forty-seven against one hundred."

"Not necessarily," I replied. "I don't know how yet, but I'm pretty sure the kids will come in handy. We shouldn't underestimate them."

"So what you're saying, from what I understand, is that we're going to risk these little kids getting killed?" Reba asked, shocked at my response.

"No. I'm saying that we are in an execution camp and they are on a list to be killed, and that we might need them to get them off that list. Just like we might not, it just depends on whatever strategy we come up with. They're going to be executed if they don't escape, so if they get killed trying, God forbid," I added, "it would have happened anyways. At least they will have died fighting back, you know."

"Yeah, that makes sense," Reba said, nodding her head in agreement.

CHAPTER ELEVEN

"What else do the soldiers do on the night of an execution?" I asked the group.

Roxane raised her hand. "The guards are always hung over the next day from getting drunk." She spoke very shyly. I had learned through earlier meetings that she didn't like being the center of attention or speaking in front of a group of people. Roxane was and still is very private and doesn't like people knowing everything about her.

"Really?" I said, slightly surprised. "That would make a lot of sense, you know, as to why we don't see too many of them the next day. Oh!" I said, as something suddenly occurred to me. "Notice whenever they leave to take the person to be executed, they always drive in the direction of the mines, and not to any of the buildings that are set aside just for them." I stopped to think, rubbing my neck. "Who here works in the mines?"

A bunch of hands shot into the air.

"Have any of you seen a passageway that could possibly lead us out of here, back the way we came in? Because it seems like the only way out is through those mines and, from past meetings, I remember people saying that every tunnel just went in circles and led right back to the entrance. This might be our only escape option, because I'm not taking any chances on that river," I took a breath and gestured widely, encouraging agreement from the crowd. "And if they're going through there to get to their execution location, there has to be at least one tunnel that leads out, right?"

"No, nobody has been through any tunnel that leads out of the mines," came the voice of a new member to the group, whose name was Jordan. He had been taken from his life along with his brother, Sam. "There is a section of the mines that the soldiers won't let us near, though. The last guy that they took to be executed snuck in there trying to escape, but he didn't get too far because he was spotted by one of the soldiers. He wound up being beaten *and* executed."

"Did he tell you what he saw?" I asked.

"Yeah, he said the tunnel went down beneath the earth and then leveled out. He also said water was seeping in through the cracks of the ceiling, as if it were raining hard. But it was a clear sunny day, so he said he thought the tunnel must have been under water."

"That's it then. That's the way out," I said to the group, my face flushed with excitement. That tunnel must run under part of the river."

Many of the people that were in the meeting nodded their heads in agreement.

"That makes perfect sense," Mao added, "which is why they won't let us work in that part of the mine."

"It sure does," Amy agreed with her friend.

"Okay," I said, nodding along eagerly. "So now we know the way out, and that the best time to escape is right after an execution. Let's look at the negatives. We have twenty kids with us and no vehicle here is large enough for us to take everybody at once. That means we'll be traveling slower than I'd like. We're going to need guns. One of the deliverers needs to find out where they keep them and how we can get a hold of them." I deliberately avoided looking at Roxane, hoping she'd understand that I didn't want it to be her.

"I will." A man named, Illya volunteered.

"Okay," I replied. "This whole plan depends on you doing this and bringing the information back, so do it cautiously. And make sure you don't get caught."

"I understand," Illya replied.

I looked at Roxane and smiled, "Guess we're getting out of here after all."

She smiled back. "I guess we are."

*****

"I'm sorry," Manuel cut in, standing abruptly and reaching out to set a hand on Gatsby's arm. "But we're going to have to cut this broadcast short. The base is under attack. Enemy soldiers are trying to force their way into Fairbanks. Apparently, two Russian choppers made it past our defenses undetected, and soldiers have parachuted in a mile out. We will continue your story later," Manuel assured Gatsby as he ushered him through the door.

Manuel rushed Gatsby out so that he could focus on getting his camera crew ready to film the impending battle for the CGX Televised News.

*****

Boom, boom, rata-tat-tat-tat, rata-tat-tat-tat. The sounds of guns firing in the distance pierced the air as Manuel Emotho and his crew recorded the battle from the roof of a nearby abandoned building. A loud sounding shot silenced the others, and a US soldier fell to the ground. The US troops started shooting in all directions as two of them grabbed the fallen soldier and took cover.

Manuel and his crew had to duck down to keep from being shot by the wild bullets. Excitement and fear rushed through Manuel—he wanted to stand up and film, but not with bullets still flying in his direction.

The soldiers were being shot at by a sniper they couldn't see, so shooting in all directions was the only way they could get to the wounded soldier without being killed.

Manuel received a call while he was on the roof, informing him that the whole east coast was under attack. Power had been knocked out across the region, and President Brooks was being evacuated to Colorado on the bullet train.

"Get this information to Tremaine Sanderson and have him go on the air with it within the hour. I'll repeat it during my show for those who miss his broadcast."

"Okay," one of the camera operators said, as he rushed back into the news studio to find Tremaine.

The crack of gunshots continued, but they were becoming more distant. The camera caught the battle on video, but Manuel and his crew kept their heads down to keep from being hit by stray bullets. When the sound of the guns became so distant that they could barely hear them, Manuel slowly raised his head and looked over the side of the studio ceiling. The soldiers were gone. He grabbed the camera off its perch to watch the video, but was disappointed to find that it had been compromised in the crossfire—the viewing screen and USB port were both destroyed, and he wouldn't be able to see the footage.

With an outraged cry, he swung the camera over the edge of the roof and tossed it down to the streets below, upset that he'd wasted all that time filming the battle only to have the video destroyed by stray bullets. "Well, that sucks," he said. "It would have been nice to have some decent footage."

"Yeah, it would have," one of the camera men replied.

"Well, let's head inside and wait to be briefed by the Army. I want to find out what went down."

CHAPTER TWELVE

Gatsby sat in the newsroom with Manuel, preparing to tell more of the story of his escape from the execution camp when, suddenly, one of the aids dashed over and thrust a note at Manuel. As he read, his face contorted with confusion and he gave Gatsby a signal to hold on a moment.

"Before you begin," he said, with a serious look darkening his face, "I have to make an announcement." He turned his attention to the mic. "Hello, everyone. This is Manuel Emotho with CGX News with an update on the president. The White House was, indeed, compromised yesterday. The President was able to get into the bunker, and from there he was able to get on the presidential bullet train, as reported by Tremaine Sanderson yesterday. The current update is that the president is now currently safe in Colorado."

"Wow," Gatsby said. His voice cracked a bit as he spoke, and he reached for his glass of water.

"He is safe. The President is safe," Manuel repeated, "and he will be addressing the nation as soon as he is rested and able to do so.

"For now, I'm going to hand over to Mr Gatsby so that we can hear some more about the heroic escape from the execution camp, as scheduled. Mr Gatsby?" Manuel gestured for him to speak.

Gatsby cleared his throat. "Uh, I'll just start with a little play back to catch everyone up. A group of us came up with a plan to escape. The plan was perfect, and we felt like there was no way it could go wrong. Within a few days, we knew where they kept the guns, and the kitchen staff was beginning to store food for the journey… today, I'm going to go into detail about Sergeant Stephen Dunham's group. The group of soldiers who found us just as we were ready to give up."

*****

Sergeant Stephen's unit were the platoon who located the first execution camp, and they were able to extract those prisoners successfully. They repeated this process three times before they met opposition, where they were ordered to retreat to an extraction point. They were told that another platoon was already in play who felt sure they were near to finding another execution camp.

Stephen and his platoon were on high alert. A sniper fired two shots into their camp, injuring two people, so the unit did what they were trained to do. They fired their guns blindly in all directions, while two of them ran in to get the injured to safety. As the gunfire continued, another of Stephen's soldiers was hit by the sniper.

"Somebody find that sniper!" Stephen yelled. Flinging himself to the ground—the safest place to gather his thoughts—he instinctively crawled his way to the sniper rifle twenty feet away, next to one of the fallen men.

Whoever was firing on them had targeted the snipers first.

Hastily examining the rifle, he found that it was the M24 sniper rifle, which happened to be his preference. It had eight-hundred-and-seventy-five yards in shooting range and fired twenty rounds per minute. It wasn't loaded, but the soldier had a clip in his hands. He was the second soldier shot and had obviously been trying to put the clip in place.

Grabbing the clip from the soldier's hand, Stephen rolled into the nearest bit of brush. A snake hissed and lunged at him as he encroached on its territory. Its first bite struck his body armor and didn't do any damage. The large cobra re-coiled, though, and prepared to strike again. As it lunged, it found its head impaled on Stephen's blade. Shaking his head and removing the remains, Stephen immediately refocused on finding the deadly enemy sniper from the cover of the brush.

He didn't have time to worry about the dangers of the insects and animals in the Congo jungles of Africa, even though he feared the giant wolf spiders that inhabited the section his unit was heading towards. The spiders were territorial and known for hiding in the tall grass; they were extremely aggressive and very fast. The glass half-full part was they didn't have webs and couldn't web their victims; the glass half-empty part was that they ate their victims alive—right away. They were native to an island off Portugal but had somehow made their way into Africa and thrived, growing into mammoth beasts that generated myth and fear.

Stephen began searching through the rifle-scope, looking for a glare from another scope reflecting back at him from the sun, or any type of movement on the ground or amongst the trees. He kept a very steady hand as he first scanned the trees and then the earth below him. He didn't see anything, and thought the sniper had gone, but still thought it best to stay hidden in the brush, just in case.

All of his soldiers had taken cover as well. They hid using their camouflaged uniforms to blend in with the jungle under the cover of the brush and trees, waiting for his order to get up. One of the injured moved. "Help!" he cried, as he stretched his arm into the air.

"Don't move!" Stephen yelled to his unit.

"Sergeant, let me get him, please."

"No," Stephen yelled back, "Wait until we confirm a kill. This ghost sniper is dangerous—we don't need more getting hurt."

"Sergeant, please help!" the soldier yelled.

"Sergeant, we can't let Bryce die like this, Sir. He's still in the open."

"Don't you move, soldier," Stephen ordered his man.

Bryce's best friend—within the unit and in life, having grown up together—heeded the order for the count of a breath before jumping up without warning and bolting towards his injured friend.

Stephen yelled, "No!" but knew it was too late to stop the soldier. He quickly scanned the trees in the direction it had seemed the shots were coming from. It took a moment, but once Bryce's friend was clearly in the open, a shot fired from directly where Stephen was looking.

Stephen placed the scope to his eye and focused on the spot until he found the sniper…

BAM!

He fired, hitting the sniper right in his Adam's apple and knocking him out of the tree.

"Got him!" Stephen yelled, his body sagging with excited relief as he made his way towards the rest of his team.

"Sergeant!" yelled another of his soldiers. "Danny Boy is down."

Stephen turned and sure enough, Bryce's best friend, Danny Boy, was lying dead on the ground beside his injured comrade. "Damnit!" He cussed, his grip tightening on his rifle. "Don't freaking move—anybody else. Bryce, stay your ass down and act dead! Don't even twitch until we can be sure there're no more snipers in the area." No one spoke, and he turned carefully to check on the others.

"Harrison!" He barked, addressing a man so scrawny that the only indication he was military at all was the full uniform that he wore. His dorky attitude and thick glasses hid him well.

"Yes, Sergeant?" Harrison waited for his instructions.

"Radio Base and tell them we need a thermal scan to see if there're any more snipers on us," Stephen ordered.

"Sir, yes Sir," Harrison replied.

Harrison radioed his orders in. "Eagle this is Ant Eater. Do we have any more snipers on us? Our coordinates are latitude –0.765251 and longitude 15.776526."

"We heard latitude –0.765251 and longitude 15.776526, confirm," a voice sounded through Harrison's radio.

"Yes, that number is confirmed as correct. A sniper has taken down four of our soldiers, and we have three soldiers confirmed dead. The fourth is injured but confirmed to still be alive. Are there anymore snipers in the area?"

Stephen set his rifle down next to him, so as not to confuse the results. It took no more than a single moment for Command to respond.

"Negative. There are no snipers appearing on the thermal scan."

"Yes!" Sergeant Stephen yelled. "Thank God!" He climbed up off the hot ground and made a show of dusting himself off as he awaited further information.

The voice came back over the radio, "However, Ant Eaters, you have been ordered to abort. You have an Army of Ants headed your way. Get to the emergency extraction point."

"Roger that. Ant Eaters confirming our orders to abort the mission and to get to the extraction point. What is extraction time?"

A new voice crackled in over the radio. "This is Anonymous—you can refer to me as General X. The Congo is massive, and a lot of it is pure jungle. If you feel the extraction route has been compromised, use all that jungle to your benefit. Stay away from the cities and be careful. Remember, you are in Africa, and in the Congo jungle at that.

"Enemy soldiers are not all you have to worry about in there. Every insect and every animal out there can kill you. You're being ordered to leave the wounded behind. Judging by these thermal scans, the Ants are nearly upon you and if you try to take the wounded, you will not make it very far."

"I can't do that, Sir. Number one rule is never leave a fallen brother behind, Sir," Sergeant Dunham replied.

"Number two rule;" the General insisted, "Always obey orders. It is not an option. That's an order. At the speed they're traveling, those soldiers are maybe nine minutes from you, if even that long."

"Sir, can you buy us time—use a drone strike or something? We cannot leave him to die, Sir. He has a family and we, as his adopted family, cannot comply with that order, Sir."

"You have a family as well, soldier. If you try to take him, they will catch you and kill you all, and none of you will see your families again. Think of the rest of this adopted family of yours—the soldiers beneath your command. Are you willing to ensure that their families will receive a flag and letter, rather than their loved one?

"He's wounded. If you leave him, it's likely that they'll only take him prisoner, and that means we can track and rescue him. But if you take him, he will surely be killed by the enemy, or killed by diseased, blood sucking insects. And that's not to mention that the scent of his blood will attract predators... there's a whole jungle full of critters out there, Sergeant—lions, leopards, crocodiles, tracking hyenas—and you guys will never be able to escape."

"Won't they be able to track us anyways?"

"No, they won't. When you get a good distance away from the bodies, use the mint spray in your bags. Don't use it all because you'll still need to use it to keep away spiders. Rub it all over your bodies. It will confuse the hyenas' sense of smell and they won't be able to track you. Now, get a move on. They're getting closer."

"Understood," Stephen replied.

"Extraction will be in thirty-eight hours. Get there, soldier."

"Roger that, Sir."

"Radio silence commenced," Stephen said as he shut the radio off. "Okay troops, you heard the orders. Let's move out. We have enemy Ants headed our way, and we need to move fast."

The Sergeant wasn't happy. He started with thirteen soldiers and was down to nine.

"Sir, what about Bryce?" Jamie asked.

"Jamie, now is not the time for compassion. Do as you're trained to do. We should worry about how *we're* going to survive, which will be hard enough. You heard me try to change this, Jamie. Command shut me down and ordered us to leave him—for our safety... and his."

"So, you would just leave me if I was shot?"

"Sergeant, please don't leave me," Bryce whimpered. "Please, Sergeant." Stephen rubbed the bridge of his nose and moved out of ear shot of Bryce. Against his better judgement, he forced himself to ignore the desperate pleas because, if he engaged in conversation, he'd soon be attempting to take the wounded man with him—everyone would be in danger.

He hated himself for leaving one of his men behind, but Command was right—they would never make it if they took him. Besides, if Bryce had obeyed orders in the first place, he would have never been shot.

The rest of the unit observed how the sergeant kept ignoring Bryce, even while in conversation with Jamie.

"Jamie, yes, you better believe I would, and I'd expect you to do the same for me. If Command said I must leave you and we were in a situation where leaving you meant the rest of us had a chance to live but bringing you would kill us, then yes, I would. And if you wouldn't do the same, then you'll never command your own platoon, because to get promotions you must first prove you can follow orders. And your job is to keep as many soldiers alive as possible, so families aren't receiving flags instead of their loved ones. Our job is to follow orders. Now, let's move out."

"They must only be minutes from us by now," Malcom, one of the soldiers, said, hinting to Stephen that they might want to discuss the rest while on the run. Stephen nodded and they began to move.

The unit gathered as light of a load as they could but kept enough supplies for their survival. They took off into the jungle at a swift run, blocking out the sound of Bryce trying to get up—the sound of their friend trying to talk them into helping him.

"Please… *Please*!" Bryce yelled, as he was left to face the oncoming soldiers alone. "Don't leave me! Please don't leave!" He began to sob but managed to drag himself to a tree and lean up against it. He pulled a crumpled cigar from his pocket and lit it, watching as the enemy approached. He pulled his rifle from his back and took aim. He did the only thing he could think to do.

"Pick it up, everyone. They'll be coming after us hard now!" Stephen yelled to his unit, as he heard the single crack of a gunshot in the distance. Soon after, it was followed by the rattling sound of many more.

They ran until they were out of breath and Stephen ordered them to stop. He kept watch, and they began pouring mint oil all over their bodies. Each person had four bottles of mint oil to keep spiders away. A quarter of one bottle covered the whole unit of nine soldiers.

"Okay, let's move," Stephen ordered as soon as they were done.

The unit was on the move again, keeping up a steady jog, just as they were trained to do. They didn't have much cover because they'd entered the desert part of the jungle. Every so often, Stephen would have one of his unit check through the sniper scope to see if anyone was following them. Each time they checked it was the same story.

Command reported that there were no signs they were being followed. The enemy soldiers did not pursue.

"They must have intercepted the message about the extraction and decided to just head to the coast and meet us there rather than chase us across the continent," Malcolm said, as they took a quick breather.

Night was beginning to fall, and they stopped to set up camp. It was not pitch black yet, but the sky had turned a dark, ocean-blue color. The moon was shining bright even though it was still a bit light out.

"Sergeant, why do you think that they're not following us? Do you think they intercepted the message? Jamison asked.

Jamison was tall and muscular, and he had hoped to be an Army ranger. But, before he was due to start school, their unit was deployed, and he ended up in Africa instead.

"That's what we're hoping for—that they intercepted," Stephen replied.

"Sir?" Jamison responded, confused.

"Well, look at it like this, soldier. There are two US bases here in the Congo Republic. Then, there's the coast. We said we were headed towards the coast for extraction to throw them off, but I assume their intelligence is at least as smart as I am, so I thought about… what if I was their commander? What would I do if I were them?

"I'd send units to the coast and have militarized choppers waiting to shoot the extraction chopper down. And I'd place more units in between our last known location and the two US bases—to intercept us."

"But, if they're covering the bases and the coast, how does that help us, Sergeant? If you don't mind me asking, Sir?" Quenshoda, another one of Stephens's soldiers, asked.

"We're not heading to any of the US bases here in the Congo Republic. We're going to make the much longer trip to the base in the central Congo jungle."

"Sergeant, but we just ran dang near thirty miles away from Brazzaville, going away from the Congo jungle!"

"We had to make sure we weren't being followed. However, myself, and the general who just told us to run through the jungle, came up with this abort plan the moment he informed me that we were being sent here to find some of the execution camps. I just didn't tell anybody, and neither did he. Easier to keep it under wraps that way.

"I left a note with the general saying if I call for an extraction, he should send a team to make it look real but abort the mission twenty miles from the extraction point."

"Sir, what if they radio the base we're headed to and tell them we're coming, and it gets intercepted by the enemy?"

"I never told Command where we would head to if we needed an extraction. As of right now, we're keeping radio silence until we get two miles from our destination. Then, and only then, will we radio our location into Command, and have Command alert the US base to our presence. Then they can meet us halfway."

"And what's the backup plan?" Valfor asked. He was a very quiet person and always kept to himself. He was tall enough and solid enough, and his tanned skin and reddish-brown hair helped identify his Russian descent. His dream was to be a Marine, but the Army drafted him before he could sign up.

Though Valfor was only twenty-one, he was very strong and could fight extremely well, which is why Command initially placed him in Stephen's unit. "I'm only asking, Sir, because we're headed to the most dangerous part of the jungle; the most dangerous part of the continent… What if something goes wrong and they don't know where we are?"

"We can radio it in," Stephen interrupted. "The minute we get in trouble, we radio it in. Understood?" He addressed the whole unit, ensuring that his hard stare landed on each of them individually.

Of those that remained, there were six men—Valfor, Jamison, Malcom, Harrison, Timothy, and Stephen—and three women—Valerie, Jamie, and Quenshoda. The four who had tragically fallen were Jerrell, Danny, Bryce, and Adrienne.

"Hoorah, Sergeant," the unit yelled in uproarious unison.

"Are we Army or Air Force?" Sergeant Stephen yelled at his unit.

"Army!" his unit yelled back.

"Are we Army or Navy?" Stephen shouted.

"Army, Sir!"

"Would you rather be Army or Marines?"

The crickets chirped, the birds sang, and a frog croaked, but not a soldier spoke.

"So you're just going to act like you didn't hear me, huh?"

"Oh, we heard you, Sir. It's just… I've been pretending to be a Marine this whole time, and now that the mission is at its peak and presenting the most danger, I won't lose hope and say I'm Army over being a Marine, Sir," Jamie said with a cheeky smirk on her face.

The unit replied, "Hoorah!" in agreement, and then all began to laugh.

A lion roared in the distance and Harrison nearly jumped out of his shoes. "Sergeant, I'm a little nervous about sleeping. I remember when I was a kid, I watched a movie about two lions that hunted people for fun, and they almost killed an entire village, Sir. And it was based on a true story and took place right here in the Congo."

"Shoot, I saw the movie *Tarzan*. I'm far more scared of the gorillas out here than anything else," Jamie cut in. "Not to mention how crazy those gorillas were in *Congo*."

"Sergeant, I saw the movie *Bee*, and I want to go home," Malcolm said, laughing as he jumped up and down, mocking the others.

The unit laughed and began to play fight each other before finally settling down to set up camp.

CHAPTER THIRTEEN

"What do you mean you lost them?" The Russian commander yelled at the African general. "If they find another one of our execution camps, you will be the next execution, mark my words! You better hope and pray that they do not find where the prisoners are being held." He kicked at the ground and clenched his fists in fury. "They've already destroyed several of our camps and freed a number of our prisoners. If it were up to you, they would find the rest!" he finished.

"Our Hyenas can track anything, Sir, but these soldiers came prepared, and five miles into tracking them, the Hyenas lost their scent."

"I do not need excuses. I will send my best tracker instead!" the Russian general yelled.

"Soldier, go get Vladkolaf," he instructed one of his own soldiers.

"Yes Sir, right away," the Russian soldier responded immediately, as he turned on his heels and headed out of the room in a hurry.

"No disrespect to you or your Hyenas, comrade, but we must find these soldiers before they find any more of our locations. Or have you forgotten that they just bombed a second secret location—the one where we did most of our live executions?"

The African general did not like the Russians taking over or implying that their tracking methods were better, but he also wanted the Americans found. If the Russians found them, then they could rest easy. If not, then the Russians would take a hit to their pride.

*****

Stephen's troop woke up to Harrison jumping around like a deranged animal. "Oh shit, Sergeant. Look!" A spider was crawling over his bag, long legs scuttling disturbingly.

"Valfor, kill it, and watch out. That's a damned camel spider. They shoot numbing poison out of their butts that will numb your whole body." Stephen looked around him and sighed. "Clean this place up! Leave not a trace that we were here. We may have fooled the Africans, but the Russians have diverse ways of tracking. More old school, less easily fooled, and even a leaf out of place will tell them which direction we're going."

While the unit spot cleaned their location, he looked through a pair of advanced binoculars that could see up to three-hundred-and-eighty yards away. He was looking for any disturbance in the brush in the direction from which they had come.

He had hoped his diversion had worked, but he wasn't willing to risk his life on false confidence, and he was wary that the Russians would try to track them, too.

If the hyenas had indeed lost their scent, any carelessness in their running ,or debris left behind at their campsites, would alert the Russians, and no amount of mint oil could keep them at bay.

Stephen was sure that his platoon left plenty of clues as to which direction they went in, and had them go over the camp with a fine-toothed comb four times before he was satisfied. They could not chance missing even the smallest thing that might give away the direction they were heading. A tracker could find with ease a bit of food wrapper the size of a small fingernail on the ground, and then they'd know that they were there. The spot they set their camp up at was dry dirt and gray rocks, with just a few small clumps of long-stemmed grass peeking out of the earth here and there. They weren't in the part of the Congo jungle filled with trees and wildlife yet, but they could see it in the far distance.

"Okay, do a food count and an ammo count," Stephen ordered his crew.

"Yes, Sir," Quenshoda replied, and the unit began to carefully check their inventory.

Some of the platoon was a little disgruntled about the order, as doing the count required them to un-pack everything they'd just put away, empty everything back out, count it, and then pack it up again. They were certain a fifth spot clean order would follow.

"Okay, Sir," Jamie stepped forward with a list in her hand, "We have nine M16 assault rifles, thirty-six mags—each clip full. We have thirty clips full for the ten M11 handguns we've got—that's including both yours, Sir.

"We have seven grenades and six flares. Food wise, we have seventy-five food bars—all the same flavor of ham dinner. We each have three aluminum water bottles filled with water, and one each that is partially drunk out of. We have nine sleeping bags, and nine four-person tents. We have three pots and two hundred and sixteen waterproof matches. We have flint and steel as well.

"We have eleven rain ponchos, nine pairs of boots, which we have on our feet, and thirty-six shirts, including those on our backs."

"That's good," Stephen said, buoyed a little by their thoroughness. "My main concern was food and ammo. I wanted to make sure that none of our fallen brothers had the food packs and extra ammo. Split everything evenly so we're all carrying the same weight."

He waited until they were all ready before he spoke again. "Now, let's also have a moment of silence for our brothers, who gave their lives protecting ours. The bullets chose them rather than us. It could have been any of us. Let's pray that the enemy has enough honor to bury them, and not leave their bodies to rot."

The platoon bowed its head in a moment of silence as each soldier focused on the time they had spent together with their fallen brethren. Whether each person were best friends or not didn't matter during that moment, because all the fallen were a part of their adopted family and had just died in their place.

As the troop prepared to move out, Stephen made them line up in single file. Whoever was in the far back of the line had the job of sweeping up their tracks. They moved slowly, so as not to rush the sweeper. As they crept along the dirt, Stephen would stop the unit every five hundred feet to give himself time to look through the binoculars, checking to see if they were being tracked.

"So far so good," he encouraged his team.

"Sergeant?" Malcolm asked. "If we threw the scent off with the mint oil, why are you worried about them finding us, Sir?"

"One, you never ever take chances, especially if other people's lives are at stake," he said, lips pressing together in a grim line as he stood before Malcom. "And two, I'm not looking for hyenas. Intelligence informed me right before we left that they have reason to believe that Russians are here aiding Africa in their fight against us. If that's true, they have some of the best trackers in the world and won't be fooled by mint oil."

"Sir, Russian trackers?" Valerie asked, eyes wide open.

"That's what I said, but I also said maybe." The Sergeant didn't want his team to be unduly frightened, just prepared. "That's why I changed the plan at the last minute. If they are here, there's no way we would we have made it to the original extraction point. He smiled "Okay group, time to stop. Get your binoculars out and let's search the area for any Russian trackers," he ordered his platoon.

"Nothing in my direction," said Jamie.

"Nothing over here," "or here," said Valfor and Malcolm.

Stephen didn't trust Valfor. When Stephen had mentioned that Russian soldiers might have been on their trail as well, Valfor avoided eye contact which wasn't good. That was normally a sign you were hiding something. In this case, it was the sign of a traitor.

Without proof, Stephen had nothing to go on, so whenever Valfor said it was clear, he double checked himself. It wasn't good to have suspicion bubbling within the team, especially in life-or-death situations, and Stephen knew he was going to have to either confront Valfor or have a little faith in him—just because he was Russian didn't make him a spy.

They looked down on the Congo jungle and its thousands and thousands of miles of trees. A lion pride roared in the distance. The entire platoon was excited and scared, and yet ready all at the same time. They began to make their way down the hill into the jungle, where they wrestled with long, green grass, ducked past tall trees, and gasped in awe at the many great rivers they could see in the distance. Luckily for them, they had just missed the rainy season.

It would have been far more difficult for them to travel if the land was swathed in water, particularly with the wet-weather wildlife having no boundaries. They'd have been forced to contend with crocodiles and hippopotamuses, anacondas and piranhas, and whatever other monsters decided to rise from the depths of their river homes.

As they neared the first tree, the lions again roared in the distance, as if giving the platoon warning not to enter. They were immediately immersed in the sounds of the jungle—monkeys shouting and chattering to each other in the trees, the chirruping and calling of a hundred different birds, the creaking of ancient timber as the tree trunks snuggled tightly together. They quickly forgot their fears and embraced the beauty of the jungle for a moment.

"Watch your step," Stephen ordered his platoon, after allowing them a moment of peace. "Black mambas love the water, and they're very poisonous."

Half the platoon walked with their guns pointed at the ground; the other half kept their guns pointed at the trees. There were many dangers lurking in both directions, and they had to walk for what felt like half a day before they found a clearing to rest in.

"Yo," Stephen said, as he halted his unit, raising his arms slowly to back them up a bit. In the tree, directly above them, was a jaguar settled on a large branch. They backed up as quietly as they could, but the jaguar heard them and lifted its head. It seemed to size them up for a minute but wound up deciding they were neither threat nor prey, laying its head back down on its resting place.

"We're good, Sergeant," Jamie said. "There're too many of us. It isn't interested."

"Okay, Jamie. I saw a jaguar fight off twenty crocodiles in the water, and he was whooping them. He lost in the end, but only because he tired out. Now, don't miss this bit. Instead of trying to get out of the water, he decided to *stay there* and fight to the death," Valfor said, eyeing the cat warily.

"Yeah, I saw that same thing," Stephen agreed. "Even if there are too many of us, we aren't taking any chances. We cannot risk firing our weapons and giving away our location."

"I hear you, Sergeant," Jamie replied.

Stephen's platoon moved slowly, hoping to find a safer clearing where they could set up camp before darkness fell. A lot of the journey seemed to be uphill, which proved to be very tiring and caused them to have to take any breaks. After trudging through the jungle for nine-and-a-half hours, they found a clearing at the top of one of the hills and set up camp.

"No fires," Stephen told his crew as he saw a few of them preparing kindling and digging around for the matches. "Not just yet." Stephen wanted to use being on top of the hill to their advantage. At night, he could use the view out over the jungle to check for fire smoke—see if they were being tracked in time to get moving again.

They set up camp, and most of the soldiers took a break, hanging out on the hill and waiting for nightfall. Stephen, however, stayed alert, watching the jungle below through his binoculars. "Listen up," he said, catching the attention of his team. "This is not your neighborhood shelter, as Harrison has already found out. While you're in your sleeping bags, zip them all the way up. We need to be in a tight circle, and we'll need to rub mint oil on the outside of the tents to keep the spiders out. We need to keep incense burning twenty-four-seven to keep away the disease-carrying mosquitos. And we'll take shifts in keeping watch for predators. Get set up," he instructed.

"Sergeant, you have to relax at some point," Jamie said.

"That is a good idea, soldier. Take watch while I take a nap. I'm going to need to be up all night," Stephen said, ready for a rest.

"Yes, Sir," Jamie said sourly. She had been hoping to talk to Stephen. He was a hard person to read, but she figured if she could get closer to him, she might be able to find out why she was so attracted to him. She knew she couldn't date him, but curiosity was getting the better of her.

She kept watch for about two hours before passing the assignment and binoculars on to Harrison and going to bed herself. It was hot outside, but she fell right asleep.

Most of the platoon sat around playing the card games or dominoes that they had brought along to entertain themselves during downtimes. Slowly, the sun began to set and the temperature began to cool. It was a beautiful sunset and, for a while, it took their minds off the grim situation. They began to bunk down for bed just as Stephen awoke from his sleep.

He stayed in his tent for a while, snug and almost comfortable, telling himself he was giving the tracker some time to set up his fire. The truth, though, was that he delayed getting up because it was cold—the temperature seemed to have dropped to what felt like about thirty degrees. Despite what he told himself, he knew that in this jungle, if you were alone, you didn't wait until the last minute to set up your fire—it was the first thing you did.

With that in mind, he slowly forced his way out of his sleeping bag, and out of his tent. He stepped out into the cool air, and the cold felt good—invigorating. He was expecting everyone to be asleep, but Jamie wasn't. She was staring through the binoculars out into the jungle, doing exactly what he had ordered her to do earlier.

"You know, you could have switched with somebody else or went to bed," Stephen said, sitting down beside her.

"Oh, I did, Sir, and I went to sleep two hours after you did, so I could be up to help you keep an eye out for trackers."

"Well, I appreciate that, Jamie. That was very thoughtful of you," Stephen told her.

Jamie blushed, though Stephen couldn't see it because it was dark. She stayed silent, knowing that if she became emotional the moment would be over.

"Well, while you were looking, did you see anything?" Stephen asked, looking over. He held her gaze just a little longer than he really should have.

"Yes, Sir," Jamie said. "There's a fire to your six."

"A fire?" Stephen said. "Trackers?" He jumped to his feet and got ready to run for his sniper rifle, but Jamie chuckled and waved to regain his attention.

"Sergeant, no. Not trackers." Jamie reached out and grabbed Stephen's hand and pulled him back down to a seated position.

"You're sure they're not trackers?"

"Yes, I'm sure. They're locals—a native tribe named by an Egyptian pharaoh."

"The Pigmy Tribe," Stephen responded, nodding. "They were called the Dancing Dwarves because their tallest person was like four feet high or something."

"Yes, Sir," Jamie said, shocked at how brilliant and knowledgeable the sergeant was.

"Yup," Stephen continued. "They're the natives and, just like back at home, foreigners came and stole their land from them. They're losing more and more of the jungle, too. The foreign African tribes come in and hunt for fun, and for tusks and hides, destroying the natural process of the jungle. And the Pigmies do all they can to continue protecting the wildlife. I saw that on the National Geographic channel." He nodded sharply.

"You're very knowledgeable, Sir," Jamie said, watching him carefully.

"I'm sure I haven't told you anything that you don't know," he replied, offering her a sly look before turning to scan the jungle once more. He could see there were no other fires lit, and there was no way they were being tracked. "Well, the good news is that we'll be able to start lighting fires at night from now on, because we're definitely not being followed," he said after a moment. "However," he continued, wondering why there was no one after them. "If they aren't following us, they most likely have an idea where we're going and are trying to get ahead of us instead. The base is supposed to be a secret, but I'll bet my bottom dollar that they know where it is. We can relax for the next few days, but we'll have to be on high alert when we get closer to the base."

After Stephen returned to his tent, Jamie settled back into to hers. She knew there was something there between them, but she would let it build naturally. She didn't want to push anything on Stephen that he wasn't ready for, and didn't want to get him in trouble, either.

*****

"Command, this is The Seeker, I have lost their trail in the Congo. What does command wish for me to do?"

"Come back. There are no bases in the Congo, and it's easy to get lost in that jungle. They're no longer our problem."

"Yes, Command. I will return," the tracker said, turning for home base.

*****

The next morning, just as the sun was rising, Stephen jumped up out of his sleep. There was a tingle in the air that made him feel uneasy, but he couldn't identify the cause straight away. Slowly, he unzipped his tent and peeked out. He could see no visible danger, but something wasn't right. "Arm yourselves!" he commanded the others, and then fired a shot through the slightly open part of his tent to make sure they were all awake.

He heard them jumping up and the clacking of safeties being released. Relieved, he went back to searching the area from his tent.

"What's going on?" Malcolm yelled.

"Stay in your tent," Stephen ordered, waiting patiently for whatever danger he was feeling to present itself. He didn't have long to wait. Within a few moments, gorillas began to walk across their camp.

"Serge!" Jamie yelled.

"It's okay, Jamie," Stephen yelled back. "You'll be okay, I promise." He smiled at her and addressed the others. "Harrison!" he yelled.

"Yes, Sergeant?"

"Can you hear me?".

"Yes, Sergeant," Harrison answered.

"Can you hear me?" Stephen asked again.

"Yes, I can hear you, Sergeant," Harrison answered again.

"Good!" Stephen yelled. "Shut up and stay in your tent."

"Sergeant, there's one heading towards my tent!" Valerie yelled in a frantic voice, "Sergeant! Oh my God! It's coming!"

The biggest gorilla was beating its chest and making violent advancements towards Valerie's tent. Valerie squealed in terror—she was already afraid of gorillas—and her fear only seemed to encourage the large animal.

Before the big gorilla could advance much further, Stephen stepped out of his tent with his gun held high. He was hoping that, with so many poachers coming through the jungle, the gorillas would know the sound of a gun and would take off. He aimed his gun into the air and fired a warning shot. The gorillas went into a rage and began to retreat. They were definitely familiar with the noise, and didn't like it.

The biggest one, which Stephen assumed was the leader, did not retreat with the others, but began moving towards him at a jog-like speed. He raised his gun and aimed again, which caused the big gorilla to pause in its charge. Malcolm, Harrison, and Jamie also stepped out of their tents with their guns aimed at the angered gorilla.

The animal hesitated. Stephen pointed with his gun into the jungle and yelled for it to go. The gorilla could sense that it was outnumbered but also that they were giving it a chance to leave, and moved cautiously back into the heavily wooded area beyond the clearing.

"Wow, that was intense," Valerie said, as she stepped out of her tent. "I'm just glad we were in a clearing and not in amongst the trees, because they could've picked us apart before we even knew they were there."

"Yeah, that's true," Stephen replied. "But gorillas, though more dangerous, are more sensible than chimpanzees. We need to be on the lookout for chimps, too. Okay everyone, let's clean everything up, and please be mindful of spiders, snakes, and insects. Even the mosquitos will kill you out here. Speaking of that, pass me some of that homemade mosquito spray."

The soldiers all had their own mosquito sprays made from beer, Windex, salt, and molasses. It smelled foul but it kept the mosquitos away.

"Sir?" Valfor asked. "How far are we from this base that you say is out here in the Congo, because when I looked yesterday while I had a shift on the binoculars, all I saw was miles and miles of jungle."

"It's close." Stephen looked at Valfor suspiciously an the whole platoon caught it..

"Serge, what's up?" Jamie asked, getting the vibe that something wasn't quite right.

"Well, to be honest, I like to trust my team, and most of us have been together for years.

Then there's Valfor here—a Russian—who just happen to conveniently get transferred to our unit for this mission. Rumor was that the Russians were here as well, but that was just speculation. No proof. At least, not until I shot that Russian sniper."

"So, you think I'm a Russian spy because you shot a Russian sniper?" Valfor asked, looking taken aback.

"Well, I'm not sure," Stephen responded. "But, when I mentioned that there might be Russians here too, you looked very uneasy... made me nervous. Now you're the only one asking how far we are from the base. Doesn't make you a spy, but two questions pop into my mind. First, how did they find us so easily? And second, why were you looking for the base when you were supposed to be looking to see if we were being tracked?"

Valfor saw the whole team was looking at him suspiciously, so he threw his bag at Stephen's feet and stripped down to his boxers and t-shirt. "Go ahead. Search through my stuff. Someone come search me," he said, holding his arms out. "I'm on your side. I'm no Russian spy."

"Serge, what do you want to do?" Valerie asked. She looked like she was starting to feel suspicious of Valfor herself.

Stephen looked at Valfor. "Well, we can't continue this journey together if there's any chance of you being a spy. You understand that, right Valfor?"

"Yes, I do, Sergeant."

"Okay. Harrison, search through his stuff, and Malcom and Valerie search his person." He made his way over to Valfor so he could talk to him while they conducted the search. "I want to believe you're family, Valfor, but

I have to make sure. You're new to our unit, and I cannot risk compromising our hidden base's location."

"I completely understand," Valfor said, as they finished the search.

"Clean, Sir," Malcolm said.

"All good over here, too, Sir," Harrison yelled, flashing a relieved grin.

"Awesome," Stephen replied. "Get your gear back on, Valfor. We don't want the locals thinking you're a stripper."

Everyone laughed, including Valfor.

"So, am I family or what?" Valfor asked, as they prepared to continue.

"Yeah, yeah, yeah," the team said.

Malcolm put him in a playful headlock. "Yeah, buddy, you're one of us," he said.

"Sorry I doubted you, Valfor, but I had to be safe. As they say, better safe than sorry," Stephen apologized, reaching out shake the man's hand.

"Okay," Stephen addressed his platoon, "We're running low on water, so we're going to go off course for a bit. Going to head towards the river. Now, what continent are we in?"

"Africa," Valerie responded.

"Yes, we're in Africa, and the river is the most dangerous part of the Congo. Anacondas, crocodiles, black mamba water snakes… there's even an itty-bitty spider that can dissolve your bones with a single bite."

"I'm sorry. What was that?" Harrison said, "Anything it bites dissolves?"

"That's what I said," Stephen responded. "And it's known as the water spider. It can walk on water and moves the speed of light."

"Sir, I'm not even thirsty," Malcolm said. Everyone laughed. "That's fine," he said, grimacing. "Go ahead and laugh. When one of you gets bit by that spider, I'll be the last one laughing."

"Nobody is going to get bit," Stephen assured the group. "Just... everybody needs to be extra watchful and careful."

The platoon followed Stephen through the jungle, and at times they were distracted by monkeys swinging in the trees, or colorful birds flying in the air. As they were watching the birds, one of them stopped in mid-air, seemingly frozen in place but not falling.

"What the heck," Jamie said, "That's weird. It's like it's frozen in the air."

It only took seconds for everyone to see what really happened. A heavy darkness filled the air, and Stephan grabbed the binoculars to check it out. He swore, and then passed them around so everyone could take a look.

"What the hell!" Valfor yelled, jumping back away from the bird.

"Colony spiders," Stephen replied. "They're various kinds of spiders that have realized it's better to hunt together than alone, and they work together to catch large prey."

"Shoot me," Valfor said, handing Stephen his gun. "Sergeant, please just shoot me. I'm not getting eaten by spiders."

"You can't even see the web," Jamie said, still in shock at what she'd just seen.

"Shoot me, too," Harrison said, also handing his gun over to his sergeant. His eyes didn't drift from where the spiders were devouring the meal they'd trapped.

"Add me to that list," Quenshoda said. "I would definitely rather be shot than be eaten by spiders, and it would be too easy to walk into one of those webs without seeing it."

Stephen wanted to press forward but he agreed on a compromise, because colony spiders' nets could stretch for up to five miles. He turned the platoon around and they walked back the way they came. A few chimpanzees scurried across their trail in front of them, pausing briefly to consider these strange new beings infiltrating their jungle. They moved on quickly when each member of the platoon trained a gun on them.

The group rationed their water the best they could, but due to their five-mile reroute, they were quickly running out.

"Okay, we need to find some baboons or we need to try making it to the river again," Stephen told his platoon as they were resting. "By the end of today, we'll be out of water. In normal circumstances, a human can only live three days without water—it's dang near a hundred and thirty degrees out here, so we've got even less time and we're still two-and-a-half days away from the base at the pace we're going."

"What will finding baboons do, Sir?"

"Well, we can dump all the salt cubes and cinnamon cubes we have stored up for food flavoring and, when they eat them, they'll get dehydrated and lead us directly to their hidden water source. I saw it on the National Geographic channel. Baboons always have a hidden water source, and it's how African tribes find water when they don't have any."

"Well, how will we find baboons?" Jamie asked. "We've seen just about every species except baboons."

"That's because they stick to certain parts of the jungle. We've actually been in their territory for the last fifteen minutes or so."

"How do you know for sure, Sergeant?" Quenshoda asked.

"You see those markings on that tree?"

"Yeah," Quenshoda replied, "I see them."

"That's how baboons mark their territory. Look on the bottom of your shoe, Malcom."

Malcolm lifted his left shoe.

"Your other shoe," Stephen said, before he could get his foot all the way up.

As Malcolm lifted his foot, the smell hit everyone like a Mike Tyson–Bruce Lee combo punch and they all covered their faces.

"Oh, shoot!" Malcolm said, as he looked for a leaf to wipe the excrement off.

"No, leave it," Stephen ordered. "You'll be able to get closer to the baboons than anyone else because of that smell."

"Okay," Malcolm said. "And, how close exactly am I getting to them, Sir?"

"Just close enough to lay the salt and cinnamon cubes where they can see it. Their curiosity will take over from there."

The group walked through the jungle looking for baboons. They focused on baboon droppings, checking if they were warm or cold, and looked for things like footprints or baboon hairs on leaves.

"Up there, Sir," Harrison said, after three hours of hopeless searching.

Up on a fallen tree was a family of baboons—about twenty of them—and it looked like there where about sixty more in the distance, combing the jungle floor for fallen fruit and other sources of food, like ants.

"Okay," Stephen said, handing Malcolm their sweet lures. "You got this. Our lives depend on us having water, so be careful."

"How close do I need to get to them?" Malcolm asked.

"Maybe thirty to forty feet away."

"Okay, Sir. Are you sure about this?" Malcom moved around anxiously.

"Quit being Air Force and act like you're Army for once," Stephen replied.

Malcolm snorted a laugh and began to walk reluctantly towards the baboons—cautiously and very slowly. When he was about sixty yards from the baboons, they went from relaxed to looking like they had rabies. They began growling and jumping up and down in a rage. At about fifty feet, Malcolm—terrified—launched the cubes at them.

It was a big mistake.

They ignored the cubes and charged towards him, their already vast number growing by the second.

"Weapons out!" Stephen yelled.

The platoon took aim and began firing. Unlike the gorillas, the baboons didn't care about the gunfire and continued their charge as Malcolm re-joined the group. The primates spread themselves throughout ground and trees, trying to surround the group of humans.

The platoon grouped itself in a circle to cover all sides and began moving away from the baboons that were still attacking them. Stephen knew if they blew all their ammo straight away, they'd be in real trouble. The number of baboons was decreasing quickly as the soldiers continued to fire. Most of them were killed, but some decided to hang back after seeing their compadres lying dead on the ground. About seventy percent were killed before the remainder retreated in defeat.

"Damnit." Stephen cursed, rubbing his neck. "Do an ammo count."

"It's okay, Sir. They might be a different type than you saw, or maybe had some young they were protecting," said Jamie, hoping to lift Stephen's mood—he was mortified by the outcome of his decision

"They must be a different breed," Stephen agreed. "I just assumed all baboons were the same, but the one I saw was by itself, and the tribal man trapped it and fed it a lot of salt. The baboon got thirsty and led him to water… it happened in the desert. I just figured it was worth a shot, and better than chancing walking into a web with thousands of spiders."

"Nobody is blaming you, Sergeant," Malcolm said, clapping his superior on the back. "Those baboons were aggressive before I even got there—that's why I tossed the cubes the rest of the way, rather than get any closer."

"No, it is my fault," Stephen said. "I made a judgement call without adding up all the factors, but that's part of the job, I guess. Some decisions pan out. Others don't. Well, let's head to the river. It's not far from here, anyway." He gave the instruction without waiting for the team to complete the ammo count and began to carelessly plunge forward through the jungle towards the river.

Jamie could see that he was still shaken up from the attack and was upset about putting the platoon in danger with an unwise decision, but she hung back. She knew he needed his space and wanted to give it to him. She hoped there would come a time when she would be able to console him, but this wasn't it.

Within fifteen minutes, they were at the river's edge. It looked incredibly deep and they were sure it would be full of crocs, but they had to get water. They all had that heavily on their minds as they approached with their water bottles.

"Keep your eyes open," Stephen yelled to his soldiers. "All kinds of animals come here. Stay the hell out of the water unless you want to become a meal."

"Sergeant," Jamie said, positioning herself beside him. "I've got the ammo count." When he nodded for her to continue, she listed off what was left of their supply.

"Thank you, Jamie," Stephen said, smiling for the first time since he got into the jungle. "Go get some water." The order was gentle, and Jamie ducked her head as she complied.

Stephen kept a close eye on her as he collected water for himself; he wanted to make sure nothing happened to her. He planned to leave the Army when the mission was over, and he was keen to see if she'd be interested in going on a date.

After they filled their cantinas, they set up a fire and poured all the water into pots and boiled it to make it drinkable. Once it was safely packed away, they set off again, walking along the river for half an hour before heading back into the depths of the jungle to find a clearing so they could set up camp. The worst thing they could do was to be caught anywhere near the water come nightfall. That was when ninety percent of the meat-eating animals would be eating and looking to drink.

They still hadn't found a suitable place after the sun began to set, and Stephen shook his head. "This isn't good," he muttered to himself before yelling to the others. "Platoon, start jogging!"

He jogged ahead and lead the way and, fortunately, they found a clearing just twenty minutes later. The sun was setting fast and time was running out to set up camp, so tensions were running a little bit high.

"Harrison, you and Quenshoda go gather some wood for a fire—and do it quickly. Everyone else!" he began, making a sweeping gesture. "We have five minutes to get set up. Let's get a move on! Let's go with just four tents this time—save some time."

They moved so fast on the tents that they had them up before Quenshoda and Harrison were back with the wood. The sharp crack of gunfire sounded from the direction they had gone, and Stephen and the rest of the platoon grabbed their firearms and sprinted through the woods to see what was going on.

"What the hell happened?" Stephen asked, out of breath.

Harrison and Quenshoda were perfectly fine and it seemed as though there was no danger at all.

"Dinner, Sir," Harrison said, pointing into the bush where a large snake lay dead.

"Oh, nice," Stephen said, with only the hint of a grimace. "Anaconda for dinner, and maybe something else too, if it hasn't digested whatever it's eaten."

Malcolm, Quenshoda, and Jamie all bent over and pretended to throw up when Stephen said the last part.

"Sir," Jamie said, "that is disgusting."

"Wait until you taste it. It's like Campbell's soup—so good, mmm. And trust me, it's a lot better than those dinner bars we've been eating."

"Sir, don't ever say that again," Valfor said, laughing.

The whole platoon laughed with him and then Stephen ordered them to carry the snake and wood back to the camp. They had an enjoyable time that night. Their water had cooled, and the snake was delicious. The discussion about tent partners was quick—after spending the day watching Jamie check out the sergeant, the soldiers silently agreed that she'd want to be sharing his tent.

"Sergeant?" Jamie asked.

"Call me Stephen."

"Yes, Sergeant—I mean, Stephen," Jamie stumbled on her words. "Ten years from now, what do you want to be doing?"

"Well, I want to open my own business selling hats and shoes—maybe clothes."

"Oh wow. That's awesome," Jamie replied.

"What about you?" Stephen asked.

"I want to be a cook. I was working as a chef before I was drafted into the military."

"A chef, really? Wow, so you can cook?"

"One of the best." Jamie smiled.

"Nice."

"What if we've lost the war?" Jamie asked. "Where will you go and what will you do?"

"Don't talk like that." Stephen straightened and fixed her with an intense look. "We will win. America always finds a way."

"Yes, Sir," Jamie replied.

"Didn't I order you to call me Stephen?" he said jokingly. "Alright, bend over and smile."

Jamie bent over and he slapped her on the butt. She turned to face him, blushing red. "You know, Stephen, I've liked you for a year now. We've known each other for nearly two. I'd like to be your girlfriend—I know you can't now, but when this mission is over, I'm going to drop out of the Army so we can be together, Sergeant—I can't help it I'm used to calling you Sergeant!"

Stephen laughed, "Its fine." He was quiet for a moment, watching her. "Wow," he said at last, dipping his head. "That's crazy because I like you to, and I considered dropping out as well—if it meant I could be with you."

"Will you stay now that you know that I'm getting out?" she asked him, her head bowed slightly.

He shook his head. “Nope. I’m going to get out with you, and then we can go pursue our dreams.”

“Sounds good to me,” Jamie replied.

She scooted closer to Stephen and leaned against his shoulder. She tilted her head so she could look at his face and, for a few beats, they were still and locked in each other’s gaze. With a tentative smile, she swivelled to put a hand on his collar, her fingers tracing the length of his neck and leaving ghost touches at his ears.

Stephen’s eyes widened in anticipation, and he reached up to tangle his hand in Jamie’s hair, tugging her closer still. He groaned and pushed her gently down to the relative comfort of their sleeping bags when she captured his lips in a desperate kiss.

She wasn’t gentle—she’d waited too long—and she made short work of his clothes, tossing them over his shoulder to pile up at the front of the tent. In a rare moment of peace, Stephen rubbed sensual circles over her skin as he relieved her of her clothes, and Jamie was quick to close the remaining distance between them. It was only after hours of passionate exploration that Stephen suggested they both get some rest.

He stayed awake long after he closed his eyes, thinking about what had just happened. He was most definitely going to resign from the military after this assignment if that’s what he could have outside—besides, he was tired of coming home from missions and checking his bank accounts to find out that he wasn’t getting all of his pay checks from the military.

When Stephen woke the next morning, Jamie was already up. She was wrapped in her sleeping bag and staring at nothing. “You okay?" he asked, eyeing her with wary concern. He hoped she wasn't regretting what they'd done the night before.

"Yeah, I'm okay," she said. "I was just doing some thinking."

"About what?"

"Well, about my parents."

"Oh." Stephen yawned. "Did you want to tell me about it?"

"No, not really," Jamie replied, still avoiding his gaze.

"Do you feel you made a mistake last night?" he asked, feeling the weight of some tension between them.

She reached for his hand quickly and shook her head. "No, I love that we finally broke the ice." She smiled. "I was just considering leaving the Army after this mission to pursue other careers, and hopefully build some kind of relationship between the two of us—but I'm a little scared, I guess. It's possible that you may not feel the same."

"I'll be leaving the military as well when this mission is over, and I would love to work on a relationship between us." Stephen replied, squeezing Jamie's hand.

Jamie bowed her head against the racing thoughts that occupied it. She had so much to say, but it didn't feel like the right time—she didn't want to distract them from their mission. Instead, they both got out of their sleeping bags and dressed, ready for another long day.

Once Stephen and Jamie were out of their tent and had endured the jokes from their fellow soldiers who'd beaten them to rise, Stephen addressed the unit. "If we jog, we can be at the base by tonight, but I'm concerned that—since the Babylonian Alliance didn't follow us into the jungle and made zero attempt to try and track us—they might know about the hidden base's location and may be looking to cut us off."

"I sure hope not," Jamie muttered.

"Do you think that they may have already overtaken the base, Sergeant?" Valfor asked.

"I don't know, but we'll find out soon enough," Stephen said, getting up. "For now, let's get everyone packed and ready to go, so we can get there sooner rather than later,"

Stephen and Jamie went back into the tent to pack up their gear. It took them less than three minutes to be ready to go. They stepped out of the tent together, but not before Jamie stopped Stephen just short of the opening to kiss him softly on his lips.

Everyone was already ready to go when they emerged.

CHAPTER FOURTEEN

Gatsby stopped speaking for a moment and chugged his glass of water. He waited until Manuel gestured for him to continue, and then picked his story back up. "We're back at the execution camp now for a while," he began.

*****

We were more than ready for our escape. One of the girls had managed to steal a map from the soldiers' sleeping quarters while she was cleaning unsupervised. The map was of Africa. We had confirmation of our location at last—we were in the Congo jungle.

I found flashlights, sleeping bags, raincoats, and a bunch of other useful stuff in one of the buildings while everyone was eating in the cafeteria. I was cleaning it as punishment for having extra lunch on my tray the day before.

"Alright, everyone. As we all know, it's getting close to time for an execution," I began as everyone gathered around. "Has anyone heard anything about what day they're planning on grabbing someone this time?"

"They're doing it in two days," a girl on the kitchen crew answered.

"Okay," I replied. "So, we begin on the day after, but we must be swift and accurate because there will still be a few soldiers here. Right… this is a rough thing to discuss, but it needs to be said: whoever is taken must not throw the rest of us under the bus. Everybody has the same goal. We're all just trying to make it home to our families and friends. They could choose any of us." I stopped speaking and a long silence filled the room, "Any of us could be the next one to die," I finished.

No one had brought it up, but it was on my mind and had to be on everyone else's. Would the person on their way to execution sell the rest of us out and give away our plan?

Only time would tell.

"Roxane, can I talk to you alone?" I asked.

"Yeah, sure. What's up?" She flashed me a worried look.

I grabbed her hand and pulled her close. "Listen. I don't know how things are going to go tomorrow, but I want you to know I love you, whatever happens."

As I leaned my head in closer and planted a soft kiss on her lips, she closed her eyes. It very well could have been our last kiss because the soldiers could have picked either of us to be the next to be executed. I was an especially likely target since I got on their very last nerve.

The kiss was the perfect antidote to my anxiety and fear, and lifted me like nothing else could. I'd say that I wish that moment had never ended and had lasted forever, but I can't because it feels like it *is* lasting forever—I feel the same every time I talk to her, see her, or just hear her name. It's always soothing, even now we're out of Africa.

*****

"I see someone is trying hard to get back on someone's good side," Manuel mouthed, laughing quietly.

Gatsby smirked and shook his head no. "I'm always on her good side," he mouthed back without a sound, making sure that the microphone wouldn't pick it up.

"Yeah, okay, if you say so," Manuel mouthed with another laugh, before signaling for Gatsby to continue with the story.

*****

The following day went by excessively fast. It seemed like we'd just gone out to the fields and then it was dark. My stomach clenched and my heart hurt. When we said anybody could be taken to be executed, that also meant Roxane and me. I couldn't sleep all night. I was glad Roxane stayed by me. We sat together on the floor and I laid my arm over her shoulder. "You better hide tomorrow—as soon as we get back from dinner," I said.

She didn't say a word but remained calm with my arm around her, making her feel safe. I was as nervous as someone could be. If they tried to grab Roxane, I didn't know what I was going to do, but I was going to do something.

The thing I hate about sleep is that time seems to have different rules than when you're wide awake. You close your eyes and wake up hours later, but it feels like only a thirty-second break from reality. When I opened mine the next morning, it was time to head to the fields to work. Roxane was already doing her job in the kitchen.

The soldiers lined us up as they always did. We ate breakfast and went to work as usual. I worked hard. I didn't need to give the soldiers a reason to place my name at the top of the list to be executed, even though it probably already was. After the sun went down, everyone ate in the dining area. It was a tense dinner, as it always was before an execution—for someone, it would be their last meal.

That night, we all stayed up waiting for the soldiers. There were about four to five different conversations going on in the sleeping quarters. I remember a specific topic that came up in our little group.

"Okay everyone," I asked, "if you're about to be executed and you know for a fact that they're going to kill you, do you fight or just obey, hoping it won't happen?"

"Fight," Jordan quickly said.

"I don't know," Mao replied, "I'm not a good fighter.

"It's going to be a lot more painful waiting for them to finish torturing you, than it would be to fight back and have a bullet kill you before you even knew it was coming."

Mao nodded. "I guess that makes sense."

"You guess?" said a kid named Jacob, raising his brow. "No, it would be easier."

"Well, what if instead of shooting you, they team up together, overpower you, and then torture you worse than they were going to in the first place?" Mao asked, effectively silencing the group.

"When you put it like that," Jacob replied, "it would kind of suck."

The group started talking about other things after that, but it got me thinking. Looking at both points, it's easy to say what you'd do, but when facing it, everything changes. You don't know what the outcome will be, and you might get too scared to do anything at all.

Surprisingly, they didn't grab anybody that night. Then two weeks passed with nothing happening. Everyone was on edge—anxious and confused.

"I thought you said the soldiers were coming," I asked the girl who, weeks prior, said that they were.

"They said they were—I heard them plain as day," the girl responded, looking just as confused as I was. "I don't know why they didn't come, but they did say they were going to."

"This is going to put a big dent in our plan," I said to Roxane, standing up to walk over to my bed. She didn't respond because she had already fallen asleep.

The next day, less soldiers were stationed with us in the fields. In fact, there were only two. The rest were stationed in the mines. I could tell something was going on, but what exactly I did not know. Three more weeks quickly flew by and, still, nobody was executed. We didn't know what was going on. They might have just decided to skip a few months, or they were possibly toying with us, making us think thank that they weren't executing us anymore—getting our hopes up just to crush them on the next execution date. We had all kinds of different guesses being passed around about the reasons for the sudden halt.

"We're almost at the next execution day," one of the kitchen workers said.

I didn't know whether to be happy or worried, because they were not letting us go, but didn't seem to be in any hurry to kill any more of us either. I couldn't help but get my hopes up somewhat, and I found myself hoping that the war was over and there was no need for anyone else to die. I considered the idea that the war was still going, and the New World

Order had seen that executing everyone, one by one, month by month, wasn't working, and decided to stop. Whatever it was, I hoped that they skipped another month.

My wishes came true. Another four weeks went by and the soldiers did not gather anyone to execute. This time, I did smile. "Maybe we don't have to escape after all," I said to Roxane. "Maybe the US made a deal with the Babylonian Alliance and someone from home is on their way to get us."

"I sure hope so," Roxane replied. "I can't wait to go back home to the United States."

"Yeah, I can't wait to go back either. Are you going to your home state, or coming to Alaska with me?" I asked because we had never discussed it.

"Really?" Roxane asked. "You already know I'm coming to Alaska with you. I don't have anywhere to go back to."

"I didn't know. I was hoping you were coming back with me, but I didn't know if you had uncles and aunts you were close to, or a grandma that you might want to stay with."

She allowed herself to smile just a little, despite the subject.

"Good," I continued. "I was hoping you'd be coming with me. If you weren't, I was planning to head to Rhode Island to be with you. One way or another, when we get out, we'll be together. I don't want to lose you or separate from you long enough for you to forget about me or find someone else."

"Aw. That's sweet Jonathan," she said, giving me a quick peck on my lips.

Everyone in the camp who happened to be eaves-dropping on our conversation began to talk about what they were going to do when they got home.

"Me? I'm going straight to Denny's," a red-haired boy said.

"Not me. I want a strawberry milk shake from Red Robins," another said.

"What's a Red Robin?" a girl asked. She had never heard of the restaurant because she was from the east coast and Red Robin hadn't extended that far.

Once our mounting fear had abated, the days began to go slower again. None of the girls were being raped either. It seemed the soldiers were not focused on us at all. We had become no more than an afterthought in the back of their minds.

*****

Manuel cut in. "You don't need to answer this question, but I wanted to pose it anyway," he began, giving Gatsby a curious look. "Did the soldiers ever rape Roxane? I only ask because you've mentioned the soldiers raping someone quite frequently."

Gatsby was quick to shake his head. "No, they didn't. I was worried they would, but it was mostly the female soldiers keeping watch over the kitchen crew and deliverers, which kept Roxane fairly safe—that and hiding when it was time to pick the next to be executed. The rape occurred mostly with the girls who worked in the mines. The soldiers in the fields never raped anyone."

Manuel sighed in relief. "That brings me to my next question," he continued. "Why did nobody else hide under their beds when the soldiers came on execution nights?"

"They did, and when they started checking, Roxane and I started climbing out the back window to hide instead."

"Oh okay, that makes sense," Manuel replied. "Okay, sorry to interrupt your story."

"It's fine," Gatsby replied. "These are the things the listeners want to know, right? He shrugged, before diving back into his tale.

*****

"Gatsby," Jordan tapped me on my shoulder and beckoned me to follow him back into the sleeping quarters.

It was dinnertime and I was hungry. "Can it wait?" I asked, just as my stomach growled.

"It can," Jordan said, but before I could walk away, he began to tell me anyway. "Anyways," he said. "I know why the executions have stopped."

I wanted to keep walking. I had two voices fighting over me—my stomach and Jordan. "Why have they stopped?" I asked.

"I overheard a few soldiers in the mines talking. The US troops found where they were taking us to be executed and decimated the place. They said they bombed it from the sky. Now they're worried that they might also know where we're being held. From what I heard, the US bombed three other execution sites as well, and then found the locations of the camps shortly after. So, they're taking extra precautions."

"Really?" I said, quickly forgetting all about my hunger. "Hopefully, they actually do know where we're at."

"It would be great to finally get back home to the United States."

"At the meeting tonight, I want you to tell everyone what you just told me. There may be some hope of us getting out of here after all," I said, more to myself than to Jordan.

We walked into the cafeteria just in time to get a plate—the servers had just started serving the food. Roxane watched us walk in, and looked at me in a way that asked me without words, "Where have you been?"

"I'll tell you later," I mouthed to her, after checking the coast to make sure no soldiers were watching me.

I sat down in an empty seat and Roxane served me my food. "Don't go getting into any trouble," she whispered in my ear, trailing her fingertip aross my arm as she put my bowl of rice and turnips down in front of me.

I pointed a finger at myself. "Me? Get in trouble? Never," I replied with a smirk.

I turned and looked at Roxane, and she was giving me The Look.

"Okay, okay, I won't," I said. "I'll tell you in the sleeping quarters why I was late coming in. It's good news." She smiled at hearing that I had good news to tell her, and went back to serving the tables.

After dinner, once everyone had gotten situated back in the sleeping quarters, we assembled for our nightly meeting.

"Jordan, you have the floor," I said, stepping to the side so Jordan could stand in the center of everyone and speak.

We always had a lookout by the door and the windows when we met as a group, to make sure the soldiers never could sneak up and eaves-drop on our meetings.

CHAPTER FIFTEEN

"Hey everyone," Jordan said, shyly. He seemed to be nervous, but a few people said hello back, which gave him a little more confidence. After clearing his throat, he began to speak. "I overheard some of the soldiers talking while we were in the mine earlier. The reason there have been no executions for the last two months is because the US Military found the location and bombed it until there was nothing left."

"Do they know where we are?" a chunky boy named José asked.

"Probably not, otherwise they would have been here by now and rescued us. But the guards probably feared that they did know, which is why they stopped executing us."

"What was the point in telling us then?" another boy asked, "You made it seem like we were getting out or something."

"I told you because Gatsby told me to."

"Also," Roxane said, cutting in, "We don't know if they know our location or not. What Jordan is saying is that he doesn't think that the soldiers holding us hostage believe the US troops know where we are. They very well could be on their way right now, even as we speak, to rescue us."

"Exactly," I said, agreeing with Roxane. "All we can do is wait and be ready in case they do come." At that moment, I felt my insides jump with excitement. Just the thought of being rescued from the month-to-month executions and slavery and what we were being put through every day filled me and the others with the sort of hope we'd long ago given up on.

For many days we waited and listened. Every moment felt as if the US troops must be only moments from discovering the execution camp and freeing us. However, nothing happened. Except one thing— the soldiers stopped everyone from working in the mines and the fields. It raised our hopes again. When that happened, we knew the US soldiers were closer than our guards wanted them to be.

Without work to do, the days began to trickle by more and more slowly. The work, at least, had made them go by faster. With that stopped, there was nothing to do except sit around and complain about the heat. They could have at least given us some books to read. The meetings were also forced to come to a stop, as we were no longer allowed to leave the sleeping quarters and two soldiers stood guard at all times—day and night. They weren't even feeding us during this period. Many stomachs were hurting.

Roxane and I sat on the floor next to my bed. It was early in the morning, maybe two or three o'clock. The stars shone brightly through the black night and, freezing, we huddled together under one blanket. Everyone had become so caught up in the excitement of possible rescue that we were no longer keeping track of the days or months. Whatever month it was, it was surely winter again. Every night and morning were freezing. It rains a lot in an African winter, and during this period those of us who'd worked in the fields kept an eye on the food we'd planted, ducking out to gather turnips as they were ready to be picked.

Roxane snuggled against me on my lap, and I wrapped my arms around her. We had a jacket for Roxane and a jacket for myself, that I had stolen from the soldiers the prior winter, wrapped around us to keep us from freezing to death. I leaned my head over her shoulder, and she quickly pushed it back, claiming my hot breath tickled her neck. I took that opportunity to sit on the floor, where I was always more comfortable.

She joined me, and we curled up together on the dirt floor, staring into each other's eyes. I don't even remember falling asleep. I just remember being woken up by Roxane violently shaking me.

It had been a very long time since the last execution. No doubt it had been months, but we had no way of knowing without a calendar and nobody kept track of the days anymore.

The first thing I noticed was light flooding the windows and illuminating the door. The soldiers marched in with their guns held high. Without thinking, I instinctively rolled over, pulling Roxane down with me, under her bed and out of sight. We were well hidden because everyone else had jumped to their feet in fear.

In front of us was a new commander. He was a tall, stout Russian man who spoke very good English.

"Her," he said without fanfare, pointing to a little girl in the corner of the room. The little girl tried to run, but she was quickly surrounded. She was seven years old. Roxane closed her eyes and cried silently against my chest. The little girl's name was Miranda.

*****

"The Russian commander and the soldiers took her kicking and screaming. About fifteen minutes later, we heard a gunshot in the distance and we knew they had executed her."

"If I may interrupt and give the details on that?" Manuel questioned.

"Sure," Gatsby said, because he didn't see what had happened to the girl. He just knew they killed her.

Manuel shifted in his seat and cleared his throat. "Okay. We were in the middle of a broadcast at the time—in North Dakota. Three thousand Native Americans had been beaten and arrested the night prior, because they refused to allow the pipelines to steal their land and pollute their rivers—never mind that the powers that be tried to sneak the pipeline through while everyone's distracted with the war." He paused to allow that comment to sink in.

"Our signal was cut mid-broadcast, and on all the TVs across the country. Once again, the terrorists appeared, this time standing beside the young girl that you just mentioned. It was their fatal mistake—the US used the broadcast to track the signal and trace you guys. But, as we watched on, the Russian commander pushed the girl's face up against the camera, then pulled her back forcefully before punching her in the face. She was brutally tortured. Her clothing was removed, and she was sliced to ribbons and drowned in a barrel of rubbing alcohol, before being revived so that they could do it all again. Finally, she was shot in the head and the cameras shut off.

"We thought that was the end of it since, before, they only did live executions once a month, but not even ten minutes later they were back with another person—an adult. He said his name was Eddie. Poor Eddie was strapped to a chair and beaten for a good fifteen minutes, and it wasn't long before there was blood pouring down his face, pooling in the creases of his shirt. It wasn't until the soldier took his gloves off that I noticed he used brass knuckles," Manuel continued, looking a little green.

"When they removed his genitals, his screams were so shrill that I had to step out of the TV room at the studio because I couldn't watch anymore. Everyone else stayed to see what happened; we knew there was no point in trying to cut the broadcast because, for a year, we had tried and failed.

"Everyone waited, glued to the TV, to see if there would be another. There wasn't." Manuel hung his head and sighed, pointing to Gatsby to take over.

"Back in the camp," Gatsby began, "we were all trying to settle ourselves. Though it was hardly our first execution, this one caught us completely by surprise.

*****

"Wow," Roxane said, her face devoid of expression. "I thought the executions were done."

I stood up but she remained motionless on the ground, staring into empty space.

"So, do we escape now like we had planned?" one of the captives asked.

"Escape with what? We weren't expecting this to happen tonight and we aren't prepared. We have no food stored up; we have nothing ready to go." I was astounded to even be asked, even though I knew it made sense.

"I still say we make a break for it and try, you know," Mao said, looking nervous. "The soldiers that are normally here watching us right now are away—we can leave."

I stood for a second, trying to decide whether making a break for it was a good idea or not, given that we had no food or weapons. After careful deliberation, I decided that we shouldn't leave straight away—it was too dangerous to wander into a jungle in Africa without being properly prepared. Hell, it was dangerous even if you were prepared. Just as I finished explaining this to everyone, the Jeep came speeding back down the road. I knew everyone was going to hide under their beds, which would make everyone open targets.

"Roxane," I whispered, grabbing her hand. "We have to hurry up and climb out the back window. The soldiers are coming back." She still had that blank look of shock on her face, but she lifted herself up off the ground, with a little help from me, and we rushed to the back window. We barely made it out unseen, as the first soldier entered the sleeping quarters faster than we expected.

Neither Roxane nor I could see who they grabbed, but we heard everyone yelling hysterically. Never had there been two executions in one night. Fear spread throughout my entire body, just as surely as it was spreading through camp. What if they were planning to execute us all, one by one, that night? Roxane closed her eyes and leaned against my chest. She was terrified and tears poured unchecked down her flushed cheeks.

"I guess this is it," she said.

I could see that all hope had drained from her. She felt in her heart that all of us were going to die that night.

"Hell no, it's not," I said, spurred on by her resignation. I waited until I heard the Jeep leave again before I ran around the building putting out the torch lights. I made a mad dash into the dining area to find some food and grab as many weapons as I could. There wasn't any food, but I was able to get a hold of a few knives. I walked in the front door with authority and demanded everyone drop everything and follow me out the back window.

Once everyone was out, I quietly but sternly demanded that everyone get on their stomach's and begin crawling towards the fields. "Roxane," I said. "We're making a break for it." She didn't say anything but nodded her head. I don't believe that she thought we would make it.

Once we'd crawled half the distance to the mines, I instructed everyone to make a run for it. As quietly as we could, we all ran towards the mines. We were still a way away when we heard the Jeep pulling up at the sleeping quarters again.

"Damnit," I said, looking back. I knew they would cut us off with the Jeep before we reached the mines. "Too late." The minute the soldiers saw that the room was empty, they rushed out and headed straight for us.

I thought we were done for. I heard a single gunshot, but I couldn't see any gunfire coming from the soldiers. What I did see made me stop dead in my tracks. The driver of the Jeep nodded slowly and slumped forward against the steering wheel. The passenger tried to grab the wheel, but another shot saw him fall forward, too. That's when I worked out that the shots were coming from behind me.

I turned around to see thirteen soldiers dressed in black standing at the entrance to the mines. I hesitated because I wasn't sure if they were friendly or not, but they were shooting at our captors, so obviously we weren't their targets. Everyone was looking at me, wondering what to do and waiting for instruction. I motioned to everyone to go, and we all sprinted towards the mines.

"Look," Roxane said, pointing back at the camp as we all stood by the mines, catching our breaths. It didn't look like we were being followed immediately. I sat down in the grass. My legs were tired. Lights on the other side of the river were rapidly turning on, and within less than a minute, there were more floating across the water.

"Take them to the pick-up spot," one of the soldiers, obviously the one in charge, said as he pointed to another man.

I had no doubt in my mind that these soldiers were there to rescue us. The second soldier did a quick head count of everyone before we began to move.

"Okay, sixty-five people with nineteen kids. This should be fun." He sighed and gave us a sour look.

"Good luck!" A few of the others joked with him, but he didn't smile.

"Shouldn't we send a few more with him, Sir?" another asked his commander.

"Look through these binoculars, soldier," the commander said. "Eighty hostiles, at least, are heading towards us. Do you really think I'm about to short myself right now?"

"What if they meet resistance, Sir? We planned for maybe nine captives, Sir, but this is way more than that."

"If they meet resistance, then Lopez failed them because his only job is to get them to that check point as fast as possible. We've neutralized the threat between them and the check point, and we're about to kill the rest of them now..."

Tat, tat, tat, tat. Bullets were being shot in our direction.

"Go, you'll be fine. If I send extra men with you, that will increase our chances of being defeated. You guys need to get out of here! We planned this long before we got here, and there's no time for doubt now. We adapt, not quit. One of us will be the guide, and the remaining twelve will hold enemy troops off until morning so they can get a good distance away from the camp. Nobody said it would be easy," the commander finished. "Get going, Lopez, before I shoot you myself.

We traveled through the mines at an extremely fast pace. Every now and then, we came across a dead soldier, who the Americans must have killed on their way through. My excitement was rising as we made our way through the cave.

We were almost free.

Our guide directed us through the part of the cave that had been off limits to those of us working in the mines. Water seeped down from the ceiling as we journeyed, and I knew this was the right way. With us jogging, it still took us an hour to reach the other side—it was a long way.

As we stepped out of the mine and onto the grass, I began to recognize where we were at once. I remembered sitting on my knees and watching the soldiers hit everyone on the back of their head, knocking us all out.

"Okay, this is how this is going to work!" the soldier began to shout. "My name is Sergeant Lopez and I'm here to guide you all to safety and to an extraction point, while my unit holds off the enemy soldiers. Rescue choppers will then fly you to safety and back to freedom. We're going to run at a slow pace. It's dark out, so if you fall behind, shout and we will come back for you. We'll jog in a chain link formation to make it harder for people to fall behind, and we will not be stopping for breaks. If my unit cannot hold those soldiers back, the enemy troops will come looking for you. Is that understood?"

Everyone nodded and murmured softly to acknowledge that they understood.

"We only have a short window to get you out of here." Without as much as a warning, Sergeant Lopez began to jog, and we instinctively followed. He was careful to keep his jogging at just above a fast walk, to make sure that the little kids could keep up.

"Catch up and grab on. Let's start forming the chain link!" I yelled to everyone. "Somebody grown needs to be at the end of the line!"

It wasn't too hard to follow Sergeant Lopez. He used the flashlight to jog on the path he and his unit had come on. After a little over half an hour, people began to start tiring. Even though he said we would not stop, we stopped quite regularly.

Eventually, we ended up just doing a fast walk, because many of the adults had grown tired and weak, and the ones that were strong were carrying the kids who were no longer able to keep up. The journey was not an easy one, nor was it short. We pushed on all through the night and into daybreak. Though we couldn't see any enemy choppers, there was no doubt that the enemy soldiers who were holding us captive would be coming for us.

Sometime in the night while we were taking a break, a soldier from Sergeant Lopez's unit came screaming over the radio. "Mission failed, last man standing—*ratatatatatatat.*" Gunshots sounded over the radio and then there was silence."

It seemed that Sergeant Lopez disliked conversation and wouldn't speak to any of us, except when he was urging us to go faster. After traveling for nine hours, we made it to the extraction point.

When we reached it, there was only a single helicopter there waiting for us. There were sixty-five of us. There was no way that we were all going to fit.

CHAPTER SIXTEEN

"What is this?" Sergeant Lopez yelled. "Where are the rest of the rescue choppers?"

"We weren't expecting so many," one of the rescuing soldiers yelled over the sound of the propellers. "We'll have to load as many as we can and come back for the rest!"

Sergeant Lopez's hands flew into the air. "Exactly how long do you think we have before they find us? They're probably moments away from finding us as we speak!" His face was contorted in frustration and anger.

There wasn't enough time for arguing, so the soldiers began loading everyone as quickly as they could. The kids were loaded first, and by the time they were all on board, there was only room for two more people. I tried to get Roxane to go, but she refused to leave my side.

"No, I'm not getting on!" she insisted, letting me know that her mind was made up.

"You have to. There's no guarantee that the rest of us will be saved."

"Jonathan, I already told you, I am not getting on!" She shot me a glare and walked away from the chopper.

"Damnit Roxane," I said angrily. "You realize that they're looking for us and are most likely going to catch up to us before the helicopters get back?"

"It doesn't matter. I'm not getting on." She stayed firm even as tears began to roll down her cheeks.

Sergeant Lopez stood by, listening to our conversation and looking at Roxane with a strange sense of pride—he was impressed by her determination to make sure that others were saved first. I was proud too, but I was also angry with her. I knew I wasn't going to convince her to go, and I felt the panic rise in my gut at the idea of her giving up what was surely safety. I had mixed feelings. I did not want her to leave me either.

She grabbed my hand and we stepped away from the helicopter. Sergeant Lopez escorted everyone else away so that the first group could take off to freedom at last.

Finding a place that could hide a group as large as ours was an impossible task. There just weren't enough trees or brush and if we stayed out in the open, we were bound to be recaptured. The options we had were extremely limited and we had no time to sit around and think of a plan.

"We're going to have to head towards the base and hope the chopper picks us up before the enemy finds us," Sergeant Lopez told the group, wiping the sweat from his brow with the back of his hand. Even though he directed his speech at the group, the Sergeant was looking directly at Roxane.

He set off in a jog and the rest of us followed. We were able to move much faster without the kids, and we jogged for forty-five minutes before taking our first rest. As we rested, Sergeant Lopez engaged Roxane in what appeared to me to be flirtatious conversation. She chatted back with him, smiling and blushing every so often, and I scowled.

*****

"Now, I'm not the jealous type, but I know when a man is flirting with my girl," Gatsby said, giving Manuel a strained look. "At that point, if I we hadn't needed him to show us to the base, I would have whooped his a——"

There was a beeping sound, and the station censored the cuss word for the listening audience.

"And so, I stayed out of it and stayed to myself. I didn't like—or trust—Sergeant Lopez, and neither did he intimidate me. I can fight extremely well, and I would definitely have fought him if it came down to it."

*****

Not usually an insecure person, the thoughts that began racing through my mind seemed foreign to me. Is this why Roxane stayed? For him? I didn't feel right. My emotions were mixed with anger, jealousy, and hate.

"What's up, Gatsby?" Jordan asked, taking a seat beside me.

"Nothing," I replied, lying through my teeth. "I'm just trying to get a little rest before we take off again."

"Yeah, my legs are exhausted." Jordan rubbed his legs as if to demonstrate his point. I waited for him to say something else, but when I turned over to look at him, he was sound asleep.

Roxane didn't stop talking to the sergeant until the rest period was nearly over. She walked over to me and sat down, blushing from cheek to cheek. Angered enough, I didn't bother to hear what she had to say, and instead I got up and walked away. That wiped the smile completely off her face.

I stared at Sergeant Lopez as I passed him. I would have liked nothing more than to hit him and break a few of his ribs, but I couldn't because—like I said—we needed him to show us the way to the base—he was the only one who knew how to get there.

"Okay," he called to everyone, "It's time to get a move on." He grinned at me as he said it. He knew what he was doing, but what he didn't know was that I was going to beat him down, as soon as we got on the base.

Those of us that were awake began to wake everyone else. The plan was to start running immediately, but too many people had cramps and their stomachs were hurting because we hadn't eaten in days. My stomach was hurting bad.

Sergeant Lopez located some ants and followed them back to their nest. He ate a few ants in front of us, demonstrating that it was okay. A few of us gave disgusted looks and some others even threw up, but in the end, we gave in to our hunger.

Instead of jogging, Sergeant Lopez decided to set the pace at a fast-walking speed. Roxane was walking right next to him. I migrated myself to the back. I thought about stopping a few times and just finding my own way, but I couldn't bring myself to do it— the base was obviously in the direction Lopez was going, so I had to stay with the group. My thoughts were all over the place. I began to think that Roxane only agreed to be my girlfriend because she thought we were going to be stuck in the camp until we died.

At some point, she turned and walked back through the crowd to me, but I wasn't in the mood to talk to her. I keep saying I'm not a jealous man, but with her I was. I think it was because I'd never felt that way about anybody else and watching Sergeant Lopez hit on her stung. The grin he flashed me every time he did was infuriating, but Roxane seemed to be fine with it. She seemed to prefer hanging out with him than me in any case.

"Jonathan, what's wrong with you?" she asked. "Why did you walk away from me earlier? Why did you go to the back of the line?"

I shrugged. "Feels good to be free, don't it?" I said, forcing a slightly sarcastic smile onto my face.

"Excuse me?" Roxane asked, eyeing me in confusion.

"Your little boyfriend's looking for you," I said, pointing at Sergeant Lopez. I couldn't help but notice that he was looking back at us.

"It is not even like that Jonathan, and you know it. Please tell me you're not going to turn into a crazy jealous type now just because we're going to be free."

"No, I'm not jealous," I said, "He likes you though. You just wait and see; I'll stay back here and mind my own business."

"No, he doesn't," she argued. "He was telling me about his family and talking about his unit—the ones that died so we could be free." She gave me a stern look as she spoke, and placed one hand on her hip, while her other was held up just below her chin level, with her finger pointed straight up towards the sky. She did that whenever she was mad, but I didn't care this time because I knew I was right about the situation.

"His wife and kids?" I asked.

"Well, no. His mom, dad, brothers, and sisters," Roxane replied. She was still trying to look mad, but I saw her eyes waver. I knew she caught onto where I was going with my statement. "His brother was abducted, and the rest of his family killed while he was in boot camp."

"Yup, sympathy; no faster way to a girl's heart," I mumbled to myself.

Roxane looked taken aback and made her way back towards Sergeant Lopez.

"Have fun!" I yelled. She didn't look back.

The rest of the walk went by too slowly. I loved Roxane, but in that moment, I felt like I hated her a little bit too. I definitely hated Sergeant Lopez—with a passion. Roxane, to her credit and despite how rude I was to her, refrained from talking to him. Instead of going back to the front, she stayed somewhere in the middle of the pack. Sergeant Lopez kept looking back at her. He beckoned her to come to the front twice, but she declined with a shake of her head.

The next break we took was at nightfall, and the night weather was freezing. Sergeant Lopez again tried to engage Roxane in conversation. "What happened to you earlier today?" he asked.

"Nothing." She sighed. "I have a boyfriend and we got into a little argument, and so I just kept to myself."

"Argument about what?"

"Well, about me spending so much time talking to you. I did some thinking, and he's right. I wouldn't want him doing the same to me, so I think it's best if we cool it on talking so much for right now. I need to work things out with him."

"Of course. If that's what you want, then that's what we'll do. You're a very pretty woman you know, and he has every right to be jealous, because a man would have to be stupid not to be interested in you." The Sergeant shot her a lust-filled gaze and waited for her to respond. He reached out a hand to place over hers where it rested on the ground, but she pulled away before they could touch.

"Okay," she said. She sounded weirded-out. She stood to her feet, turned, and walked away from him.

I was half asleep near the spot where they'd been talking, but I heard every word that was said. I was proud of Roxane. She walked around the group looking for me and I raised my hand to help her find me. When she laid down beside me, it was all I could do not to gasp. Her eyes seemed to be sparkling in the moonlight and her hair was hanging beautifully, halfway down her back. I rubbed my hand gently down the side of her face, and then I softly touched her crusted lips—she definitely needed some chap stick. I made a joke about cutting myself on the dried skin, and she chuckled.

CHAPTER SEVENTEEN

"Hold on a second. The supposed hero soldier rescuing you guys tried to hit on your now fiancé, even after she told him she was with you?"

"That's correct," Gatsby answered. "Now, despite me being right, after our little romantic moment she let me have it. She told me that if I was the jealous type that we wouldn't work, and that the only reason she stopped talking to Sergeant Lopez was because he made her uncomfortable."

"Wow, that's crazy. Not something you'd expect from someone rescuing you. Besides that, what has me confused, I guess, is that everyone claimed that you led them to freedom. They didn't mention a soldier?"

"That's because he walked out on us," Gatsby explained to Manuel. "We had walked for a few days, and he kept complaining that our group was slowing him down. When another one of the girls told him to go to hell after he tried to flirt with her, he took off and we were left to fend for ourselves."

Manuel's eyes grew wide. "Well, I'm sure that if he made it back to the base, he definitely got punished for showing up without you guys. Was that the only reason he walked out, or is there more?"

"Well, more, obviously. He kept complaining that certain members were moving to slow. After jogging for two hours straight, a lot of the group needed a rest. He wanted to keep going, but we united against him and rested. We also needed to eat, so we found our own ants and feasted on them. He was mostly pissed that he—and these are his words—had to 'babysit us because the government didn't send enough rescue choppers.'"

"That's not a reason to walk out on the people that you're supposed to be saving! Inexcusable if you ask me," said Manuel. "Well, Gatsby. I know you want to get home to your soon-to-be-wife. So, tomorrow same time?"

"Sounds good to me," Gatsby replied, getting up from his chair.

Manuel bid America goodnight. "Tremaine, you got it," he said to his colleague as he walked off the set.

*****

"Hello, America. This is Tremaine Sanderson coming to you live again from CGX News, reporting *truthful news* and *only* truthful news.

As of this morning, there have been a large number of racist and prejudiced atrocities committed overnight. Seventeen African Americans, thirteen Hispanic Americans, fourteen members of the LGBTQIA+ community, thirty-three women's rights activists, and thirty-two Muslims were found hanged from trees. With each incident, there was a burning cross left at the scene of the crime. The Ku Klux Klan has also hung their flags over the porches of each victim's house.

"Many neighborhoods woke up to this, and riots have taken over streets across the country. Police are doing the best they can to break it up, but with the Army—including the National Guard—

occupied, there are just too many people involved for the police to be able to do much of anything. For now, it seems that nobody will be breaking these fights up. People from both sides—minorities and non-minorities—have been killed, and more have been hospitalized.

"If this country would stop protecting racists and kick them out, as they are so determined to do with 'illegal' Hispanics—who've been in America for nineteen years without ever having committed a single crime and working to send money to their family—this country would be great! Then those bigots could go ruin another nation! That goes for racists in all races!

"In further news this evening, as most of our listeners know already, the country has moved the White House from the east coast to Colorado after an attack was made on it. The enemy were defeated in the end however, and the White House and the east coast are still standing strong. What bothers me is that enemy soldiers breached the White House in the first place. It's hard to wrap my head around the fact that this country is so racist that it started a civil war while we're in the middle of World War III and defending the White House!

"What in the hell is wrong with people? You know what? If we can't let go of hate towards one another in a time such as this, it just might be time for us to lose this country.

"When I say 'civil war' I'm referring to the out-of-control riots. They might not have quite descended into war yet, but my sources tell me that both sides are forming their own armies. There is even rumor of many minorities heading towards the northern states and non-minorities gathering themselves to the southern states, as they form their armies.

"There are literally social media ads saying, 'Join the New Confederate Army today!' and, 'Sign up to fight for our right to live in a country free from human–animals.' I've seen another one going around for the minority Army, saying, 'Enlist today in the Free Nation Army, and fight for your right to live in a country free from oppressors and white laws set against you and your families.'

"This is crazy, and that, my friends, is the first step towards a full out civil war. Of course, in the New Confederate Army, it's all non-minorities, but in the Free Nation Army it looks to so far—according to my sources—be composed of a mixture of races and ethnicities, so it seems there're far more soldiers in the Free Nation Army… I don't think this is going to go particularly well for those lonely confederates! They might want to take into consideration that the bible does say history repeats itself.

"More states need to be like Alaska. Alaska sought out their racist citizens and booted them out; they wanted nothing to do with this rising civil war. They were not going to have any riots happening in their state! I give a big congratulations to Alaska for being an example to America on how to avoid such nonsense.

"It's not like we don't know where the hate—rising to the point that it has—is coming from though. All the fake news stories being put out, all the violence from police towards civilians, and a decades-old hate between races is fueling what's going to be one heck of a fire.

"Now, back to the agendas being pushed on social media. An FBI agent, Agent Smith, has been arrested. He confessed to the Secret Security Agency and to the local police that he, along with Russia, worked to hack into the government's system. They hacked the elections and sent out subliminal messages through social media to cause an uproar between civilians and government. Agent Smith was killed an all-out fight-out with Secret Security as they tried to arrest him at the hospital."

.Tremaine paused for a moment while an aide handed him a slip of paper. "We have an update, folks. The entire west coast is now being targeted by enemy troops. It appears that they're being hit with everything short of atom bombs, and my guess is that's only because they plan on occupying America after they snatch it from us, otherwise I bet they'd be pleased to wipe it out."

*****

"What's up?" Gatsby said to Roxane as he walked into the house. "Miss me?"

Roxane eyed him with a smirk. "No, I don't believe I did," she answered, blushing as she smiled. She turned the radio off as she reached out to wrap him in a warm hug and dropped a kiss on his lips.

There was a fire already blazing in the fireplace and the room lights were dimmed. They sat on the living room sofa—Gatsby tired and struggling to keep his eyes open. Roxane didn't care. She wanted to discuss the wedding.

"Your mom and I already picked out the dress that I'm going to wear, and the tuxedo for you, but I need to go over the guest list with you… and a few other things."

"Well, we don't really need a guest list. Let's just do open invitations."

"No," Roxane interrupted. She looked completely taken back, as if he'd had suggested to invite people from the prison or a halfway house. "I'm not going to have a bunch of strange people at our wedding!"

"I hate to tell you this, but we're in Alaska," he teased. "It's a long way from Rhode Island. You don't know anyone around here yet, and most people I was friends with are serving in the war.

"I guess if you want a big wedding with only people that we know, we'll have to wait until the war is over to get married. Or we're going to have to let strangers come, you know," Gatsby said hoping that she would see his point and agree.

"I guess," she answered, with an exasperated look on her face.

"Now, what else do we need to discuss?" Gatsby asked. "You said there was more to talk about."

"We need to decide on what food we want your mom to do—she's catering, of course. We still need a location, a preacher to marry us, a DJ for music, and decorations."

"Goodness gracious, that's a lot—it might be out of our budget."

"Do you just want to wait until we can afford a wedding then?" Roxane asked, her voice loaded with disappointment and a bit of frustration.

Gatsby just looked at her for a moment. The wedding seemed to be driving her crazy. She was almost nothing like the girl he had met and known for the last two years.

"Roxane, do you think you would have married me back at the execution camp, if I'd asked?"

"I don't know. I guess I would have. Why?"

"Well, because we're in the middle of a war. We just got back to the United States and I don't have a job. I have no money except what we're being given by the government for the time we spent as captives, which we need to save because we don't know how long it will last. I don't want to have to wait to marry you, but how can I pay for it all with no money in my pockets?

"Who cares if we can't afford a big wedding right now! Let's marry now with what we can get, and we can remarry in a few years, after we have money, and then we can have a fancy wedding. What do you think about that?" I asked.

Roxane looked disappointed, but agreed with a small smile. "Yeah, I guess I was being a bit selfish and got carried away with wedding ideas. I'm sorry, Jonathan. I didn't think..."

It hurt Gatsby to see her with such a defeated look in her eyes. He knew he couldn't ruin her dream wedding, so he had to find a way to make it happen for her. She had confided in him at the execution camp about everything that she wanted her wedding to be. Gatsby considered her desires for a moment and thought about their conversations over the years. He made up his mind to find a way to give her everything she dreamed of.

The next day, Gatsby showed up early for his session with Manuel Emotho. He had decided to put his pride aside and ask him for help.

"Hey," he said, waving to Manuel as he walked into the newsroom an hour early. "Do you have time to talk in private?"

"Yeah, I do. What's on your mind?" he asked, leading Gatsby into a small room and closing the door behind them.

"Well, I have a problem… and I've never been really good at asking for help." Gatsby looked at the ground, wringing his hands.

"Okay, go on," Manuel encouraged.

"Well, you know that I'm marrying Roxane in a month, and I have no job yet… Well, in the camp she told me about her dream wedding. She wanted beautiful decorations and many people to help her celebrate. She wanted a beautiful dress and, more than anything, she wanted to get married inside a big church.

"When I told her yesterday that we would have to settle for a cheap and small wedding, she agreed but I saw the hurt in her eyes. I was—I was wondering if you could use some of your pull around town to help me get a job, so that I can at least attempt to make her dreams come true."

"I see," Manuel said, his face impassive.

"She's not putting pressure on me for it, but I know that if I can come up with something nice, I can make her happy," Gatsby continued. "It's bad enough that her dad isn't alive to walk her down the aisle, which I know will be hard on her, and I don't want to take any more away from her than I absolutely have to.

"To me, making her happy is my number one priority in life. I'm not asking for money, but for work so that I can make the money myself."

"Have you tried applying for a job since you've been back in the US?"

"Yeah, I have, but the businesses won't hire me because I have a record. I've applied at just about every business in town."

"Don't worry about it," Manuel said. "I'll pull some strings, and she'll have that dream wedding. I can't afford to have you working right now—at least, not until you finish your interviews! After that, I can get you a job here at the news station. Does that sound like a deal?"

"It sure does!" Gatsby said, grinning as he shook Manuel's hand.

Gatsby and Manuel walked back into the waiting area for the CGX News station. Gatsby sat down on one of the comfortable leather recliner chairs, and Manuel moved about the station. It was a wintry morning; around thirty below zero with an ice fog to go with it, which made it feel ten times as cold. Gatsby wore six pairs of socks, five t-shirts, three pairs of pants, three sweaters, two jackets, and a t-shirt around his face to keep his nose from running. Even with all that on, on his walk from the house to the newsroom he'd still felt the extreme cold against his body, and his toes and fingers had been numb.

Now that he was inside a building, all the clothes were not necessary and he asked one of the janitors for a large garbage bag, went straight into the waiting room's bathroom, stripped out of all the extra clothes, and warmed his hands and toes in the warm sink water. Once he was comfortable, he left the bathroom and went back to sitting in the recliner, the large garbage bag of clothes set down neatly beside him. He fought to keep his eyes open as he relaxed a bit, and the next thing he knew was the studio staff attempting to wake him up.

"It's time for you to go on with Mr Emotho," the staff member told him as he stretched and yawned loudly.

"Thank you," he said, as he grabbed his clothes and moved himself into the recording studio he'd grown so familiar with.

"Enjoy your nap?" Manuel asked, with a smirk across his face. He frowned. "And… why do you have a garbage bag?"

"I needed somewhere to put all the extra clothes I had on this morning! It's freezing outside, but it's great in here so I had to take them off."

"Yeah, I almost had to do the same thing. I had to get a ride to work this morning because somehow I forgot to plug my car in last night and it froze." Manuel chuckled as he told his story.

As usual, the camera crew counted them in. "Three, two, one, go."

CHAPTER EIGHTEEN

"Hi, I'm Manuel Emotho with CGX News, and as always we are bringing you the news first from around the world. This war has been quite costly and many countries are pulling out as we speak. The war may seem like it's ending, but as they say, 'don't light your cigars until the fat lady sings.' The war is not over until it's over. Yesterday, it seemed like the war was intensifying, but now it seems that was more of a finale for the enemy because, after failing to breach the coast as they did on the east before they were fought off, they pulled their armies out and their war ships are heading away. Missiles are still being fired from across continents, but none are getting through.

The sad part is, as Tremaine mentioned during his broadcast, even if the world war ends, we're heading into a civil war. News that came in last night that suggests that, while we're going into civil war, other countries are going to war with their governments, and from what I'm told, they're being supplied with funding and weapons by the Nationberg Group. Even after all the news came out about that group, people around the world are still siding with them—carrying out their agenda of destroying governments around the world. I feel that this cannot possibly end well.

"Today, as always, we have Mr Gatsby here to tell us more about his escape, and how he saved many others from the prison camp. With that, I introduce the man of the hour once again! Gatsby was telling us yesterday that Sergeant Lopez, who was supposed to be rescuing them, was not only sexually harassing women but walked away from his duty and left these young lives at the mercies of the Babylonian Alliance. The floor is yours," Manuel said, pointing to Gatsby.

Gatsby nodded and cleared his throat. "As I did yesterday, I'll start with Sergeant Stephen's platoon, since we're getting close to where they find us, just about dead in the jungle."

*****

"Everyone, let's hurry up!" Stephen yelled. "Today is the day."

Those who were in their tents packing began stepping out with the rest of their gear, ready to go. The sun was just beginning to rise and the brightness of it was blinding, yet intensely beautiful. Everyone was buoyed by its warmth, and the tents and sleeping bags were put up in no time.

"Okay soldiers, here's the deal. We can be at the base by the end of the day if we jog at a steady pace. This is what we trained for. When we get close to the base, we'll stop and then radio command."

"Hoorah!" The platoon yelled in unison.

"Okay, everybody. Do a quick spray down of bug repellent and then let's get moving."

A lizard ran across the campsite as they were spraying themselves down, and a few vultures flew over their heads.

"Well, that isn't a good sign," Valfor said.

"What do you mean?" Quenshoda asked.

"We're about to head off right as a lizard runs through the camp—it was probably running from something. Vultures are worse; they represent death, and only hang around when death is hanging around..."

"Okay Valfor, since you can read the future by watching animals, you can take the lead," Stephen said, laughing as Valfor's eyes widened. "We're still going to jog, and if we run into any problems, we'll do what we do best!" the proud sergeant said. "Okay, let's move out!"

The platoon was hot and tired from running through the jungle for a long period of time, but they were getting closer to the US base and that was all that mattered.

"Halt!" Stephen yelled, and everyone stopped running and dove to the ground with their assault rifles pointed into the air, in case the sergeant had seen something, or they were in danger.

"Harrison!" Stephen barked.

"Yes, Sergeant?" Harrison yelled back.

"Call in to Command and let them know that we've made it to the base."

"Yes, Sir!" Harrison responded with excitement. They were about to finally be saved.

"Eagle, this is Ant Eater. Do you copy?" Harrison spoke into the radio. "Eagle, this is Ant Eater. Do you copy?" he asked again. There was nothing but silence.

"Something isn't right." Stephen looked around warily. "Guns out!" He relaxed a little when he heard the radio crackle to life.

"Ant Eater, this is Eagle."

"Eagle, we have made it to the Lion's Den in the heart of Africa and are ready for extraction. I repeat we have made it to the Lion's Den in the heart of Africa, and we are ready for extraction."

It was pitch black, and their only source of light were their flashlights, until Stephen made torches from branches and clothes.

"An extraction team will be there soon. Sit tight, Ant Eater."

"Roger that," Harrison said back to Command. "Also, we need confirmation—requesting permission to enter the Lion's Den."

"Contacting Lion's Den now to confirm, Ant Eater."

Harrison and the rest of the platoon waited for confirmation. Stephen was ready to give the order to go in and relax. Everyone was looking forward to finally having a cozy place to protect them for a while, with furniture, and out of the open jungle.

"Ant Eater, this is Eagle. We have confirmation that the Lion's Den is an empty cave. Wait outside the cave and extraction will be there in one hour. I repeat the Lion's Den is empty. Wait outside for extraction in one hour."

"Roger that," Harrison replied, and then cut the radio off.

"Wow, we're here and still have to wait outside. This really bites, Sir," Quenshoda said, frustrated and desperate to get comfortable.

"We could go in for forty-five minutes and come back out and wait the other fifteen," Valfor suggested. "What do you say, Sergeant?"

"No," Stephen replied. "If command is telling us to stay outside, there's a good reason—maybe the base is rigged to blow inside in case intruders found it."

"Oh, yeah let's stay outside then," Quenshoda said, changing her mind. "But cut the radio back on in case they need to contact us for any reason." She leaned against a tree trunk, trying to keep the urge to sit down at bay for a little longer.

"Yeah, good point Quenshoda. Cut it back on in case base needs to contact us," Stephen ordered.

Harrison complied.

"This is Base to Ant Eater. We know you just made it to the base and are waiting for extraction, but the team from the Lion's Pride sent in a message with a soldier who said he was the last man alive, and he was shot in mid speech. That was a few nights ago, Ant Eater. They were rescuing the survivors from the final execution camp. The survivors got out safely, and a few of them were extracted, but not enough choppers were sent. The group of survivors are lost in the jungle with only a Sergeant Lopez guiding them, and we need them found as of yesterday. When the chopper went back for them, they were not there waiting, so we believe that they're attempting to make it to your location on foot. There was no evidence of enemy soldiers having been there, nor of any kind of chase or struggle."

A few of Stephens's soldiers groaned in disappointment. They were looking forward to heading home, and now they had another mission.

"We're on it, Sir," Stephen replied into the radio, gritting his teeth. They were tired and hungry and didn't even know where to start looking for the survivors and the soldier leading them.

"You may rest for two hours, Ant Eater, but after that we need your team out there searching. They've been on foot a long while already, and the jungle is no place for anybody, with or without training."

*****

"I'm switching back to our group in the story now," Gatsby said into the microphone, to let Manuel—as well as the listeners—know that he was jumping back to talking about their part of the story.

*****

We—well I—decided to keep traveling in the direction that Sergeant Lopez had been leading us towards. Roxane stayed close to my side. I was silently appointed as the leader—probably because I'd taken on that role in our plans to escape. I knew I had no idea where I was going, but no one else did either, and I trust myself better than anyone else, so I accepted the responsibility.

"Jonathan," Roxane whispered to me as we walked. "I have to use the bathroom."

"Okay, just go over…" I paused to search the area for a good spot. "Right there, behind that tree over there. I'll keep watch for you."

After Roxane took her turn, it seemed that everyone in the group had to use the bathroom, so I reluctantly kept watch for them all as they went, one at a time.

"Okay, everyone!" I yelled. "Is everyone ready to go?"

The group nodded and settled into step behind me. I couldn't tell if we were walking in a straight line or what, but I knew we had to keep going. With no food or water in the open part of the jungle, we were bound to die from dehydration or from going crazy in the heat if we were stuck in it for much longer. There were a lot of trees, so we had to be extra careful. My biggest fear was running into wild animals.

We walked for an entire day. Several times we had to stop, due to people in the group fainting from the heat. By the end of the day, it felt like we had gotten nowhere. I looked to my left at someone who was having trouble breathing from dehydration and felt a sharp stab of panic in my chest. I had to find some water, or we all were going to die.

"Stay here," I told Roxane, and went out in search of water. I knew not to go too far because I didn't want to get lost. After about two hours, I came back empty handed and settled down next to Roxane to die. She was in worse shape than I was, already blinking in and out of consciousness. I truly felt that we were about to die, and I wanted to hold onto her tightly. I knew, though, that it would only make us hotter.

I had given up hope and so had everyone else, and it felt like nothing short of an act of God when, out of nowhere, it began to rain. It began to cool rapidly and then, further improving conditions, clouds began to form, giving us shade from the sun. It still was warm, but it was not hot anymore. Within an hour, Roxane, myself, and many of the group were hydrated enough to get on our feet and begin walking again.

We saw a few monkeys swinging from the trees, yelling loudly as they passed high above us. We also saw a few smaller animals run across the jungle floor, probably enjoying the drop in temperature as much as us we were. They would stop and look at us, and then scurry along. Some of the group liked seeing the little animals—they thought they were cute. I, however, did not. Where there is prey, there's bound to be predators, and we had no weapons to defend ourselves with.

We wanted to try to gather some of the rain, but had no vessels to collect it in. We decided that we'd worry about that later. In the moment, we were going to enjoy the shade and drink all the water we could. To our great joy, it continued to rain the next day, and we continued to walk in it. Roxane had the biggest smile on her face, and I understood. Just when we thought that we were going die, miraculous rain saved us. The rainy season had begun, just as we were done for, it seemed.

The day after that day, however, the rain ceased and we were back in the dry heat. I did not like this, particularly because we'd made it out into the desert and were surrounded by rocks and sand. Without the cover of the trees the heat became unbearable.

Luckily, the sandy landscape didn't last for more than a day, and soon we were walking through grass. The tall grass made us nervous, though, as it was certainly tall enough for a predator to hide in.

We all knew we were bound to run into a lion or jaguar or something else intent on eating us, eventually. We did, and this is the part of the journey where we lost most of our members. We became so concerned with not being able to bear the heat that we were not properly keeping an eye out for wild animals.

As we walked through thick grass, I quickly wished we had stayed in the desert. A pack of lions sprawled lazily in the grass, watching our group closely as we passed. Two of the lionesses were pacing back and forth, growling. They did not attack. I watched them carefully as we walked by and noticed that the male was not with them. I knew he must be out patrolling his territory—the territory that we were trespassing on—and waiting to tear anyone who stepped foot into his kingdom to grizzly shreds.

"Thank God they didn't attack," a group member said as we walked.

"Don't get too happy yet," I responded. "Lions are lazy during the day but are wide awake at night. If they're going to attack us, that's when they'll do it, because at night is when they hunt. We need to find stuff that we can protect ourselves with, in case they do decide to attack us," I continued. "We need heavy branches and anything sharp that we can use as a weapon. We'll have to stay together at night, because the way they hunt involves separating one or two animals from a group. It's far easier for them to kill those that are alone than it is to tackle many at once."

"You sure know a lot about lions," Roxane said, a worried look clouding her face.

"Yeah, I used to watch National Geographic all the time. Kind of wish that idiot, Sergeant Lopez, had at least left us his gun to defend ourselves with."

As we walked, we looked for sharp objects and for long and solid branches in case the lions came after us. We had to take care to avoid being bitten by poisonous snakes and giant spiders, and we ended up with nothing. I knew we'd be in trouble without any weapons, but I suddenly remembered we had knives in the bag I was carrying—from the kitchen back at the execution camp. I quickly opened my bag, and in it were fifteen kitchen knives in various sizes. I grabbed two for myself and passed out the rest to people that I handpicked.

As nightfall approached, we all became very paranoid. We'd already lost six people to dehydration, and only eight of us had knives. Once it was dark, we decided that we would just keep walking. I had ordered everyone to huddle in a group if we saw a lion, and the people with knives were to do their best to stay between the lions and those who were left unarmed.

As we walked deep into the night, the group began to tire because we hadn't slept in God knows how long. I pleaded with them to keep going, but they were unable to go any further without rest. After a long debate, I agreed to rest, but only because I was tired too.

That soon proved to be a big mistake.

People put their knives on the ground and closed their eyes to sleep. I knew what we were doing was dangerous, so I slept in the middle of the group with Roxane right next to me. If the lions were going to take anyone, it was going to be the people on the outside of our sleeping circle.

I was in the middle of a dream and, out of nowhere, people began screaming. I immediately opened my eyes. Four people from the group were screaming at the top of their lungs as the lionesses were dragging them off. In the distance, we could hear their final shrieks as the lions ripped into their flesh. Roxane was in a state of shock. I did my best to calm her, but I had to calm down a lot of the others as well.

I knew the lions would not be back anymore that night, so I ordered everyone to sleep, explaining to them that the lions took all the meat that they could eat and, for a while, we'd be safe. The next morning, we took off at a more rapid pace. We wanted to put as much distance between ourselves and the lions as we could.

The rain began to pour again, and I hoped that this would cause the lions to lose our scent. We began eating bugs to keep from starving.

Some of the bugs tasted okay, while others were disgusting. When you bit into some of them, you could taste their gooey intestines squirting out, onto your tongue. Three days went by before the next attack and I was beginning to think that the lions had lost our scent, but they hadn't. They were following us—but from a distance."

The next time they attacked, it was during the day. The rain was still pouring, and we were growing weary. My body was irritated and itching from being wet for such a long period of time. We were now walking through a lot of tall grass. Nothing was comfortable about this journey. If we were already itching from being stuck in the same soaking wet clothes, having to wade through wet grass made it ten times worse.

Just as I thought things couldn't get any worse, a lioness leapt out of the tall grass, grabbing one of the boys by his neck. We hadn't even seen the lioness as we walked past her. Roxane and I were in the front of the group, and the first person who was attacked was no more than six people behind us.

I felt Roxane cave to her knees beside me. "No!" she screamed at the top of her lungs, almost hysterical as she jumped at me. She wrapped her arms around me, hugging me extremely tight, and she didn't let go for a long time. She didn't see it, but I watched on helplessly as three more members of the group were snatched from the line ruthlessly by the lions.

I was breathing heavily; that very easily could have been Roxane and me. The knives were useless to us; we were in a hopeless situation and there was nothing we could do to defend ourselves against the lions. We were like the people in a shark movie who were left out in the ocean—knowing with certainty, after the first bite, that they were dead as hundreds more surrounded them. We had no choice but to accept that now we were on the lion's fast-food menu.

We continued our journey, hoping that we were going the right way. Even as nightfall came, we continued to walk, scared to sleep with the lions so near. It seemed the bugs were seeking shelter from the rain and no longer walking around, so we weren't able to find enough for everyone to eat.

I heard a noise and reacted. "Everyone down," I said very lazily, as I slowly got down, too. In the distance there was a jet flying overhead, and I didn't want the pilots to see us in case they were enemy troops. I soon realised there was more than one, and as we hid in some tall grass, they flew over us, and just kept flying. I don't believe that they saw us. After the jets had passed, people began getting up, but one look to the right and I made everyone get back down. A little way away were two cheetahs. Luckily, they never attacked. I believe, because of how small they were, that they weren't full grown adults. I made everyone crawl for a few hours, until we were clear of the teenage cats.

"I can't do this anymore. I need something to eat now, and it needs to be some meat," one of the girls in the group yelled in frustration.

"I know. I'm dying of thirst, too, but we have to keep moving," I said, hoping that I'd be able to encourage her to not give up.

"We're lost, aren't we?" A woman named Kiara asked.

I hissed in frustration—the last thing I needed was for everyone to start panicking

"No," I replied. "We got off the path when the lions attacked, but I led us back onto it. We're fine."

"How do you know? It's not like you've ever been where we're going, is it?" I knew Kiara wasn't trying to be vindictive or give me a hard time—she just really wanted to know whether I knew where we were or not.

"Well, if you pay close attention to the positioning of the sun at its highest point, and the position of the moon, it can help you work out where on earth you are. I paid attention to that, even before that idiot soldier abandoned us. So, I first noticed we were walking crooked the other day, when the sun was at its highest point, and I began leading us back towards the path.

"Also, I made this," I told her, holding out a leaf contraption for her to see.

She eyed it as though it were completely alien to her. She probably thought I'd gone crazy, but I explained to her that I used the rain and a small twig to make a compass.

"Nice," Kiara said, finally smiling. At last, she seemed satisfied.

We all walked and talked with each other to take our minds off our hunger. Eventually, we were fortunate enough to find thousands of ants, and everyone began shoving them into their mouths like popcorn at the movies. When you're as starving as we were, taste buds don't exist—only your hunger.

We ate all the ants we could, and drank from the rain until we could drink no more. We decided to rest for a while and hold a group meeting to regroup.

"That's it," one of the girls in the group said. "We've been walking for who knows how long now, and don't seem to be any closer to a

US military base, or any base at all. I'm sick of eating bugs. They taste like crap. And I'm tired of having to wait for it to rain to get a drink of water. I say we turn ourselves in at the first base we come to, whether it be a US base or an enemy base."

"I'm with you on that," Jordan said, as he found a spot in the grass to sit.

Most of the members were for the plan, including me, but Roxane had other ideas. There was no way she was going to turn herself into anyone but a US military base.

"No." She almost stomped her foot, and the defiance in her expression made me feel alive for a few seconds. "You guys can turn yourselves in, but I didn't escape just to go back and be killed," she told the group, while looking at me to change my decision and support her.

I nodded my head. "I've changed my mind," I began, but was interrupted.

"You're just changing your mind because you're dating Roxane," one of the girls said, sounding out the syllables in Roxane's name with disgust.

With one hand on her hip and the other pointed directly at the girl's face, Roxane angrily replied. "No one is stopping you. You can go to whatever base you like, but I want to live. I didn't escape to be recaptured, raped, and killed; I could have gotten on the darn helicopter, and already be in a warm place eating regular food, but I stayed with the group for Jonathan, so I will be darned if I let him get recaptured now."

The girl didn't respond but stood in place. She was almost incandescent with anger.

The rest of the group said they were sticking with me on whatever decision I made, so I told them that as far as I was concerned, we were free and we were going to stay that way, but that they were also free to do what they wanted.

The rain was annoying and just kept coming down; I could barely see in front of me at night. We were grateful to the trees then—at least they were giving us some shelter.

I growled in frustration, and it took everything I had not to pound my fist into the nearest trunk. "Where the Hell is the base at?" I yelled. We had traveled in the same direction that Sergeant Lopez had been taking us in, but I began wondering if maybe there was a turn that we were supposed to have taken somewhere that we didn't know about.

Gathering myself, I sighed. "We have to keep going this way," I said, using my jungle made compass. I know it's the right direction; I can feel it.

"I sure hope so," Kiara said, as she released a hopeless sigh.

"Get away from the trees!" I yelled to everyone, as lightning streaked across the sky.

"What's that?" Jordan asked, pointing at lights that seemed to be moving towards our group.

They were still in the distance, but they were moving towards us fast and there was no way to escape. At first, they only seemed to come from in front, but before long we were surrounded. There was nowhere that we could run. Fear raced through my body. We were going to be killed right here, and there was nothing I could do about it.

"Get down," I whispered to Roxane, even as the two of us fell to our stomachs. I didn't hear any gunshots, but everyone around us began to fall violently to the ground, unconscious. What am I going to do? I thought. I couldn't let them capture either Roxane or myself, and I didn't want to see anyone else recaptured, either.

Once everyone in our group was down, the soldiers rushed in. I expected them to start checking the bodies to make sure that everyone was dead, but they didn't.

"These aren't soldiers," one of them finally spoke, after a long silence. "Some of them are just teenagers. They look American, don't you think? My guess is these are the ones we're looking for."

*****

"Sergeant, what do you think?" Valfor asked.

"We need to get them to the base," Stephen replied, nodding to his unit. The unit looked at the sergeant as if he was crazy.

"Sir, there are only nine of us and at least forty of them. How do you plan on getting them anywhere, Sir?"

Stephen didn't say a word. He stared at his soldier.

"Got you!" the soldier yelled to him, as he jogged off.

I stood to my feet. I wasn't a hundred percent sure yet that we were safe, but these soldiers were speaking English and, in my mind, I knew that they had to be US troops.

"Do not move an inch," one of them yelled at me. He stood right above me, gun drawn and pointed right at me.

I stood frozen as rain poured on my head. I didn't move. I just looked at all the bodies on the ground—the bodies of everyone who had been traveling with me. It looked like they were all dead, but there was no blood on the ground. Then, I thought, maybe there had been blood and the rain had already washed it away. I was scared, but I managed to slip my hands into my pockets and wrap my fingers around the hilts of the knives I had hidden there. I wasn't going to be killed without a fight.

The soldier in front of me had the draw on me, but I wasn't going to let him hurt Roxane. I glanced at her as she lay on the ground, looking up at me with eyes wrought with fear. She thought as I did—that these soldiers were going to kill me as they had everyone else.

"What are you doing here?" the soldier asked fiercely.

"Trying to get home!" I yelled over the sound of thunder. The rainclouds were gathering, and a storm was rolling in.

"What's your name and where are you from?" the soldier continued with his questioning. His voice sounded menacing in my fear.

"My name is Jonathan Gatsby, and I'm from the United States of America. I was taken, along with these people that you've just killed—"

"They're not dead, just stunned," the soldier interrupted me.

I was giddy with relief, and I was starting to feel my glimmer of hope grow into something stronger. "We were being executed, one at a time, once a month. We escaped. I don't know how long ago exactly, but we're starving and cold. Please. If you're US soldiers, please help us," I begged, as I fell to my knees.

"What state and city are you from?" the soldier asked. He was still sharp but beginning to calm down.

"I'm from Fairbanks, Alaska, and I just want to get home."

We're going to run a check on your name but relax a bit while we confirm your story.

"Okay," I said. My heart wanted to jump. These were the people we'd been looking for, and once they'd confirmed my identity, we'd be properly free.

"Can my girlfriend get up, Sir?" I asked the soldier, feeling safe for the first time.

"Yeah, she can," the soldier helped Roxane to her feet.

"Thank you." She looked exhausted, but she smiled politely.

"You're welcome, Miss," the soldier replied, before turning back to me.

"It's confirmed!" a soldier named Jamie yelled at the top of her lungs, "His name is listed as one of the captives. We did it! We found them! Our mission is complete now! Does this mean we can all finally go home, Sir?" Jamie was almost bouncing in place, and her eyes lit up brightly as she spoke.

Stephen chuckled. "No, I think in this case, they found us," he said, correcting his officer as he allowed himself to smile, "And we'll find out for sure when Command briefs us, but I sure hope this means we're getting out of here." He paused and held Jamie's gaze for a minute. "Thank you, Jamie," he murmured.

It seemed they were just as tired of the jungle as we were, and they were ready to go home as well.

Once everyone who had been stunned had finally come-to and were up on their feet, the soldiers led us to the almost mythical US military base, which wasn't far from where we were at all. It was a forty-five-minute walk in the direction we were already headed—we'd nearly managed to make it to safety ourselves.

It was a relief to have Sergeant Stephen's platoon to usher us over the ground that was still between us and the base.

*****

"The soldiers talked with us the whole way to the base, and I held on tight to Roxane's hand. I was scared that if I let it go, I'd wake up still at the execution camp, waiting to be executed. It felt so surreal that it was easy to think Roxane and I escaping together had only been a dream." Gatsby looked exhausted—almost as if he were reliving the experience through the telling of his story.

"That's amazing," Manuel said. "What a story of survival, listeners. They had no food; they had to eat bugs while there were enemy soldiers on the lookout for them. They almost died of dehydration, had lions attacking them, and were ditched by their rescuer because of his lack of romantic options. Perhaps worst of all, they were taken from their families and forced into what they call an execution camp.

Manuel shook his head, still trying to process what he'd been told. "While waiting to be executed, Gatsby here found love in his soon-to-be-wife, Roxane.

"This is Manuel with CGX News. To all the listeners that tuned in, I hope the story of Mr Gatsby and the survivors might be as inspirational to you as it has been to me. For those who missed it, you missed a real treat." Manuel signed off.

CHAPTER NINETEEN

"Now how about that job?" Gatsby said, shaking Manuel's hand.

"Not wasting any time, I see," Manuel said with a warm laugh "Come back tomorrow around twelve, and I'll get you started on your assignment."

"Really? Awesome. I can't wait!" Gatsby looked as though his face might split in two with the force of his eager grin. "Do you know what I'll be doing?"

"Just come tomorrow and you'll find out. Oh!" Manuel caught Gatsby by the shoulder as he was about to head out. "Before I forget, this is from the studio. Three hundred dollars for coming every day and doing our show—sharing your story."

"Wow, thank you." Gatsby was almost overwhelmed with gratitude. He and Roxane really needed that money. "Okay, I'll most definitely be here tomorrow, and—thank you," he said, and almost slipped over in the studio doorway because of the rush he was in to get home and tell Roxane the good news.

"Hey, Roxane!" Gatsby said, walking into their new, empty house with a thirty-inch TV that he purchased at the store. His face was alight with excitement.

"Wow, somebody had a good day today," Roxane said as she wrapped him in a welcoming hug and gave him a kiss on the lips. "What's with the TV?"

"Sure did!" he said, grinning. "I got a job at CGX News" —he held up his hand to stop her interrupting him in excitement— "and as I started walking home, I changed my mind, caught a cab to the store and bought this TV. I got a DVD player, too. Then I stopped by my mom's house and grabbed a bunch of movies."

"Wait, what?" Roxane asked, leaning in for a second hug. "You got a job at CGX News? Wow, that's really awesome, Jonathan."

"Yeah, it is." He nodded and flashed her a smile.

"Did they say when you start?"

"Well, not exactly. They just told me to be in tomorrow at noon, and said they'd give me the details then."

"I'm really happy for you, Jonathan. We should celebrate tonight."

"Yup, we should. What do you say—we can play a movie on our new TV, and I can make some spicy Italian sausages... or what do you want?"

"Sausages will be fine," Roxane replied. "No soda though. Let's have some apple juice."

"Apple juice sounds good to me!!" Gatsby replied.

"That's good, because it's all we have," Roxane said playfully.

Gatsby laughed, "Well, that will change soon. No more struggling and not being able to afford stuff. In fact, let's go to The Turtle Club to eat tonight."

Roxane smirked, "Really? And exactly how are we paying for this?"

"CGX paid me for the interview today. They gave me three hundred dollars in cash."

The Turtle club was the fanciest restaurant in town, and he was really craving their prime rib. It was a difficult choice because he was also craving duck from Pagota. It had been so long since he'd been to his favourite restaurants.

"Wow," Roxane said. "That was nice of them, but no need to rush. We'll get to go there in time, but it's probably best to save that money for now, because you never know when we we'll need it."

Gatsby felt a little taken aback, but he knew she was right. He didn't know how often he was going to be paid, or even how much he'd be making. "You're right," he said after a moment's thought.

"Yeah, I know I'm right," she said jokingly. Her face was lit up by her beautiful smile. "That's why I said it."

Gatsby went to work on making the spicy Italian sausages and broccoli, while Roxane prepared snacks to go with the meal. She poured a bag of Doritos into a bowl, and apple juice into the cups. Within fifteen minutes, they were sitting down on the couch ready to watch the movie.

"So, what do you want to watch? Action? Or adventure? Or comedy?" Gatsby asked, leaning into Roxane as he pulled the movies out.

"*Titanic*." She looked over at him with that brilliant smile.

"Really? You want to watch *Titanic*?" he asked, frowning. "You sure you don't want to watch *Die Hard*? It's a very romantic movie."

She sighed. "Fine, we can watch *Die Hard*, again, for the thirtieth time since we got back, I swear that's the only thing we watched at your mom's house," she said, laughing.

"Yes!" Gatsby was excited, but as he skimmed through the movies, his fingers brushed across *Titanic* and he pulled it out instead. He threw it in the DVD player without telling Roxane, knowing she'd be grateful for the surprise

She let out a throaty chuckle as she realized what he'd done. "Aw, thank you," she said, snuggling in tighter to his side. She wrapped her arm around his waist and laid her head on his chest. They were both asleep before the movie was even close to being finished.

When they woke up a little while later, Gatsby began to clean up their snacks and tidied the kitchen. Roxane was the type of person who, if she saw something needing to be done, would do it without a word of complaint, so he'd made it his new mission to try to beat her to everything. He was just finishing up with the mopping and sweeping when she walked into the kitchen stifling a yawn.

When she saw how much work he'd done, she made a point of slapping his butt as he walked past her. "I'm the luckiest woman in the world," she said, leaning into him.

"You're damn right," he replied with a light laugh and a tired smile.

She laughed with him. "Or is it *you* who's lucky?" she asked, as he held her tight.

Roxane could hear him breathing heavily from where he stood behind her with his arms settled around her stomach.

"You might not believe me," he whispered against her neck, "but from the moment I saw you in the van, I was in love with you. I totally forgot I was a prisoner and, at that point, all I knew was that I had to get to know you."

"I believe you," she assured him. "And it took me awhile, but I fell in love with you at the camp, maybe even before I should have."

CHAPTER TWENTY

The Nationberg Group met as normal, but they noticed a key member was not present. Where was President Brooks? They had made it clear to him upon joining that missing meetings was not an option. President Brooks had been handpicked by the Nationberg Group twenty years prior to him running for office. They had him slated to run and win the presidency. He was to be the last male president, as the Group had laid the groundwork to ensure that the one to follow him would be a woman; they'd chosen someone just two years after they'd chosen Brooks. She would be instrumental in dissolving the government and turning their country, along with many others, over to the elite members of the Nationberg Group, who intended to rule the world themselves, under a single government banner.

Any nation that fought against them would be destroyed.

"Call President Brooks," demanded one of the leading members, standing imperiously and shooting the other members an irritated scowl. "This is not allowed. Being late to meetings, or just not showing, is never permitted."

Six members of the Nationberg Group all reached for the phone and the youngest queen amongst their party was the first one to get through to President Brooks' cell phone. It rang a few times before it clicked off, indicating that the president had declined the call.

*****

President Brooks sat in his office, looking at his phone and wiping the sweat from his brow. He was watching the speech of a former President—one who'd been assassinated for his words.

President Brooks listened very closely as the former president spoke.

> *"I have been silent for too long," the speech began. "I made choices to advance myself, not understanding the price that I, along with this country, would pay." The crowd at the press conference remained silent as he spoke.*
>
> *"My duties as President are not to attend secret meetings, nor to submit to secret societies. Neither are my duties to perform abominable rituals each month to satisfy the sick minds of secret powers that be.*
>
> *"The press has released information that should not have been released. Dangerous information. Information like missile launch times, locations of bases that were supposed to be secret, and a great deal of sensitive data. If the press had known we were at war, I know that they would not have released such information, as it could be used by any enemy, foreign or domestic, against our great nation.*
>
> *"The press will destroy the president every day of the week during times of peace, and that's okay. It is also true, though, that during times of war, the press has always worked*

alongside the government for the sake of our country, and I stand here to tell you today that we are at war.

"Secret societies, secret powers—those that others before me have warned us about—prey on our country during times of peace and stand against us in times of distress. These bankers and financial powers are greedy and evil beyond comprehension. We must, as a nation, stand up against these secret societies that look to own the universe and enslave even the stars."

President Brooks stopped the tape. He took a heavy breath. The press was in the next room, but he knew that two presidents before him had been killed within a week of their enlightening speeches. He knew that his decision not to attend the meeting that was presently taking place within the Nationberg Group would mean he was severely punished—perhaps even left a marked man.

He had seen other rulers punished for missing a meeting by lashing, burning, and awful forced bestiality. President Brooks was about to outright tell the country about the Nationberg Group and their damning connection to the Illuminati and the Masons. They were going to kill him, just as those presidents and music stars and dissidents before him had been killed. They might first take him to one of their personal facilities for "mental illness" where they utilized methods developed in Nazi Germany to break their prisoners. One may be subjected to having controlling substances forced upon them, and forced to endure continual hypnotism or brutal torture. In the end, everyone broke.

******

"He is not answering," the young queen stated, reiterating the obvious in her frustration.

The middle-aged money man who'd ordered the call was furious. "Fine," he said. "If he wants to break his contract with Lucifer, we will break him for it. Send our best assassin after him. I want him dead by morning. Make it look like a heart attack." He finished his sentence and calmly returned to his seat.

"Let us not be so hasty to kill him! If you remember the plan, we were going to make him look crazy before replacing him, anyway." A member of a similarly old family, known as The Speaker, spoke, and several other attendees nodded their agreement.

"Sir!" The Special Security director yelled, interrupting the meeting. All the well-known intelligence agencies acted as personal security for meetings held by the Nationberg Group, the Illuminati, and the Masons.

"What is it? One of the members stood up upon seeing something in the agent's hand.

"Sir, the president of the United States is getting ready to make a speech."

The Speaker sighed and pinched the bridge of his nose. "Play it for us on the big screen," he ordered the Special Security director.

"Yes sir," the director responded, and did as he was asked. Within seconds, the screen was playing the sitting President's speech.

> *"Today is a sad day for our country, and for many other nations." The President looked decidedly green. "I have a confession to make, and I feel I better get right down to the point, before a bullet comes flying at me. I know that, today, my life is in as much danger as the lives of the presidents assassinated before me were."*

The crowd was silent, but when the president mentioned the previous assassinations, some of their faces were struck with horror. Many others scooted to the edge of their seats to listen better, while some showed no emotions at all. Secret Service agents edged their way towards the president, but he motioned for them to back off.

> *"To get right down to it," he said. "The entire platform that I ran on was devised for me by a secret association. All the promises and the policies were designed by them, and not me. If it were up to me, Flint, in Michigan, would have water; there would be no wall even being considecxred between the US and Mexico. Racism would be a crime with the penalty of exile. What you must understand," he implored them, looking boldly over the press crowd, "is that this is the same group that previously assassinated presidents have tried to warn you about. I am here today to again warn you of their dangerous intentions."*

"Sirs, should we cut the nation's signal to stop the broadcast? The Secret Security director asked, addressing the heads of the controlling families.

"No, just pause it on our TV so we can continue watching it in a second."

"I think we should cut the broadcast." The most powerful of the Chinese delegates stood as he spoke up.

"No," The Speaker replied. "This is perfect and it's going to fall right into our favour."

"How is this perfect?" the other family head asked in outrage. "He's about to expose our society!"

"Simple. Fake news is such a big thing right now—we've been putting out so many edited videos over the years, shown that videos *can* be edited—and with the president already having a low rating, we can make it look like he's losing his mind, just like we planned. We won't have to kill him. He's doing it himself, at least in the eyes of the United States citizens.

"We've got Congress and the Senate in our pockets—they'll assist us in making President Brooks look deranged." He turned to the representatives for both sectors. "The Nationberg Group requires you to move for his impeachment. Is that understood?"

They all nodded their heads, knowing there were hefty prices to pay for refusal to cooperate.

"Well, how do we plan to make him look crazy?" The Speaker's cousin asked.

"Let us not worry about that now. This was set to be his last year anyway, if you remember. We set it up for Brooks to be accepted as President by including subliminal messaging in popular media. Do you remember what happened in 2000, when we had him appear as the president on an episode of The Blackout Show?" A large portion of the gathering nodded silently. "Well then, you'll probably also remember that in a following episode, we showed that he'd only serve three years of his term. So what if we cut him out a year early? We're prepared for the next President right now. She also got an episode on The Blackout Show, didn't she? We've already told the world that Brooks will be followed by a woman." He turned and gestured towards a woman seated against the wall. "Hernandez, please step forward."

Hernandez stepped forward confidently.

"During this year's television awards, I want you to announce that you're running for President."

"Wait, what about Hillary?" the older queen asked, clearly not too comfortable with an African American woman being placed as President of the United States.

The speaker looked at the queen with disgust. "I do very much despise being interrupted. Take her into the dungeons; we'll deal with her after the meeting." He nodded to several Special Security agents and they stepped forward to oblige.

"No, please, I'm sorry, I didn't mean to say anything untoward!" the older queen begged. "I just thought that we were using Hillary as the next President! Please, no! No! NO!" the queen yelled as the agents her off. She kicked and screamed all the way down to what they called the dungeon, where she would await punishment.

The Speaker resumed the meeting. "Speaking of presidents, how's our candidate holding up in the Russian elections?" he said. "The sooner we can regain control of that country the better."

"I'm holding up fine, Sir, Porsiea Karvia'k responded. "The current president is putting much, much pressure on me and has made two attempts on my life but, so far, he has failed to get me out of the presidential race for our wonderful country of Mother Russia."

"Okay, no problem. He knows our procedures—being a former hit man for our organizations. We will not have him killed though, for the sake of our plans. With all the leaks, and now President Brooks' speech, our society is no longer so secret. The best thing we can do for now is to make the rumors seem false and show the world the corruptness of their current governments. We can show them that that a One World government, through our organization, is what is needed to save us all. That's also, coincidentally, the reason I've decided not to kill President Brooks.

"Besides, we're the least of his worries. Breaking your agreement with Lucifer will bring his wrath on you, and I, personally, would rather be dealt with by the Group than have Lucifer punish me. What we plan to do is to show the world that, with every country under one government, there will be no more wars, because there will be no more opposition. We will use the Masons to form protests around the globe, targeting the current governments. When we step into the light as the solution, the Masons will switch from protest to support for our One World government idea."

"Do you think that they'll be able to draw enough of the world's support to accomplish this?" the leading Turkish delegate asked.

"Of course," The Speaker's cousin replied. "The Masons and the Freemasons are over five million strong, and that's not including the women's sect, The Eastern Stars. It'll be easier than using a microwave. People always go with the crowd, and with the protest being so big, they'll happily join in."

Syria's head delegate raised his hand. "You," The Speaker pointed at him. "What is it?"

"It is more of a question," the delegate said. "But since we make up most of the world's government, why can we not just shut our governments down ourselves?"

"Because if we force it, we'll meet a strong resistance from the people, but if we win over their support and their votes, we'll only meet a small resistance. That will be far easier to stomp out, and we won't have to worry about it drawing others to its cause.

"We really must show each group what they desire to see. We'll target their social media by noting their political preferences. We'll target the poor neighborhoods and make them see that their government is only destroying them and wants to rid themselves of them, and they'll see that is why they need us. We can use this very same method of destroying governments to build up ours.

"We will leak information out, with videos of each government ordering military strikes on their own people to start wars. We will release documents and videos of governments poisoning their citizens and putting drugs out on the street to reduce their populations. And when our Masons begin their mass protest in each country, many will run to the cause."

The head of the other family nodded. "I'm in full agreeance with this plan," he chimed in from his seat, smiling from ear to ear. "This has been in the works for years, and now it's time to put our plan into action. So, we need to regain control of Russia, we need to gain control of North Korea, and we need President Brooks, his vice president, and their staff out of the office. Instead of allowing The Speaker of the House to take the post, we need to get Hernandez to run for President. She really has the people on her side with the commotion she's made amongst Congress.

"Unless anyone from the two ruling houses have any amendments to this meeting let's put our plan into action immediately. Let's make what we've discussed here happen, and with haste. This meeting is adjourned," The Speaker announced. Those of you who wish to stay and watch the rest of Brooks' speech are welcome to." He turned to the Secret Security director. "You can un-pause it now."

The President's speech continued.

> *"The group that you all have been warned about and these secret groups that you have recently heard many celebrities speaking out against—before being killed by—are all part of the same organization. These three groups are all different branches of the one organization, with our two most notorious wealth-controlling families at their heads. These three groups are the Illuminati, the Masons, and the Nationberg Group."*

Some people in the crowd thought he'd snapped, but others believed him and paid close attention to everything he said.

"Right now," he continued. "You do not pay taxes to the United States Government but to one of these families. We have to shut down the Federal Reserve and start printing our own money. They have the power to freeze everything any American citizen owns right now, at the push of a button.

"Their plan is for a One World government. Who do you think is leaking private, encrypted government documents? No hacker can hack into any encrypted computer without being directly on that computer. I believe that the FBI agent, Agent Smith, who was killed by Secret Security had no affiliation with the hacks or collusion with the countries responsible. He must have gotten to close in his investigation, and they killed him so he couldn't speak out.

"Our intelligence and other government spy agencies work for the Nationberg Group! They are members of the Illuminati! You'll see, then, why I find it so odd that he confessed to, and was killed by, the Secret Security, rather than just confessing to his FBI bosses.

"For your information, the Nationberg Group does not have to hack into the system, because they have all the passcodes—our Senate and our Congress are all a part of the organization. It's very real! Every President has had to join, in order to get elected. You, the American citizens, might vote, but trust me when I tell you that these powers look at your votes and laugh at your ignorance to what is really happening with the election behind closed doors. Then, they declare their person the winner, regardless of what the votes say. They want a One World government, and they'll do whatever it takes.

"I can say with confidence that no government,no matter how bad, could be worse than a One World government.

"I have a surprise for everyone. I actually lost the election by a lot of votes. I was not even close to winning... Some of you must be wondering how that's even possible. Well, the simple truth is that they fixed it so I won. I admit that our government is corrupt! There is no excuse for it, but the next person elected will be just as corrupt as I was. I say again! No government at all can be worse than a One World government ruled by one evil, corrupt governing body, from which there is no escape, because it is worldwide."

The people who were in attendance at the press conference had no idea what to think about what they were being told. Here was the president telling them that their government was all part of a big conspiracy, and that they had been coercing and lying to the American citizens.

"Look under your seats," the president told everyone as he put his speech on hold.

Everybody looked under their seats and found a thick paper packet. The president began to speak once more, enrapturing most of his audience.

"Inside the packets you are about to open," he continued, "you will find the full documents outlining the circumstances of the assassination of the last president to try to warn the people. The proof is right there. It was the Secret Security Agency. The partial documents we gave you two years ago were forged and fake. These are the real files. Look for yourself.

"You will find the assassinations of other great leaders were performed by the Secret Security Agency also. These assassinations had nothing to do with race but everything to do with them not joining the Illuminati when they were approached. It's all right there in

those files. Some were even killed because of their refusal to fill their movies with hidden messages that push the organization's agenda.

"I have no doubt that you, the press and private citizens both, will review the documents for authenticity. I have no doubt, either, that you will do the right thing and inform the world about the agendas of these secret societies."

*****

"Okay, you can turn it off!" The Speaker yelled at Secret Security director angrily. The screen went dark. "Well, he certainly has said a mouthful. Now," The Speaker gave a pointed look. "Release the video we made him do upon joining our group."

"Which one? The lead delegate of Nigeria asked. He hated America and was looking forward to the turmoil that he knew was about to occur in the United States.

"Use the one that shows the little girl that he raped—the one we kidnapped. She was screaming a lot in that video," The Speaker said. "His country will likely assassinate him themselves, after seeing it." He sat down with a furious expression etched all over his face. "They found her dead under a bridge shortly after, all drugged up. It will look like the president killed her to keep her from ruining his chances of getting elected. Oh! And also show the one where he and the vice president performed the donkey ritual earlier this year—the one in Ontario, Canada. Not much will rile the citizens like a tag-team donkey rape committed by their fearless leaders."

"Nice," the Turkish delegate said, leaning back in his chair with an evil grin.

"Yes, sir, we'll get right on it," the Secret Security director responded as he left the room.

CHAPTER TWENTY-ONE

Gatsby walked into the news studio, excited and curious about his new job. "Hello," he said to the janitor as he walked by.

The janitor gave a slight nod of his head and said hello back.

Gatsby didn't know if he should just sit in the waiting room, which wasn't as warm as the rest of the building, or if he should go into the studio. As he was trying to decide on where to wait, Manuel walked through the door, carrying a few boxes. He rushed over to help him. "Here, let me help you with that," he said, grabbing two of the three boxes out of his hands.

"Thank you," Manuel said. "I could have gotten them, but I appreciate the help."

"You're welcome."

He followed as Manuel walked down a hall and into an office that Gatsby had never been in before. Pictures of Manuel's family and awards that he had received were hung on the walls. *This must be his office*, Gatsby thought to himself.

Manuel took off his coat and hung it up in a small closet, and Gatsby sat down, patiently waiting for him to get settled.

"How has your day been so far?" Manuel asked, as he set his briefcase down in front of his desk.

"My day's been good. I didn't do much—just went for a walk and then came here," Gatsby replied.

"How's your family? And how's Roxane?"

"They're doing well, and Roxane is doing great. She was really excited when I told her that I now have a job here," he said, hoping that Manuel did indeed still have a job for him.

Before Manuel was able to reply, there was a knock on the door. "Come in," Manuel said, very calmly, as though he had been expecting a visitor. "Awesome," he continued when a tall man walked in. He stood to shake the man's hand, so naturally, Gatsby did the same, so as not to appear rude.

"This is my boss, Mr Hoggsby," Manuel said, by way of introduction. "He's here to explain your job to you."

"Why, hello, Mr Gatsby. First, let me say you did an excellent job in keeping the listeners tuned in for your story. More people tuned in during your biography hour than they have during any other time, including before the war began. Now, to get right down to business, we want to keep the listeners tuning in like that, so Mr Emotho has brought a wonderful idea to me. Would you be interested in co-hosting a show with Manuel? Instead of telling a story, you guys would be going back and forth discussing news topics."

"Yes, sir. I would love to do that," Gatsby replied, with a big grin on his face. "And I'll do my very best."

"Oh, you just keep doing as you were doing before, and I'll remain impressed." Mr Hoggsby chuckled. "Now, next thing is pay. You'll only be on air for one and a half hours per day, but you'll have to do research on topics and bring topics to the table—there's a lot of prep work. You and Manuel will always give each other a heads up about anything you want to discuss the day before a show, if you plan to bring up a topic not on the prior list."

"Like for instance," Manuel said. "Tomorrow, we're going to be talking about the president and his current administration, his policies, and his role in the starting of World War III. That was the planned topic, but the president has just finished addressing the nation on national television. He's revealed that our most notorious keepers of wealth are also behind three secret organisations, which is going to be a hot topic. So, we would inform Mr Hoggsby about the planned topic, and let him know that we'd like to add that subject to the list for tomorrow."

"So, I start tomorrow?" Gatsby asked, unable to hold in his grin.

"Yes, you do," Manuel replied, giving him a slap on the back.

"Is there a computer here I can use to research stuff?" Gatsby asked, ready to take on the role.

"Yes, there is, but you'll also have your own company laptop to work from, so you won't have to stay here."

"Nice," Gatsby said.

"Now, as for pay," Mr Hoggsby cut in. "As I had started to mention earlier, we will pay you a hundred dollars per day, and your show will air five times per week. Can you handle five hundred dollars a week?" he asked.

"Yes, Sir, I believe I can," Gatsby replied.

"Okay. All right then. The job is yours." Mr Hoggsby shook Gatsby's hand.

Gatsby remained standing as Manuel made his way around the desk to shake his hand as well.

Once the formalities were out of the way, he rushed home with his new laptop in its case, access to unlimited internet, and a new company phone. He finally felt like he was back on track.

"Roxane!" he yelled as he entered the house excitedly. "Roxane!"

She came down the stairs in a blue dress, with her hair done and her purse hanging from her shoulder.

"You going somewhere?" Gatsby asked. Somehow, he got the idea from the way she was dressed that Manuel had already informed her of what his new job was, and how much he was going to get paid. He shook his head and decided to play it off a bit before he told her. "Well, I didn't get the job, so we might as well just move back in with my mom so that we can save what little money we have left until I can find another one somewhere," he said, schooling his facial expression to show frustration. He balled his fist up and bit his lip to make it look more convincing.

"Wait. What?" Roxane said, her bright smile faltering. "I have the feeling that you're not being honest with me..." Her smile reappeared quickly.

"No," he shook his head again. "They were going to give me a co-hosting job with Manuel, until they found out I never graduated high school. Manuel said the station will give me a few hundred dollars more next week, to help us out, but that's the best they can do."

"Are you serious?" Roxane asked, her face flushing with growing anger. "That's messed up, because clearly they thought you were qualified before they found out you didn't graduate." She reached out to comfort him. "Well, we'll be okay even without your show, because I found a job today. I can support us for a while."

"Wait a minute. You found a job. Where? And when did you even apply for a job?"

"Well, I went out today looking for one, so that we both could be working. Not just you. Those stone age days are over, and I believe women should work just like men." She waited for a response with her hands on her hips, her head tilted to the side, and a look on her face that dared him to argue.

"What?" he asked, laughing. "You'll get no argument from me. I feel the same way. I just asked where... And when did you apply?" he asked again, still chuckling.

"I got a job at the college as a teacher's aide."

"Wow, that is awesome, Well, now that we both have jobs, we're going to have it made. Gatsby smiled flirtatiously at Roxane.

"I knew you got it, you jerk." Roxane blushed as she stood by the steps that led to the second floor of their house. "So get ready! Quick now."

"Get ready for what?" Gatsby asked, confused.

"Um, we both got good jobs. We're going out to celebrate."

"To the Turtle Club, I'm assuming?" Gatsby asked, hopeful.

"For once, your assumption is correct," she replied. She slapped his butt as he walked up the stairs to change into something more formal.

"Alright now. Don't get me aroused or we might not make it out the door," he said jokingly.

Moments later, he came down the stairs in the only suit he owned. He took it from his brother Mark's closet when he saw it the day he and Roxane were moving their stuff into their new house.

They took a cab to the Turtle Club, where they waited for the hostess to seat them, looking as fancy as could be. It was a very fancy restaurant, with the namesake, turtles, being represented by green coloring. Each table had white tablecloths, and there was a large tank with all kinds of sea life in it.

The place was packed, and they were lucky to get a table as fast as they did. It probably helped that Gatsby tipped the hostess fifty dollars to move their names to the top of the list. They sat down and placed their orders—both ordering the prime rib.

"This place really is nice," Roxane said as she looked around from her seat. A band was playing in the background and a few couples were up dancing to the swing music.

"I can't dance," Gatsby said to Roxane, laughing, as he saw her looking back and forth between him and the dance floor.

"Please just one dance?" She asked, offering up wide eyes and a pleading face.

"Alright, fine, but if I embarrass us, this is completely your fault."

"Okay," she agreed easily, jumping up and pulling him towards the dance floor.

Fortunately for Gatsby, the song changed into something slow the second they stepped on the dance floor. He gently took Roxane's hand into his right hand, and then placed his other around her waist and pulled her in close. She rested her head on his shoulder as they danced in circles. A few times, she looked up and found his eyes gazing back into hers. She closed her eyes, lowered her head back down, and finished the dance resting snuggly against him. She still couldn't believe that they were free from the execution camp and back in America. At times, she felt it was a dream and was scared she would eventually wake up and find them still in the camp.

Once the dance finished, they walked back to their table and waited for their food. They talked about Roxane's teaching job a bit, and then about Gatsby's new radio job.

"Speaking of that," Gatsby said. "Remind me to get on the laptop and study when I get home. I have to read up for tomorrow's show."

"Okay," Roxane replied. Just as she was getting ready to say something else, the waitress appeared with their food.

"Oh, wow!" Roxane said, brimming with excitement. "These are huge."

Gatsby agreed. "I told you," he said. "Wait until you taste it."

When they'd finished and packed up the leftovers onto to-go plates, Roxane called a cab using Gatsby's work phone, while he used the bathroom.

"Don't forget to do your research," Roxane reminded Gatsby when they got home, as she caught him sneaking upstairs and heading towards their bedroom for a rest.

He snapped his fingers. "I knew I forgot something," he said, turning right back aground. He was tired, but it needed to be done.

He opened the laptop, logged on, and searched YouTube for the president's speech. He watched intently, picking key words out of the speech to focus on. He studied the Nationberg Group and the Illuminati quite intensely and couldn't believe what he found. The President had just given a speech on their corruptness, and they had a recruiting page looking for young talent. The page read "If you want to take your career to higher levels, join the Illuminati today and advance in ways you have never dreamed possible."

The Nationberg Group seemed to have orchestrated many wars and other events throughout history. Gatsby found evidence dating back to President George Washington, who spoke of them in code. After hours and hours of research on many subjects, he finally made it to bed around eleven o'clock, exhausted and ready to sleep.

Roxane wrapped her arm around him and kissed his forehead. He was surprised that she was still awake and leaned in to kiss her in return. He ran his hand over her belly a few times, before closing his eyes and falling asleep.

He woke up at around three in the morning, head swimming with thoughts about what he'd discovered. He jumped on his company laptop again, as he'd decided to research a few more subjects to talk about. There were so many things to choose from. The hard part was researching factual truths, because the media had become partial in their facts, depending on what station you watched. They picked sides rather than reporting the whole truth. So, for each topic, he had to look at different media pages to see what they each said, in order to tie everything together to find out the truth.

That's when it hit him that what they needed to talk about was the media's role in the wars being fought. How did everything get so bad? And what events took place that led them into the war? Somewhere around five in the morning, he went back to sleep, hoping to be well rested for his first day of work.

*****

"Hey," Gatsby said to Manuel as he walked into the office.

"Hello," Manuel replied. "Did you get a chance to research our topic for today?"

"Yes, I did, and it made me think," Gatsby said, taking a seat. "I don't know what you have planned for the rest of the week but, at some point, I'd like to discuss with you—on air—what's brought our country to the point that we're at now, especially as there's a civil war and a world war being fought at the same time."

"What do you mean?" Manuel asked, clearly curious about the topic.

"Well, as I was trying to research the facts on each topic last night, I had to go through twenty different websites per subject to get the whole truth on each one. It made me think about how this war began—it began with the media pushing agendas for certain secret societies, like the presidents stated during their speeches. I feel like—"

"The media definitely has been lying to the people," Manuel finished his sentence for him. "Which is why we always state that we're truthful news, because we take no part in that."

"Yes," Gatsby replied. "This is why I would like to discuss this on the show at some point. I thought it would be a good idea to get your story, leading up to this massive war, about the struggles you had competing against false news from mainstream media." He leaned forward. "Today is my first day and I don't pretend to know anything, but you guys told me to come up with topics and this is the first one that comes to mind."

"Personally, I actually love the idea," Manuel replied. "Let's talk about the president and his speech for today, and then tomorrow, we can begin to talk about how we got to this point, and how the false and twisted stories that were being put out by other mainstream media contributed."

"Okay, sounds like a plan to me."

They headed into the newsroom, where they sat and rehearsed for a while.

"For example," Manuel said, "I might say, 'well the president must find a way to bring us back from behind, because currently we're losing this war. How do we come back from being this far-gone?'" He gave Gatsby a moment to think. "Now, how would you reply to that?" he asked.

"If this was live it would be easier but, just off the top of my head, I would give some ideas, like 'yes, we are behind, and it's not just because of the enemy, but because half our country was more willing to help the invaders because of the race wars that are going on.

"Half the minority didn't like the president because he ran on a racist campaign. Most African Americans wouldn't fight for our country, because the country would not charge cops in the killings of their unarmed people.

"'Most Mexicans wouldn't fight because President Brooks launched an outright purge on them, even though he said he was only going after those that were here illegally.

"'Those from Asian nations, or of Asian descent, wouldn't fight for our country because of the things the president was saying about them—as countries and as people. And the Native Americans wouldn't fight because we kept breaking treaties with them and stealing more of their land. The pipeline had been halted in North Dakota, but as soon as the president took office, he allowed it to go through Native American territory, even though that broke treaties that had been made as early as 1968.

"'He dragged racial issues to the forefront, and not in a good way. The media helped it skyrocket by showing any hateful act between races that was caught on tape and causing race wars and riots between a diverse America. It started with minority rallies and protests, where the Skinheads, Nazis, and the KKK began physically attacking minorities who were protesting. The minorities united and fought back against the racists in this country, and against the racist government who has set so many laws against the minorities. People thought they could pretend that it wasn't happening, and the racists thought they were really winning something, but ended up finding out that for every action there is a reaction.

"'There were constant race riots, even after the war officially started. So, when the draft was put out most minorities refused to sign up, because they refused to fight for a country that wouldn't fight for them.

"There were some that did, including two of my brothers, but most didn't. The president would have to apologize to each race, and make reparations to them, if the government wants minorities to fight in this war. That's what he would have to do, in my opinion, but an apology alone wouldn't be enough. The President will have to put laws in place to guarantee that minorities have access to wealth, giving everyone a fair chance, and he would have to put a member from each race in Congress and in the Senate.

"'They had Muslims and Mexicans locked up in concentration camps, and locked up an average of forty-three percent of Black males, generation after generation because, somehow, they always fit the description of a wanted criminal. Some of them were lawyers, doctors, and business owners—dressed in suits—so what exactly does a criminal look like?

"'Now, from my research, now that I've seen video evidence of warnings from our President and discovered a few things online, I'm starting to think the evidence might actually show that Russia may not have hacked our elections at all!'"

"Okay, that was a lot," Manuel said, laughing. "But it was good, because that is why the country is losing—because most minorities won't fight. I'll save the other questions for the set—we have only a few minutes before we go on, and that's exactly the kind of stuff the listeners want to hear, so you have nothing to worry about. Well done, Gatsby. That was good."

"Thank you," Gatsby replied.

As Gatsby and Manuel sat in their chairs, they were both given hand-held mics, and exactly as it was when he'd been giving his interview, they were counted in.

"Hello, everyone. Welcome to the CGX. I am Manuel Emotho, and tell them who you are," Manuel said, pointing to Gatsby.

"Good morning, I am Mr Emotho's new co-host, Jonathan Gatsby," he said, and rubbed the back of his neck as he waited nervously for Manuel to take over again.

"During this hour of news, we'll be talking about current and past events, and we'll be keeping you, the listeners, in tune with the real news." Manuel began. "To start things off, we've got some big news from the president. Last night, the president declared Colorado as the new location for the White House. He believes that the White house should remain far, far away from any coast." He gestured to Gatsby. "What do you think about the decision?"

"Well," Gatsby began, "I think it was definitely a smart one. I mean, other than for historical purposes, why would you have the White House right next to the coastline, where it's an easy target? Colorado, which is towards the middle of the United States, is a much more secure location. As I understand it, when the first president was elected America had not yet extended past the east coast and the weapons were nowhere near as advanced as they are today, which is why the White House was located where it was. But at some point, you'd think that intelligence would have thought it wisevto move it further inland."

"I agree," Manuel replied. "Being located on the coast, with all the advancement of weapons, doesn't seem like a smart move to me. We almost asked for what happened to the White House to happen. ROX News posted a fake news article saying that the president plans to move it back to Washington DC, but if you listen to this clip, it disproves that story entirely." Manuel cued the station to play a clip of the president announcing that the permanent location of the White House would be in Colorado. "Now you've heard from the president himself, listeners—he did not, in any way, say that the White House would be moving back to DC.

"That's ridiculous," Gatsby cut in. "And people shouldn't have to check and double check to see if the news is real. What's worse," he continued, "is that ROX News was a fact check site, meaning it was one of the sites people went to, to check *facts*. Now where can people go to? With the bias in so many news sites, and most outlets not reporting one hundred percent truthful news? ROX News? NBGCS News?"

"That's an easy answer," Manuel replied, sounding a little smug. "They need to come here to hear the truth. This is exactly why we're rated number one in the news market right now."

"Has he stated any plans yet, other than the relocation of the White House?" Gatsby asked.

"He says that he has no plans but will be meeting with his generals and intelligence to decide what to do. He said he does plan to meet with representatives from the Latino, African American, and Native American communities that are still refusing to fight, and instead forming their own armies. He was quoted last night saying a civil war must be avoided at all costs."

"Well, the question is, why should they fight for a country that wouldn't lift a finger for them?" Gatsby replied. "Muhammed Ali said it best, 'Why should I go and fight overseas for you when you won't even fight for me right here at home?' I hear people ask, 'How can they not fight for their country?' and I reply with this question. 'Was the country theirs when the pipelines forced their way onto Native American land? And while the police were assaulting Native Americans, who were peacefully protesting—hosing them with powerful water hoses, beating them with night sticks, blowing their arms up with grenades, shooting them with rubber bullets—in a now historical event known as Standing Rock?' The country showed the minorities what they thought about them when they made the Blue Lives Matter page, defending cops killing unarmed African Americans. They've killed individuals from almost every race, sure, but they specifically targeted African American males who, most of the time, had no weapons, more than anyone. I can't fathom why you'd shoot to kill an unarmed man. That makes you a murderer, not an officer of the law.

"They showed the minorities what they thought of them by voting in a President who called any Mexicans that illegally came over—trying to earn a few dollars to send home to their families—rapists and drug dealers. Most didn't come the legal way because they were in a rush to escape the cartel, who were taking over Mexico—anyone who did not submit was killed. They didn't come the legal way because they didn't have the money or couldn't meet the requirements, because most of the average citizens in Mexico are living in poverty.

"They showed the Blacks what they thought of them when they attacked them day and night, until many Caucasian military vets formed a large group, five thousand strong, and stepped in as a shield, protecting the protestors from the police. Then, the country stepped in because to them *military* lives mattered, not Black lives.

"Yet this country has the nerve to tell all its minorities that 'This is your country too, it's un-American for you not to fight.' Well, actions speak far louder than words. Then they said, 'If you don't want to live here, leave.' *News flash*—Hispanics, and Native Americans were here first, African Americans have no home but here, because their ancestors were stolen from their land and brought here, so if you can't stand to live with other races here in this land of many nations, *you* leave, because you are the only immigrant to this land!

"Video after video surfaced of police beating and killing every race, but mostly unarmed Blacks that were showing no aggression. Yes, more whites were killed by police overall, but they were usually assaulting—or even shooting at the cops. Blacks were killed for running stop signs, or for just happening to be the wrong color in a store. When they tried peacefully protesting, they were called thugs. When they wouldn't stand before the flag, they were insulted and had their jobs threatened, and police continued killing more and more of them, because they saw the overall community did not care. Therefore, some African Americans resorted to rioting, and then they were called animals.

"So, no matter what they did, this country wouldn't say 'stop killing Blacks.' Instead, they made excuses for the cops, so Blacks started killing cops in return. To the majority, these cops mattered more than all the Black lives that'd gone before them, and the country grieved for them; made the Blue Lives Matter website for them.

"So, the country showed African Americans, from the slavery days all the way to the present, how they felt about them. I ask you—does that paint a picture that shows them it's their country, too?

"In the first six months of his presidency, the president rounded up every Mexican and every Muslim and put them in concentration camps. He tried to send all the legal and illegal Mexicans back across the border. However, Mexico would only accept those who were in America legally. Rather than just letting them return to their homes, the president kept every legal Mexican in concentration camps, along with the Muslims. Tell me, how in the hell does that show them that this is their country too?

"You can't treat people like horse manure and expect them to be grateful and go out of their way— risk their life—for you."

"Those are some very good points," Manuel said when Gatsby stopped for a moment. He nodded his head approvingly. Gatsby was doing very well for his first day on the job. "Now, let's talk about the speech the president just made. What are your thoughts on what he said? I'm certain you've got an informed opinion on that."

Gatsby grimaced. "*Wow* is the thought that races across my mind. The way he starts his speech off alone is disturbing enough, and then for him to not only imply that he knew who was behind the presidential assassinations, but to also give real, physical proof to all the people present? It was big. It's scary to think that he's frightened to say certain things because someone monitors what is said and will kill even the president of the United States if he says something that they do not like."

"I'm going to agree with you on that," Manuel stated. "I watched the speeches of each of the former presidents who have been assassinated, and each one was killed shortly after giving a speech about a secret organization preying on our nation. The timing of their deaths is just too precise for it to be coincidence."

"Yup, I definitely agree with that," Gatsby threw in, as Manuel continued to talk.

"So, for the first time, these secret organizations have been named. Former presidents would only refer to them as secret societies, but this time, President Brooks has said their names—the Nationberg Group, the Illuminati, and the Masons. What are your thoughts on these groups?" Manuel was eager to hear Gatsby's opinion.

"Oh, I have quite a few thoughts," Gatsby replied with a grimace.

"I figured you would," said Manuel jokingly.

"Well for one thing, I find it strange that the only two nations that everyone is looking to conquer in this present day are the only two whose income the power families do not own.

"Every other nation is in debt to them and, in return, their central banks are all owned by them and they pay their taxes to them and not to their governments. Russia paid them every last nickel that they owed them in gold, and then banned them from Russia.

"North Korea would never allow them access, but if they can get North Korea and Russia to submit to them, they will own all seven continents, which effectively means they own everything. That includes the continents, of course, but also the people, the oceans, food, water, electricity, religions, and everybody's money.

"I did some research and environmentalists have said that the world is beginning to run short on food. So, if these families, by way of their secret societies, control all the food in the world, we are royally screwed."

"That's a very good point," Manuel said. "Now, let's talk about this Nationberg Group real fast. They're composed of the most powerful people in the world, including the power families. I did my own research last night, and they seem to be linked to every major catastrophe the world over. Several of their members are actually currently wanted for war crimes, but out of fear of the Nationberg Group, no nation attempts to detain them and prosecute them—"

"From what I found," Gatsby cut in, "there's a reason for that. Each nation's leaders and most powerful persons are in this group, and they know that to go against it—as our President just recently stated—is to put your life in danger. They will kill you. Now, from what I found, the three groups that President Brooks mentioned are all one organization, just as he said. They seem to be different levels. The Nationberg Group is made up of the world's most powerful leaders. The Illuminati are the next level under Nationberg, comprised of the most influential people, and the Masons are the level beneath that.

"It's said that the Illuminati, along with the Nationberg Group, practice Luciferian worship.

Many celebrities have given accounts of what they saw happen at the inductions into this group—things they were forced to do. Of course, they were all also coincidentally killed after revealing such secrets. They mentioned that initiation included some of the most grotesque things I have ever heard of. They sacrifice a baby for every new member, and they force the person joining to eat the heart. Once a month you, each member is required to commit an abominable act. Listen to this, though. Part of the rituals they enforce upon the members include bestiality, involving the rape of a donkey."

"That's disgusting," Manuel replied.

"Yeah, I know," Gatsby answered back. "Even Presidents and royalty are not exempt from the rituals. In fact, they're actually expected to do worse things.

"This is how the chains work, according to my research. All members of the Nationberg Group are in the Illuminati, but not all members of the Illuminati are in the Nationberg Group. All members of the Nationberg Group and the Illuminati are in the Masons, but few of the Masons are allowed in the Illuminati or Nationberg group."

"Well, what are the requirements that help determine which group you can be a part of? I'm asking because you seem to be well versed on this subject," Manuel said.

"Well, anyone can join the Masons or the Freemasons, but only influential people such as major actors, speakers, leaders, and such people who have really significant influence over others can join the Illuminati. Only the world's most powerful people, the people who really run the countries behind closed doors and bankroll everything—pretty much only the wealthiest people in each country—are freely allowed to join the Nationberg Group."

"I see," Manuel said, leaning closer to Gatsby, enraptured by what he was learning.

"Now, here's a theory of mine. I find it weird that the agent in charge of investigating the hacks into our country admits he was behind them—along with Russia and North Korea—the day after his parents are murdered."

"Hmm," Manuel said thoughtfully.

"Knowing that Russia and North Korea are the only two nations not controlled by Nationberg..." Gatsby continued, "and being sure that the agent was getting close to uncovering something—as the president said in his speech—because the last statement he made to his boss was that it didn't look like our system is being hacked, but rather used by somebody with access to it, makes me wonder.

"To me, that looks like he got too close, they killed his parents as a warning, and then probably threatened to kill his wife and two kids if he didn't take the fall and blame Russia, who is avidly denying any involvement in the hacks. Right there, they can kill three birds with one stone.

"I will bet you anything that President Brooks will not finish his presidency, and that he will be replaced by a woman."

"What makes you say that?" Manuel asked with a strange look on his face.

"Well, The Blackout Show predicted that Brooks would be president in an episode they made in the year 2000, I think. They also predicted that the next president after him would be a woman. It's right there in everyone's face."

As Gatsby spoke, both he and Manuel received an email.

"Wow," Manuel said, looking at his phone and then holding it up for Gatsby to see. "It looks like you may not be too far off. The Congress and the Senate, as one, have just called for the president's resignation—and not just the president, but also his entire staff, including the vice President—over a few videos that have surfaced—there's one of the president raping a young girl who went missing a long time ago, whose body was found in Canada, and a second one that shows the president and vice president performing sex acts on a donkey. That only makes it weirder, because you just mentioned that exact scenario with the donkey."

"And then the producer just sent this as well. Hernandez just announced at an awards show that she would like to run for president in the next election. That TV show sure is good at making predictions. Either that, or since we know the Illuminati runs the media, maybe it was more a plan than it was a prediction, and they—knowing how dim-witted we humans are—put it in our faces, knowing that we would never figure it out."

"We will see soon enough," Manuel stated. "More news will be coming to you in just a moment, on the *truthful new*s with Tremaine Sanderson. My name is Manuel Emotho—" Manuel pointed at Gatsby.

"My name is Jonathan Gatsby," he said, putting his microphone down.

"—and that is our show for the day. May you all have a goodnight and be sure to tune in tomorrow at this same time to catch myself, Manuel Emotho, and my new co-host, Jonathan Gatsby, as we bring you the news.

There was a short commercial break, and then Tremaine Sanderson took over.

"Well, hello everyone. Today is a great day as always. I am Tremaine Sanderson coming to you today with more *truthful news*. Today really is a great day. It seems the war has become a stalemate. While we had troops stationed overseas there were casualties on both sides, but as of yesterday, our last troops abroad have returned home. At this point, there's a stalemate here at home. We're firing missiles pointlessly at other countries, and they're doing the same to us.

"With modern technology, everyone has a missile defense system of some kind, and if they don't, their allies are using theirs to shoot our missiles down before they can reach their targets. It's the same here in America—all missiles are intercepted before they can reach land. Hopefully, this war will come to an end soon. Most countries are wasting money in fighting it; all they're doing is going broke, and all they'll manage is to wind up in bankruptcy."

Gatsby was listening in, and he realized that, if countries went into debt because of the war, they would end up in even more debt to the power families. He called Tremaine's caller line.

"Hello caller, this is Tremaine with the *truthful news*. Can you state your name and the reason you're calling?"

"Hey, Tremaine, this is Jonathan Gatsby. I'm sorry to interrupt your show, but you just said something that caught my attention."

"Oh, no problem," Tremaine said. "What was it I said that's so interesting?"

"You said that this war was set to put many countries in debt and in bankruptcy."

"Yes, I did. Now what's your take on that?"

"Well, when you said it, a lightbulb went off in my head. What if the Nationberg Group is behind this war, and the sole purpose is to bankrupt North Korea? I mean, think about it. Other than Israel, most of the countries are focused on attacking North Korea. I mean, how are there more countries after North Korea than there are after the United States? If they bankrupt North Korea, all they have to do is get rid of Russia's current leader, and they'll own all seven continents!"

"Wow, I didn't even think about that," Tremaine replied, thinking deeply about what Gatsby had just said. "That makes perfect sense," he said finally, after a moment's pause.

"Okay, well, that was all I wanted to say before I forgot it, and while you were still on that topic." With that Gatsby hung the phone up.

*****

On the surface, America began to become normal again, with the exception of the president, who was in the process of being impeached. Gatsby and Manuel were doing five live shows per week. The people in America, as they always are, were divided on what to think about the Nationberg Group. Many posts were popping up on social media supporting a One World government.

Gatsby wasn't surprised, and neither were Tremaine or Manuel. Humanity had been lost since the day after it existed. Very few posts spoke against the Nationberg One World desire. Most pointed out that with one government, there would be no more wars, which went over well with many nations, particularly following the recent bloodshed.

It seemed that exposing the Nationberg Group only made them more desirable.

Finally, the day of impeachment was upon the nation. The president walked out of the White House, along with the vice president. Secret Security agents walked closely behind on high alert, because the president was under arrest for the rape and the murder of a young girl who turned up missing during his stay in Canada.

The president kept his eyes on the ground. He knew the power of the Nationberg Group, so he knew that he was going to prison and there was no way out. The Nationberg Group and the Illuminati were just too powerful.

The people booed as the former president was sat in the back seat of the Secret Security car. Some threw items at him, disgusted at what they'd seen in the videos. He had embarrassed the country and had taken the life and peace of a young girl. People were calling for the death penalty. Some were even calling for a permanent government shutdown.

*****

Hernandez approached the podium for her first press conference as a candidate for next President.

To be continued...

Coming Soon

The Quest for the Forbidden Book

Book Two

Follow Jonathan on Facebook to be the first to know when it's released.

https://www.facebook.com/AuthorJonathanGatsby

ABOUT THE AUTHOR

Jonathan Gatsby was transported from his troubled youth into unknown lands and the exciting tales of our favorite heroes when two of his early high school teachers broke from the mold to encourage him. They instigated a voracious love of reading that opened up new worlds and opportunities that had previously felt unreachable.

Born in America on August 4th, 1984, Jonathan's youth was rife with the difficulties of the time. He is dedicated to using his experiences to nurture and care for others through the various passions that have spanned the course of his life and inform his writing today. He has spent time as a professional boxer, recording artist, preacher, church pianist and, most importantly, a dad.

Jonathan's love of boxing and music led him to open a boxing gym and piano school. Having been a writer since the age of fifteen, it was a natural progression for his love of words to eventually lead him into authorship and the inclusive and escapist fantasy worlds he inhabits today. Despite his colorful life, Jonathan still feels he doesn't fit in much anywhere, so he keeps to himself, entwined in a world that he has created.

ALSO AVAILABLE NOW

The Wars Between Angels and Gods: Book One
Middle-Grade to Young Adult Mythological Fantasy

THE BEASTS AND THE 4 DEMIGODS

Strength. Invisibility. Telepathy. Teleportation. Weapon Mastery.

Is it enough to defeat the gate keeper of the realms, Leviathan the mighty dragon?

Having superpowers is a gift but, as John, Jasmine, Marcus, and Ho Young discover the hard way, it can also be a great burden. The world of the gods is in deep unrest, and an unlikely Chicago foursome have been bestowed with the power to end the troubles for good. In the first of seven tournaments, they must take on a most fearsome array of the gods' beasts in order to prevent history from repeating itself and putting human civilization at risk.

Working alongside Michael, Gabriel, and his wayward band of fallen angels, the group learns to traverse their teenage landscape of friendship, love, and self-discovery when they embark on a journey that leads them to an exciting revelation. They're left to dig deep and find out more about the mythology they're reading about in class, and how it links to their own long-lost heritages.

Can't wait to find out what John, Jasmine, Marcus, and Ho Young get up to next?

The Wars Between Angels and Gods:
Book Two

Middle-Grade to Young Adult Mythological Fantasy

FORCED INTO HEAVEN'S WAR

Coming Soon

www.ingramcontent.com/pod-product-compliance
Lightning Source LLC
Chambersburg PA
CBHW030335310726
48979CB00001B/48

* 9 7 8 1 7 3 6 1 7 6 9 3 1 *